HECKLER

HECKLER

DAN BARTON

THOMAS DUNNE BOOKS
ST. MARTIN'S MINOTAUR
NEW YORK

MYSTERY
BART
a

THOMAS DUNNE BOOKS.
An imprint of St. Martin's Press.

HECKLER. Copyright © 2001 by Dan Barton. All rights reserved. Printed in the
United States of America. No part of this book may be used or reproduced in any
manner whatsoever without written permission except in the case of brief quotations
embodied in critical articles or reviews. For information, address
St. Martin's Press, 175 Fifth Avenue, New York, N.Y. 10010.

www.minotaurbooks.com

Design by Heidi Eriksen

Library of Congress Cataloging-in-Publication Data

Barton, Dan.
  Heckler / Dan Barton.—1st ed.
    p. cm.
  ISBN 0-312-27183-2
  1. Comedians—Fiction.   2. Las Vegas (Nev.)—Fiction.   I. Title.

PS3552.A76785 H4 2001
813'.6—dc21

00–045779

First Edition: April 2001

10 9 8 7 6 5 4 3 2 1

To my sister Jean,
the other comedian in the family

Acknowledgments

I'd like to thank the people directly involved with the publication of this manuscript:

First, attorney Robert Youdelman, for his legal counsel and words of encouragement; Matt Bialer, my agent at William Morris, for giving this book the thumbs-up; and Ruth Cavin, senior editor at St. Martin's Press/Minotaur Books, for her positive comments and editorial input. Julie Sullivan at St. Martin's was also of great help.

I got valuable feedback from my mother, Nancy, on character and story. My father, Richard, aided greatly in continuity and plotting. As of this writing, he and I have the manuscript pages on a picnic table spread between us for one last read. Also, thanks to Barbara Barton, my stepmother, for her input on this and other works in progress. Lisa Bradley was among the first to read it and like it, and she is always right about these things.

I'd also like to mention a few folks who helped me promote the Biff Kincaid mystery series from the start. Especially of note are my friends and coworkers at E! Entertainment Television, where I've worked for many years. I'd like to thank John Rieber, Gary Snegaroff, and James BigBoy Medlin for their support. Edward Zarcoff proofread the final manuscript before I sent it off.

My gratitude also goes out to the southern California chapters of Mystery Writers of America and Sisters in Crime. Their fellowship has been a good antidote for the hours spent laboring in solitude and silence.

I got some valuable Internet promotion from Brian Whalen and Brian McKim of sheckymagazine.com, Kate Derie of Clue-lass.com, Cathy Gallagher of the mysterybooks.about.com site, and the perpetually hip Kastle Waserman, editor of music, clubs, and fashion at the *Los Angeles Times* calendarlive.com Web site. Thanks.

Support your local independent mystery booksellers. They're the ones who know what they're doing.

Go see some live comedy tonight.

HECKLER

PROLOGUE

Comedy is my business. Laughter is my profession. Name's Kincaid. Have jokes, will travel.

The club scene isn't what it used to be, but I still work the road. These days I try to spend at least half my time in Los Angeles, working the same clubs as guys that have their own sitcoms. I like the sense of competition it brings to the stage. You can get seen in L.A. People can get to know you, start thinking that you have something going. A funny guy can go far here.

Comedy is a world parallel to the one most people live in, with its own honors and crimes. Personal risks are involved. Not everyone is going to be a star. I've found out there are deep shadows surrounding the stage, some into which no light shines.

I tried to catch such a shadow once, one made in the shape of a man. He killed many people for reasons no one understood. I was left alive to know and tell.

I'm in it. It's my story, too. I'm the guy who found the Heckler.

ONE

I was driving west on the Sunset Strip when I got paged. I was headed into the Comedy Store. It was Monday, almost two in the afternoon. I was going to pick up my paychecks for last week's spots and give my avails for the coming week. The sky was clear, and so was the traffic. The first week of September. Billboards for the Christmas blockbuster movies had just gone up. The weather was still warm and the women were dressing lightly. Ah, California. After I stopped in at the Store I might drive all the way to the beach just to look at the water.

I had just rounded the curve by the Chateau Marmont when I felt the black plastic of my pager vibrate against my hip like a hummingbird. I unclipped it and checked the number. The area code was 702. In my line of work, that meant only one thing:

Vegas.

I pulled into the parking lot of the Comedy Store just minutes later and walked in through the delivery entrance. Past the bar and in the hallway where a pay phone was located, just outside of the Original Room, where I'd done a spot not even twenty-four hours ago to a Sunday night crowd.

3

I dialed in the number and punched in my home billing code. I didn't know exactly who I was calling back. I'd played a couple of rooms up there.

"Comedysino," a male voice answered.

The Comedysino was a club located inside the Palace, a gigantic hotel and casino on the Las Vegas Strip. I'd been there less than six months ago. The booker's name was Rick Partino. I didn't recognize his voice. Maybe it wasn't him.

"Rick?" I said.

"No, but may I ask who's calling?"

"Biff Kincaid," I said. "Someone paged me."

"Oh! Great! Biff! It's Dave! Hold on. Let me get Rick."

"Great." Who was Dave? I couldn't remember. Did he run the door?

I held for the briefest of pauses while listening to a snatch of Palace Muzak in the form of British ceremonial marches, then Partino picked up the phone. "Kincaid! Thank God you called me back."

"What's up?"

"I need a headliner," he said.

"When?"

"Now. Tonight. Two shows. I know it's short notice, but can you make it?"

I checked the time on my pager. It was now seven minutes after two o'clock in the afternoon. Las Vegas was two hundred and eighty miles away. I ought to know. I'd driven every one of them. "When's your first show?"

"Seven-thirty," he said.

"Second show still at ten?" I asked.

"Right," Rick said. "You do this for me and I swear I'll book you back for two weeks headlining anytime you want."

"I can do the when and where," I said. "How much?"

"Three hundred," he said.

"Maybe I'm not your guy," I said. "I got more than that last time."

"Yeah, but that was for all week—okay, three-fifty."

"That's gonna cover my plane ticket," I said. "But even on Southwest, with a same-day purchase . . ."

"Four. Cash from the bar. Plus room and board and two drink tickets from your favorite waitress."

"Done," I said. "You got yourself a comic."

"When can you be here?"

"Last contract you gave me said a half hour before show time," I said. "Showered, shaved and ready to perform."

"Good."

"Why the one-nighter?" I said. The Comedysino usually booked for a week solid. "Someone get sick on you?"

"Uh, yeah. Something like that. He's in the hospital."

"Who?"

"Tiger Moore."

I did a double take to the pay phone. "I know Tiger," I said. There, in the back of the Comedy Store, I found his picture among the hundreds of comedians' headshots that hung there. Tiger had a thin face, with large eyes and an eagle nose. His blond hair was in a buzz cut. His ears stuck out from the sides of his head. In his headshot he was making a face, as though the camera had surprised him.

The first time I'd seen that photo was five years ago, at a club in Lawrence, Kansas, called the Comedy Classroom. There'd been a few more gigs together since, all of them a good time and a good show.

"What'd he go to the hospital for?" I asked.

"Long story."

"I'd like to hear it."

"Don't you have a plane to catch?"

"Tell me when I get there," I said, and hung up.

I left my paychecks sitting at the Comedy Store. I went straight from hanging up the phone to my car and headed back on Sunset the way I came. So much for the beach. So much for anything else. Now I had a gig.

I live in Beachwood Canyon, the hillside community right below the Hollywood sign. I stopped at my apartment on my way to Burbank Airport and packed a bag and my backpack. There I phoned for a flight and gave my credit card number.

5

Burbank Airport is charming because it looks like it belongs somewhere else than five miles from Hollywood. It's about the size of a single terminal at LAX. I parked in the B lot, took a shuttle in and got my ticket at the Southwest counter. By the gate were cardboard cutouts NBC had put up of their hit sitcoms. That reminded me.

I dropped a quarter at the telephone bank and called the Comedy Store to take care of unfinished business.

"Comedy Store."

"Manny, it's Biff Kincaid."

"Talk to me."

"I just got booked tonight in Vegas," I said. "Tuesday through Saturday, I'm open for anything."

"Tuesday through Saturday. Gotcha, Biff. Call back Tuesday at five and I'll have the schedule."

"One more thing."

"What?"

There was someone who would want to know about Tiger Moore being in the hospital. "You got a number for Louie Baxter?"

Louie Baxter was the latest success story to come out of the L.A. comedy scene. He had a sitcom—*Baxter's Place*—that NBC had prominently positioned on Tuesday. He played a comedian who lived in the basement of his favorite comedy club and worked as a bartender. It was a top twenty hit and climbing.

"Uhhh . . ." Manny said. "Let me see. He just did the Main Room two weeks ago so . . . hold on a minute."

I held, turning around with the pay phone to my ear so I could look at the cardboard cutout of Louie that had prompted my call.

Louie Baxter was a big beefy guy from Chicago with curly brown hair, a face-splitting grin and a taste for food and partying that had made him tabloid fodder during the first season of *Baxter's Place*. Over the summer he'd cleaned up and slimmed down. The second season premiere was less than a month away.

"I got his home number," Manny said, sounding surprised at that fact. "You know Louie?"

"We played La Jolla together two years ago," I said. "Before he got the show."

La Jolla was just north of San Diego, a beautiful seaside resort. I play the Comedy Store branch down there at least twice a year. That weekend Louie was the headliner and he rocked the house with his quick-change characters and over-the-top physical comedy. The tabloids compared him to John Belushi and Chris Farley. He reminded me more of Jonathan Winters. He had a bit where he opened two beer bottles with his teeth while playing the "Star-Spangled Banner" on the kazoo. (He was pretending to be the world's biggest football fan.) Then he stripped off his shirt to show his bouncing flabby belly with team colors painted on it and smeared himself with hot dog chili when he didn't like the referee's call.

This was his opener. This was the first thing he did onstage. He went on from there. The next night the manager made him use drop cloths.

Since then, Louie had dropped his props-and-food shtick for material, just as loud and boisterous. I hadn't seen him much since he got the show, although I heard he still dropped by the Store.

"It's area code three-one-oh . . ." Manny said.

I opened my address book and wrote down the rest next to Louie's old home phone number. The last area code was 818. The Valley. Now he'd moved closer to the ocean.

I'd last seen him before the summer, when he was honing his act to go on tour. He'd been playing the big clubs and casinos. With the show renewed for a second season, he was moving up to thousand-seat theaters. We'd watched each other's acts and chatted out in the parking lot for about twenty minutes.

One of the topics of discussion was Tiger Moore. They were friends, buddies from the road. Things were breaking big for Louie and he wanted to see if he could throw Tiger some action. Maybe now he'd give him some help.

"Thanks, Manny."

"I got my other line going, Kincaid," Manny said.

I hung up.

Louie had gotten Tiger Moore a showcase at the Comedy Store within the last year. (I'd seen Louie's name next to his on the Sunday lineup of new talent.) Not that it had done him any good: I hadn't seen Tiger around the Comedy Store lately.

Now I was filling in for him while he was in the hospital. Maybe I'd phone and see if he needed anything.

I snapped my address book shut. My flight was being called. I picked up my bags and started walking toward Vegas.

TWO

My plane touched down at McCarran Airport two hours before show time. I took a cab in to the Strip. It was Monday, so traffic was light. Vegas had changed over the years I'd been playing there. When I started, it was fading from its Rat Pack Glory like the cover of an old Sammy Davis Jr. album. Now it had been redone so it looked like a movie backlot. The MGM Grand. New York-New York. The Monte Carlo. Wow. And more were being built.

The taxi dropped me off in front of the Palace, one of the newer themed megaplexes to have opened in the City of Sin. Its gimmick? The decor was that of British Royalty, slicked up and dumbed down to appeal to everyone from Oregon to Osaka. I carried my own bags in, slung over my shoulder. I shrugged at the bellman, dressed as a Beefeater. He was sweating in that getup. It was still summertime in Nevada, and hot as hell.

The lobby looked like Buckingham Palace, with royal standards and paintings of reigning, deposed and deceased monarchs along the walls. The Royals had denounced the Palace when it was built and the management had defended it as bringing British culture to the world. The hotel hired Sarah Ferguson to do ads for the place, but only after it nixed plans to open a Princess Diana Beauty Salon.

I presented myself to a desk clerk, who was dressed like a London bobby. "Good afternoon, sir," he said in his best fake BBC accent. His name tag read Edward. "How may I assist you?"

"The name's Kincaid," I said.

He tapped that into his computer keyboard. "And your first name?"

"Biff."

More tapping. "I'm not showing a Biff Kincaid, sir."

"Try Brian Francis," I said. "Biff's my nickname."

A frown. "I'm not showing anything under a Biff or Brian Francis Kincaid."

"I'm one of the comedians performing at the Comedysino," I said. "I have to go onstage in less than two hours and do two shows."

"I see."

"Can you give me a room now and we straighten all of this out later?" I asked.

"I'm afraid we're full up, sir," Edward said. "Packed to the coach houses."

"Could you call Rick Partino?" I said. I had flown all the way here on short notice and now I didn't have a room. Great.

"Rick Partino?"

"He's the entertainment manager of the Comedysino," I said. "A fellow employee of yours."

"The Comedysino is a vendor," Edward said, "so he's not a fellow employee."

"Just get him."

"I can put you in touch with the Comedysino's business office."

"Fine."

He pointed over my shoulder to a house phone. "Just pick up the line and you'll automatically ring up a Palace operator and tell her what you want."

"A room," I said. "That's what I want."

"Cheers," Edward said. His eyes were already reaching over

my shoulder to the next guest. "May I be of assistance to you, madam?"

I turned away before I did something very uncricketlike. I found the house phone. It was in a red British telephone booth, next to a restaurant called the Double Decker Bus. Serving bangers and mash, no doubt.

"Comedysino."

"Dave?"

"Yes."

"Biff Kincaid."

"Biff! Where are you?"

"In the lobby," I said, "without a room."

"Oh, right, Rick wanted to talk to you about that."

"He better talk fast," I said. "My return ticket's burning a hole in my pocket."

"Just a second," Dave said. "Rick's right here."

I held for a little longer than one minute and forty-five seconds. I timed it. At two minutes I was hanging up and heading for the bar.

"Biff, it's Rick," Rick said. "You get here okay?"

"I don't have a room," I said, "and they're full up. What—?"

"Right. We're giving you Tiger's old room," Rick said. "The maid's done it up. I brought some of Tiger's things to the hospital today, so there's still a suitcase or two in there but otherwise it's perfectly fine to use."

"Okay." My temper went down a notch.

"Where are you?"

"In the lobby," I said, "right next to the Double Decker."

"I'll be there, with the key, before you hang up the phone."

I hung up and stepped out of the booth. A dozen Japanese tourists were busy taking pictures of each other in front of a ten-foot-tall portrait of Winston Churchill. Hello? There's a call for Historical Irony on line one.

Almost immediately I spotted Rick Partino. He was short and barrel-chested with black hair swept back from a forehead that had gained a few sun creases since I last saw him. He was wearing white khakis, a loud shirt, gold chains, rings and white shoes. He had a mustache, saggy brown eyes from too many after-hours rounds of blackjack and stained teeth from too many cigarettes. Mister Vegas. I didn't know him well enough to not like him, but I knew him well enough to not know him any better than I already knew him.

"Biff!" He had a crushing two-fisted handshake, taking me by the wrist and elbow. He had changed colognes, but was still using too much of that, too. A man of fashion excess. His chains clanked when he stopped. "Am I glad you could make it!"

"Got my room key?"

From his shirt pocket he produced a flat plastic card with the Palace logo on one side and a black magnetic strip on the other. "Right here," he said. He looked around as he palmed it to me. "I'll take you to your room." He looked down at my two bags. "This it?"

"I headed straight here from the Comedy Store," I said.

"Is that where you were calling me from?" he said. "The Comedy Store?" He had a light East Coast accent. Somehow, this didn't clash with the motif of a British castle in the desert. I think he was from New Jersey. A lot of guys from the East Coast had this thing about the casinos. It was their idea of real show business. Never mind movies or TV.

We crossed a drawbridge in the lobby, hung over a moat stocked with live fish. The concrete bottom was painted green and lined with pennies.

"So how's Tiger?" I asked.

"Not good," Rick said. "They wouldn't let me see him."

"Why?" I stopped in front of a motionless costumed palace guard. A group of kids were trying to get him to smile, making jokes in English and their own Arabic tongue. No luck. "What happened to him?"

"No one's sure yet." Rick wanted to move me along and change the subject. "Hey, have you eaten? They got a buffet here, that—"

"Rick, I'll do the two shows," I said. "I want to know what happened to Tiger."

"Not here," he said. He led me past a row of slot machines that were remodeled into barrels of ale, porter and stout to signify nickel, dime and quarter machines. The arms were wooden handles.

We silently waited for an elevator and rode up to the twenty-second floor with four drunk German youths, who were laughing over something that had happened with a waitress.

The elevator chimed and we stepped off on the twenty-second floor. There were two floors still to go. High-roller suites.

We walked down a hallway decorated with velvet purple wallpaper. "Like I was saying," Rick said, "they got a buffet here I can get you comped into. They got everything. I know you eat healthy, so you'll like the salad bar and the . . ."

He slowed and then stopped, his voice doing the same. "Oh my God," he said.

"What?" I asked automatically. I looked where he looked.

Rick didn't answer. He just picked up speed until he stopped in front of the room that matched the door key. It had a big yellow X of police tape across it. "I thought they weren't gonna do this."

"Who?" I said. "Do what?"

"The cops," he said. "They told me it wasn't a crime scene. That they caught the guy."

"What guy?"

Rick turned to me. He looked away and blinked, trying to think of a cover story. He couldn't, so he told me the truth.

"Tiger's in the hospital because someone broke into his room last night and tried to kill him," he said.

"How?"

"By stabbing him in the neck," Rick said. "Dammit." He looked down at the plastic card still in my hand. "We're gonna have to get you another room, Kincaid."

THREE

This is what happened to Tiger Moore.

Last night was Sunday. Two shows. Second to last night of the gig. Tiger headlined, put his free drink tickets to good use after the second show, then hit the slots for about an hour. He'd gotten sweet on Linda, one of the cocktail waitresses at the Comedysino, and was trying to get her to go gambling with him after midnight, but no dice. Around one o'clock he played a few hands of blackjack and headed up to his room.

Someone was waiting for him inside.

The guest in the room next door said he heard sounds of a struggle. Tiger yelling. Tiger's neighbor called security, then started pounding on Tiger's door. The door opened and he was knocked down by a masked man carrying a bloodied knife.

The masked man with the knife headed for a stairwell exit. The stunned neighbor went into the room and found Tiger crawling on the floor, one side soaked in blood. The intruder had stabbed him in the shoulder, right at the neck.

Rick told me this story as we took the elevator back down to the lobby. "Tiger get a good look at this guy's face?" I asked. "The stabber, I mean."

Rick shook his head. "Tiger passed out before the paramedics

got there," he said. "I don't know that he's regained consciousness."

"What about the Good Samaritan next door?" I said. "Did he
get a make on the attacker?"

"Said he was wearing a mask of some kind."

"A mask?"

"Yeah. Like black leather or thick cloth."

"A black mask?"

"Yeah. Or a hood. It was like over his entire head." Rick
shrugged. "He only caught a glimpse of the attacker when the
guy knocked him down."

We stopped at the fifteenth floor. A middle-aged couple with
Gallic accents asked if we were going up. I shook my head. Down.
They must have pressed both buttons. They began to mutter to
each other in French as the doors closed and we descended.

"Tiger know why anyone would want to kill him?" I asked.

"Might be a while before we hear," Rick said. "When I went
to the hospital this morning he was still in intensive care. I
thought the police had arrested a suspect. Maybe he was the
wrong guy."

Then we reached the lobby, the doors opened up and we
headed for the front desk. All the regular rooms were full, so I
ended up with a high-roller suite on the twenty-third floor, with
a balcony that overlooked the Strip. I left Rick at the front desk
having an argument with Edward over whether or not the Comedysino was going to have to pay extra for this room. I just wanted
a place to eat dinner, watch the news and go over my act. I had
worked up some special Vegas material over the years but it
was in my files back home. I was going to have to try to pull it
out of memory.

In my suite, I watched the daylight fade from the Vegas skyline and the city lights started to burn brightly as the night
settled in. I brought up a salad from the buffet and munched
thoughtfully as the TV kept up a low level of chatter and I stared
at a blank piece of hotel stationery with a pen in my hand.

I couldn't concentrate on my material. Not after what Rick
Partino had told me had happened to Tiger Moore.

Now here I was sitting upstairs in my luxury accommodations unable to think about anything else than what had happened last night, just one floor below me. The best clues were behind a bunch of police tape.

I had an hour to go before the first show, thirty minutes before I checked in at the club. Time enough for a look-see. I grabbed a washcloth from the bathroom to wipe away fingerprints. Disturbing a crime scene was against the law. That wouldn't stop me from trying, but I still didn't want to get caught. I finished my salad, left the news running and took the elevator down a floor, to Tiger's old room. In my pocket I still had the card key that Rick Partino had given me. No one had asked for it back. That might still let me in.

I got off on the twenty-second floor. From the elevator, there were five corridors. I checked them all for security cameras and personnel. Clear. I walked down a hall, nodding at the only other person I saw.

Tiger's room was down the northeast wing, toward the end on the right-hand side. There was a stairwell at the end. Perhaps that's where his thwarted intruder had gone. It wasn't far: less than twenty feet. Next to it in the hall was a picture window that looked out on the nighttime Nevada landscape of desert and hills. It was dusk and beyond the festive city limits it looked like the world just dropped away.

I made it quick. I looked right, looked left and slid my card key through the slot in the lock. The little red light next to the slot flashed green and there was a soft click. I pulled out the washcloth and turned the knob and wedged myself through an opening in the X of yellow tape marked with POLICE LINE: DO NOT CROSS.

I was inside. I closed the door behind me.

I was in complete darkness. The drapes were closed. There were no lights on. It was dark. For all I knew there was a dead body in there.

I stood motionless for a minute until I could see the barest glow from the lights outside seeping around the edges of the drapes. I reached out with my right hand, still using the washcloth, and felt for a light switch. I found one and moved it up. The bathroom light came on.

The room was much smaller than the suite I was in, but a copy of the last one I'd stayed in when playing the Comedysino. A dresser with a mirror over it. A TV on a stand. I couldn't see around the corner from the bathroom, but I'd bet money there were two double beds with a nightstand between them.

I took one step forward and stopped.

There was blood on the carpet.

Dried blood, not fresh. The rich crimson had turned rusty brown overnight, and there was a lot of it. The knife wound in Tiger's neck had cut deep. No wonder he was still in the hospital.

I stepped forward, staying to the left of the trail of dried blood. I found another light switch and flicked it. That turned on the nightstand lamp, and it threw odd shadows from a low place. As I rounded the corner I saw why. It had been knocked to the floor between the two beds. A heavy brass lamp, two feet tall, lay on its side, the shade at an angle that filtered out most of the light. It made the room look frozen, like a snapshot. Crime scene was right.

Then I saw what had been written on the wall.

It was just above the bed where I guessed the attack had taken place. That bed looked slightly unmade, and on the bed-spread right by the pillows there was a dark pool of blood so thick I could smell it from where I was standing, right at the foot. Blood had gushed all over one of the pillows, soaking the pillowcase and flowing across the bedspread, patterned with a design that suggested various coats of arms and other instruments of knighthood and heraldry.

A framed map of England from a few centuries back had been placed between the bed and the adjoining wall to the bathroom. I looked at the wall above the bed and saw a bare hook and the faintest outlines of the frame faded into the wallpaper. Someone had taken it down from the wall and put it by the bed. In the ensuing struggle, the glass had been cracked.

In place of the map, someone had taken a can of black spray paint and—with careful precision—written a message, meant to be read presumably after Tiger Moore's body had been found. There would be Tiger, his throat slashed, the eyes wide-open and staring, the police baffled, the press looking for an angle. Well, the self-styled killer knew all that. He wanted everyone to know that this was not a crime of opportunity or a simple burglary for ready cash. This was something else. Anyone wanted a clue, he was going to give them one, in large letters.

GET OFF THE STAGE, it read. YOU SUCK.

FOUR

When I got to the Comedysino showroom Tiger Moore's picture was still up in a glass case on a stand outside the ticket booth, underneath a sign for the Comedysino bearing the slogan "The funniest place in town!"

Below that was another headshot of a mustached cowboy with an ear-to-ear grin, wearing a pearl-buttoned shirt and a turquoise bolo tie and a stalk of hay in his teeth. His name was Bobby Lee Garnett. Below his name, set in cursive quotes, read: "The Comedy Cowboy." Yee-haw.

It was a half hour before show time and there was a small line of about twenty people, loosely assembled in front of a bank of nickel slots. Men with bellies hanging over their belts under striped polo shirts and women with handbags the size of spare tires. Tourists.

The electronic ringing and pinging of gaming filled the air like a calliope, punctuated by the occasional sound of a jackpot: metal on metal, when a handful of coins hit the tray of the slot machine. One of the men in line was lighting a cigarette. That reminded me of an old bit about how Vegas was where Californians came to smoke indoors. I made a mental note to use it.

A weathered blond woman in her fifties was working the ticket booth and she didn't see me deftly unhook the maroon velvet rope guarding the curtained entrance to the showroom. She was too busy counting out cash. She had a cigarette dangling from a corner of her mouth and one still smoldering in the ashtray.

Past the curtain I stepped into the showroom and immediately spotted Dave. I'd spoken to him when I first returned Rick's page. I remembered him now. He was the floor manager and, true to tradition, had worn a tux to seat the audience for the first show. He was in his late twenties but looked younger because he carried about twenty-five extra pounds and had a cherubic face that always seemed to be smiling. He wore thick-lensed black-rimmed glasses and his black hair curled around his ears and eyebrows in a modified shaggy Afro. He looked like Weird Al Yankovic's little brother who needed to go on a diet, except Weird Al was a lot taller. Dave came up to my chin.

"Hi, Biff!" Dave said, enthusiastically shaking my hand. He wanted to be a comedian. Last time I was here he'd gone on and done five minutes about getting beat-up all the time as a kid. Truth in humor. "Glad you could make it!" He reached into a pocket of his tux and pulled out some paper squares. "Here's a drink ticket for each of the shows. You remember where the bar is?"

I nodded to the left, toward some double doors. "Out that exit and to the left."

Dave nodded so hard his hair shook. His name tag read D. TYLER. That was his last name. Tyler. "I also threw in a coupon for the breakfast buffet."

I pocketed the miniature paperwork. "Thanks."

"Anything else I can do for you?"

"Yeah." I reached into my backpack and pulled out a head-shot. I carried about half a dozen with me at any given time, along with some résumés and a bio. Never knew when you'd get a last-minute call to head to the airport. "Could you put this up outside for me?"

"Oh, yeah! Instead of Tiger Moore's. Sure." I went outside with him while he did it.

"How soon you going to start seating people?" I asked.

Dave glanced at his watch. "In about five minutes."

Time enough for me to get a little information. "Too bad about Tiger, huh?"

"What?" One of the cocktail waitresses had walked by in a cutaway mock tuxedo outfit that emphasized the legs and cleavage. He was temporarily distracted. "Oh, yeah."

"He still in critical condition?"

"Last I heard. He lost a lot of blood." Dave motioned me toward him. "Did Rick tell you what happened?"

"Someone broke into Tiger's room last night and stabbed him in the neck."

"I mean before that."

"No," I said, dropping my voice. I didn't take my eyes off Dave but listened for anyone else entering the showroom. The waitress had gone through the swinging doors that led to the bar. "What happened before?"

"Rick didn't tell you?"

"No," I said.

"Tiger got a note," he said. "A written threat."

I remembered the writing on the wall of the room: GET OFF THE STAGE. YOU SUCK. "What kind of a threat?"

"It was slipped under his door two nights ago. Gave him the creeps."

"What did the note say?"

"I don't know," Dave said. "I just heard about this after he got attacked."

"Who did you hear about it from?" I asked. "Tiger? Rick?"

"No," Dave said. "Linda."

"Who's Linda?"

"She's a waitress here."

"Is she the one he talked to last night before he got stabbed?"

Dave nodded. "He showed her the note. Wanted to know if she had a jealous boyfriend." Dave had a high-pitched voice. When he whispered, he sounded like a choirboy. It emphasized his unfortunate image as a eunuch.

"Why?" I said. "They dating?"

Dave snorted. "No. Tiger wishes. We all wish. You never met Linda?"

I shook my head. "She new?"

23

"To here, yeah. She used to dance in one of the shows in town."

I tilted my head to one side as if to say, that explains it. "What's she look like?"

"You'll know her."

"I take it you mean she's attractive," I said. "That doesn't narrow it down much here in Las Vegas."

The weathered blonde stuck her head through the door and croaked, "C'mon, Dave, I gotta open the doors."

"Okay, Dolores," Dave said. He turned to go, straightening his black bow tie. "If you haven't found Linda by the end of the second show, come see me. I'll recommend a good eye doctor."

I didn't want to tell him that wasn't very helpful and I was more interested in what this note had to say than who the cutest waitress was in the club. The Comedysino had never been short of fine female forms, but I had a rule: no waitresses. Very strict. I'd only broken it fifty or sixty times.

I walked through the showroom and hopped up onstage. Vegas was good to the live performer. You get a big stage, a great sound system, a free room and a decent paycheck. I liked it here. The whole town had a history of respect for live entertainment. I tapped the mike a few times, scuffed my feet on the black polished stage. The mike, the lights, the crowd, the show. As George Carlin used to say, Welcome to my job. I felt a little tingle between my stomach and my spine and pushed back the gold curtain to step backstage.

There was a small round black cocktail table and four chairs set up backstage like a small café. There was a dressing room that doubled as a bathroom. There was a clock on the wall and gray metal boxes that house the electrical workings of the house. The controls were far from the stage, in a booth along with the sound equipment.

Sitting in two of the chairs was Bobby Lee Garnett, the Comedy Cowboy. He was wearing a black Western-styled shirt with leather piping and pearl buttons, a straw-colored hat tilted forward across the bridge of his nose, faded tight Wrangler jeans and gray shiny boots made from the skin of some dispatched reptile. He had his arms folded as he sat in one cane-backed chair and his feet propped up in another. He looked like he was sleeping. I couldn't see his face.

There was a watercooler by the dressing room with an opened tube of plastic cups on top of it. I fished out a cup, let some pure aqua spill into it and drank it empty while I stood there. It had been a long day. I poured myself more water and sat down on the other side of the table from Bobby Lee Garnett.

"Yew the big headliner they flew in from Holly-wood?"

His voice was low and rumbling and came from underneath the hat. It was flat and nasal and twangy. My guess was West Texas.

Before I answered, he took a deep breath and unfolded his arms to cock his hat back on his head and look at me with baggy eyes. He was over thirty, like me, but it was a hard over thirty. A whiskey-and-cigarettes over thirty. He had red hair, but a darker shade of red than mine. I'm more of a strawberry blond, with light freckles and blue eyes and even as a kid I had the sense to avoid sunburns and play in the shade. Bobby Lee Garnett had sun-blasted his fair complexion into a ruddy mask that was going to bloom into a variety of skin cancers by the time he was fifty.

His hair was cut in a country shag, like a singer's. He had a handlebar mustache grown out over his upper lip the color of a rusty bicycle chain. He looked like Yosemite Sam, if Yosemite Sam had a drinking problem. His eyes were rheumy with a hangover. He had a half-empty glass of whiskey and water with the ice starting to melt sitting on the table beside him and we hadn't even done the first show yet.

"My name's Biff," I said. "Biff Kincaid."

"I don't know why the hell Rick felt he hadda fly in a big fancy headliner from Holly-wood," Garnett said, taking his legs off the chair and scooting it aside with a bootheel so hard the legs made a honking sound on the floor. I heard music start up out in the show room. Faint jazz. People were coming in, taking seats.

Bobby Lee Garnett stood unsteadily and turned the chair he was sitting in around and sat back down so that the cane back spread his legs apart. "I told 'em they had a headliner sittin' right here," he said. "Whyn't they just let me close the show tonight?" He pronounced the last word *ta-gnat*.

"Rick booked me just this afternoon," I said. I felt like I was in a Western, facing down the local gunman. Mister, I don't want no trouble. I'm just a sheep rancher. Trying to feed my family.

He drained the whiskey and water and reached down to the floor to pick up a blue plastic bucket, the kind the Palace dispensed to keep coins in while feeding the slots. Dark noxious liquid sloshed in the bottom. He'd been spitting in it. Ech.

"That peckerwood Eye-talian sumbitch got his haid so far up his ass he can't pick his nose without a roll of toilet paper and a tube a' Preparation H," Garnett said. He reached into his pocket and pulled out a tin of snuff. He put a pinch between his cheek and his gum. I saw the mottled pocket of tooth enamel and lip lining his favorite spot to park his dip. I'd seen healthier gums in a dog pound. "All week long I been tellin' him that Tiger Moore can't follow my act. When that stupid fucker got hisself stabbed, I thought there was mah chance."

There's no people like show people. They're all heart. "How'd he get himself stabbed?" I said.

Garnett hadn't been looking at me much. People who talk all the time rarely wonder who's listening. He focused his bleary brown eyes on me with some effort. "Whut?"

"You said he got himself stabbed," I said. "How'd he do that?"

Bobby Lee spit a mouthful of bug-colored juice into the bucket. It hit bottom with a *pank*. "Who the hell knows?" He turned to me and smiled, his lips and teeth stained with chewable carcinogen. "Mebbe it was one of my rabid fans."

"Let's rule out that highly credible scenario as being too obvious," I said. "Tiger say anything to you about anyone with a grudge against him?"

"Naw."

"He have problems with a heckler or anything like that?"

"Some. His biggest problem was followin' me onstage," Garnett said. "I'm out there practically gettin' a standin' O every night 'n' he's followin' it with his lame-ass Hollywood bullshit."

"Thanks for the review," I said. "I'm more interested in why someone attacked him."

Garnett shrugged. "Just lettin' you know what you're in for workin' a show with me."

"Did he say anything about receiving threats of any kind?"

"What are you, the fuckin' cops? Shit, I already tole them I only knew about that one time." He pronounced it *tam*, as in *tam-o'-shanter*.

"What one time?"

"The time Linda's boyfriend came here and told Tiger to lay offa her."

"Linda the waitress?"

Garnett nodded. "You seen her?"

"No."

"Make a tadpole slap a whale, that one. Fightin' stares off with a stick, as my grandaddy used to say. She got it all when they handed good looks out, and she got all there was to git."

"So who was this boyfriend?"

"Some bodybuilder-lookin' dude." He held his hand up high over his own head. "I mean big." Another bucket spit. Another *pank*. If he kept that up, I was going to barf. "Used to dance with Linda in a show where he played a gladiator and she played a Roman maiden." He leaned in close and I could smell the chaw on his breath. His freckles looked baked on. "I heard she showed her titties in that one."

"What was this guy's name?"

"Lucky or Larry . . . but he didn't call himself Larry. Lawless. That was it."

"Lawless?"

"Yeah. Sounds like a biker, don't it?"

"When did Lawless show up?"

Bobby Lee Garnett tilted his head back like the answer was written on the ceiling. The skin on his neck looked like it belonged on an iguana sitting on a rock in the desert. "I thank it was last Friday night," he said. "After the first show."

"What happened?"

"Whatever happened, it happened while I was on stage," Garnett said. "They had a few words and Dave out there had to go get security to put Lawless outta the showroom. When I get off, Dave goes onstage to bring Tiger on and Tiger's so rattled he forgets his first bit. Takes him a while to git started. This, a course, after I killed."

"Anything happen to Lawless?"

"I hit the bar outside for a drink and saw Linda having it out with Lawless in the middle of the casino. Least it looked like him."

"What's Lawless look like?"

Garnett snorted. "Like Conan the fuckin' Barbarian," he said. "Big. I mean like, six-four or six-five. And wide, too. He had on one of those bodybuilder sweatshirts that cuts off at the sleeves and comes up short at the belt to show off his guns and his washboards. Long hair, all the way down to his shoulders. Tan. Good-lookin' guy. You can see what he was doin' with Linda. They musta kept each other busy on- and offstage." He shook his head. "But she must have sugar down there 'tween her legs 'cause he got hisself one bad crack habit." He chuckled. "Hers."

"You said they were arguing," I said. "Did you overhear anything either of them said?"

"Man, I was headin' for the bar," Garnett said. "I got my eye on that bottle a' Jack. I ain't stoppin' to hear some guy argue with his squeeze."

Dave popped his curly head through the curtain. "Five minutes, guys."

"Who's on first?" I asked. "I haven't met our opening act yet."

Dave looked at me. "Biff, Rick has me open and emcee all the shows now."

"Good for you, Dave."

"What do you want in your intro?"

I named a couple of TV shows. "And a regular at the Comedy Store."

Dave nodded and left.

"You think he's a choir?"

"Do I what?" I said. "Do I think he's in a choir?"

"No," Bobby Lee said, pronouncing his words as if I was lipreading. "Do-you-think-he's-a-choir."

He was saying the word *queer*. "You mean, do I think he's gay?"

Bobby Lee nodded. "Looks like a faggot to me."

"I have no idea," I said. "I never thought about it."

"Don't make no difference to me," Bobby Lee said. "I just was wonderin'." Bucket. *Pank*.

I'd had about enough of Bobby Lee Garnett, the Comedy Cowboy. I'd decided to become interested in something somewhere else when he beat me to my feet with his half-empty glass in one hand and his spit bucket in the other. "You want anything from the bar?" he asked. "I'm gonna get me a refresher."

I waggled my water cup. "I'm fine."

He left through a side door that led out directly into the casino, his bootheels stomping down the steps. I could hear the crowd noise through the curtains. It was twenty-four hours ago that Tiger Moore had been here, sitting and waiting, ready to do two shows on a Sunday night. He'd had a note left for him under his door, and later a message written on the wall where his dead body was supposed to have been found. He had a jealous body-builder threaten him. He had a middle act gunning for his slot in the show. In thinking about who had stabbed Tiger Moore and why, it wasn't a question of where to start. It was a matter of where to stop.

Dave popped his head back in and looked at his watch. "Where's Bobby Lee?" he said. "We need to start the show."

"He went to the bar."

"Wow, what a surprise." He shook his head. "Every show I have to go and get that guy from the bar or the blackjack table or—" He ended his sentence with a sound of aggravation: "Agh! I'm sick of him! Thank God tonight's his last night."

"Want me to help round him up?"

"No, thanks."

He ducked out. Thirty seconds later the side door opened and Bobby Lee Garnett walked back in, a whiskey and water in a highball glass with a red straw in it. He'd lost the spit bucket. I didn't want to know where.

"Dave was looking for you," I said.

Bobby Lee spread his arms in a gesture of universal misunderstanding. "I'm right here," he said. "They make such a big fuckin' deal outta havin' to find me afore the show, and I'm always right here." *Rat cheer*. He picked a chair and sat down in it. "You wanna go find him and tell him I'm here?"

"He'll come back," I said.

Bobby Lee fumbled in his shirt pocket, found a hard pack of Marlboros, packed a cigarette down by tapping one end against the flip-top and lit up. He drank, he chewed snuff, and he smoked. This guy was going to be in chemo by his next birthday.

He scooted his chair back and stomped on his wedge-shaped heels over to the dressing room. He walked in empty-handed and walked out with a guitar. He began to strum a few chords, then fished a pick out of the frets and started tuning with moderate ease.

"You play music?" I asked.

He didn't look up at me. He just nodded while he started picking out a tune.

"In your act?"

This time he looked up at me and smiled. "I close with it."

"Uh-huh."

"Told ya Tiger Moore had a hard time followin' me," he said.

I turned away from the guitar. Guitar acts, keyboard wizards and magicians were the bane of my existence. I had nothing against them other than they were hard to follow. Here an audience had just seen a guy pull flaming rabbits out of his ass and then I went up there and talked about real life.

"You want to switch?" Bobby Lee said. "You go on first and I close the show?"

"Not on your life," I said.

"It's your funeral."

Dave came backstage, bouncing on the balls of his feet. "Okay guys, here we go."

I nodded. Bobby Lee set down his guitar. I heard a taped intro begin, welcoming everyone to the Comedysino. It laid down the rules: no excessive talking, no flash pictures and tip your waitresses. And now . . .

Dave was rolling his neck around on his shoulders with two fingers touching the curtain's part. Bobby Lee had put down his guitar and begun to shadow box. The preshow jitters were kicking in. I stayed where I was.

The intro ended with a blare of brassy big-band music and a spotlight hit the stage and Dave bounded through the curtains.

Showtime.

"By the way," Bobby Lee said, nodding in Dave's direction. "He sucks."

FIVE

Dave Tyler did a weak opening five minutes about being chubby and having a high voice and not getting any girls. Little laughs here and there. Heh-heh-heh. Pity laughs.

I'd left backstage and gone out into the casino to enter through the showroom. Rick Partino was minding the door.

"Biff, everything okay with the room?"

"Great," I said. "It's a suite."

"Really appreciate you flying up from L.A. to fill in at the last minute like this."

"About that."

"Yeah?"

"Did Tiger Moore ever—"

A party of five came in behind Rick and he had to seat them. I'd save my question for another time.

I found a dark empty booth in the back of the club and sat down to watch the show. Half the tables were full, those mainly toward the front. The seats were spacious and spread out, the tables large and covered with white tablecloths. Through the sound system, even Dave's voice sounded smooth and mellow. The spotlight made everything on stage kind of glow. This was what I came to Vegas for.

I saw a long-legged lovely waitress, six feet tall, her maid's costume racily modified to even further show off her plentiful assets: full deep cleavage, tan skin, perfectly shaped long legs that shifted effortlessly as she sashayed through the club carrying a tray full of drinks. Her long thick curly dark hair flowed over the muscles in her back, swinging slightly as she walked heel-toe, heel-toe, like a dancer. Men watched her go by and kept watching. I didn't see her face but I knew who it was. Linda.

She brought a drink to one young couple, leaning over as she set a beer down in front of the man and a wineglass in front of the woman. Then she turned around, her face still in shadow, and bent at the waist as she figured out the check. The man looked a little too long at Linda's heart-shaped ass packed into her skintight costume and his date gave him a slight smack on the arm. Linda seemed to be good at starting certain kinds of arguments.

Dave ended his set to weak applause and a little more music courtesy of Dolores, the sun-baked ticket seller now working the sound booth. I had yet to see her without a cigarette parked in the corner of her mouth.

"And now it's time for your feature entertainer, please welcome, all the way from Lubbock, Texas, the Comedy Cowboy, Mr. Bobby Lee Garnett."

Some more applause. Bobby Lee came stompin' out, the cowboy hat parked jauntily on his head, the guitar slung over his shoulder, a drink in one hand and a guitar stand in the other.

Before the applause ended, he had his guitar off his shoulder and on the stand, waiting for him, as full of promise as a magician's trunk. "Thank you, thank you . . ."

First joke: "Great to be here in Las Vegas, so's I can practice my only three job skills . . . drinking, gambling and divorce."

Laugh.

"In that order."

Laugh.

"See, one leads to t'other . . ."

Laugh.

"I love gambling. You know why? Now I got a reason to be broke."

Laugh.

"When I git drunk I'll bet on anything. Took me thirty minutes ta realize the el-e-va-tor wasn't just a really shitty slot machine."

He acted it out, playing himself drunk on an elevator, weaving slightly, punching buttons, looking at his wallet. Long laughs.

"Still don' know where I won that fifty bucks from."

Laugh.

And he just kept it going from there. His material was tight, economical and very polished. He played up the cowboy character for all it was worth, doing jokes about his hometown, his granddaddy, growin' up in Lubbock and he slipped right into that groove of everyman identification and stayed there. He waited out applause breaks by taking a drink of whiskey. I was impressed. He'd done this a lot.

Then he picked up his guitar. "Ya'll wanna hear some music?"

They sure did, and let him know with cheers and applause. He spun into a series of country song parodies and original novelty tunes, all very short and very clever. I checked my watch. He was closing. I better get backstage. I was going to have to work to follow this guy.

I went out the door and around the Palace showroom inside the casino and entered the backstage door marked PERFORMERS ONLY. I had some notes in my pocket on some new bits I was working on and I glanced over them. I heard the laughs building into applause as Bobby Lee ended another song and went into his closer. I found a spot on the wall and used it to mentally focus for the show. It didn't matter what Bobby Lee had done, good or bad. I was going to go out there and make it my show. They were my crowd and this was my night. When I got up there I was going to own that stage.

Bobby Lee left them at their peak, clapping, whistling and wanting more, a lot more. Of him. He charged through the curtain, his forehead dripping with sweat, breathing heavily, and kept going. He went into the dressing room and put down his guitar and came out with a towel in his hands, his hat off, wiping his face.

"Good set," I said.

"Thanks," Bobby Lee said. "They're a goooood crowd."

We both heard Dave asking the audience for another round of applause for Bobby Lee. He got it.

Bobby Lee finished wiping his face and set the towel aside. "Good luck out there," he said.

"I'll take it," I said. "You're funny."

"Thanks, man." He kept walking around and pacing, still in the high of the show. With his hat off I could see he was losing his hair up front. Thin strands were plastered to the sides of his head in a U.

Dave started my intro. Bobby Lee and I looked at each other. "My turn," I said.

"See you when you get home from work, dear," Bobby Lee said, and I laughed. He smiled and winked.

Then Dave said my name and I walked out onstage into the lights and sound.

I shook Dave's hand and let him go. I asked for yet another round for Bobby Lee Garnett, not because I thought he deserved it, but because after three sitting ovations, these people subconsciously would think okay, okay, he wasn't that great. Now you do something.

The applause wasn't nearly as long or as loud as the first two rounds. Good. I'd worn them out on Bobby Lee Garnett.

I went right into my act with a light tie-in to Bobby Lee: "Ladies and gentlemen, I'm not from Texas. I'm from Hollywood, California . . ." I started off with tight, close combinations, making short segues into obvious conclusions. Hollywood. It's a weird place. Here's how weird it is. L.A. It's a big city. Traffic's so bad . . .

There weren't a lot of Californians in the audience, or people from other big cities. Once I was working in Oklahoma City and the headliner was from *Saturday Night Live* and all she did was talk about riding the subway and taking cabs. People in Oklahoma City didn't do either of those things too often.

I was getting the same kind of response now that she had gotten then. Mild laughs off of delivery and presentation, but no acknowledgment that this was something that happened to them personally. No recognition. No "oh, yeah!" factor.

I realized I'd made a mistake. I was following a country comedian with big-city material. Not a great choice. I had to do something.

Current events. Not what had happened in today's news, but recently there had been another Washington scandal, this one tinged with more sex than usual. I threw in some not half-bad impressions of major political figures and the crowd bit big.

I kept at it. I used that as a springboard to launch into a ten-minute bit I did about news, both local and national, especially about coverage of tornadoes and hurricanes. I left earthquakes out of the equation.

Now I was off, picking up speed. I glanced at my watch. I was twenty minutes in. Less than halfway through my forty-five-minute headliner act. As I was delivering the last of my news bits, I started rifling through my mental material files to pick out something else, quick, quick, quick.

Nothing. I was blanking. It's the worst thing that can happen to a comedian on stage. He can't think of where to go next. No ready bits. No natural cues. I was headed toward a brick wall, with thirty seconds left to go on my current routine. Then I was just going to have to stand there and think of something to say.

Right then I saw Linda come slinking down the main aisle, carrying two bottles of imported beer. By the time I finished up my last line to a small applause break, she was front and center, with her back to me. All the better. The audience could see who I was talking to.

"Hi," I said, looking at her.

No response. She didn't know I was speaking to her. She was making change. But I got a laugh. She was too obvious a presence to ignore.

I turned to a side table. "See? She's flirting with me. I can tell."

An even bigger laugh.

37

"Watch this," I confided to another table. "If she doesn't respond at all, I'm in."

I turned back to Linda. "Howya doin'?"

Linda thanked her customers. One of them—a man—slipped her a few bucks, smiled, said something and pointed over her shoulder up at me. She turned her head to look.

I hadn't seen her face before, not full up close. She had bright green eyes that were unnaturally light. Even in the dim club atmosphere they glowed like a jungle cat's. Her cheekbones swept up the sides of her face, and her jaw was long and leonine. She had a high forehead and naturally full lips she had colored a deep red. No one had been kidding when they talked about her. She was gorgeous.

"Hey there," I said and the audience fell apart.

It wasn't what I said; it was that I'd gotten her to look at me. A few seconds before I'd been blanking and now I'd created something that was purely improvisational. An audience can tell when you're working in the moment. I call it comedy jazz.

Linda didn't say anything. She just slowly blinked her long dark lashes and smiled, showing a row of perfectly white teeth.

"You're Linda," I said. "Aren't you?"

She nodded. Another laugh. Not as big as the last one.

"Yeah," I said. "I heard about you." The way I said it got a good response. "As soon as you walk into this place, you're asking 'What time's the first show?' and they're all saying, 'Forget that. Have you seen Linda yet?' "

Linda herself got a laugh by cocking her hip flirtatiously and holding her tray up on one hand.

"You do that so well," I said. I was playing the part of the horny guy, but it was time to let it go. "Thank you, Linda," I said. "Lovely having you here." That was her cue to go and she took it, moving herself artfully through the tables. And then just to make sure the other waitresses didn't get mad, I reminded everyone to tip. Then I did a bit about tipping and that led to a bit I did about working temp jobs and I started to kill again and all of it came back to memory, all my material in its polished form and I totally made them forget about Bobby Lee Garnett and when I ended the show it was to applause just as big as when he got off. I closed the show and Dave came up applauding and smiling.

Now it was my turn to plow through the curtains and wipe my face with a towel. I didn't see Bobby Lee Garnett anywhere, but Dave wrapped it up quick and came backstage to congratulate me. "That was great, Biff," he said. "Hey, did you see my act?"

"No, sorry," I lied. I wasn't in the mood to give a critique to a newcomer. You never tell them what they want to hear. "I was back here talking to Bobby Lee."

"Oh." Dave was disappointed. "Maybe you can catch my set next show."

"I'll try." I'm not a good teacher. I don't have the patience to coach up-and-comers. There's only one classroom, and that's up there in the spotlight. Your instructors are sitting in the audience. The only advice I give is to keep at it. You'll either get better or quit. Class dismissed. "Where's Rick?" I said. "Out front? I wanted to talk to him."

"Probably. Hey, why don't you see if you can find Linda?" Dave said. "Follow up on that little bit of business you did with her."

"I'll take a number," I said. I walked with him out into the casino area.

"Well, look who's gambling," Dave said, pointing.

I followed his finger. Bobby Lee's cowboy hat was bent down over a blackjack table, a cigarette and drink going in the same hand as the dealer laid down the cards.

"He gambles until he's broke," Dave said. "He's tried to get Rick to advance him money off his next booking, but no dice. Right now I imagine he's working off a cash advance from his credit card."

As I watched, Bobby Lee nodded for another card and didn't like what he saw. The cowboy hat tilted even lower.

"There's Rick," Dave said. "I'm going to grab a bite to eat. I'll see you at the second show."

Dave left and I crossed over to Rick. He was having an animated discussion with a yellow-haired portly gentlemen in his fifties with a florid face and fleshy neck that billowed out over the collar of his white shirt, dark blue suit and red silk tie. He had blue eyes the same size, shape and warmth of shirt buttons. His pale skin was reddened at the cheeks and nose. He was in need of a haircut. I could detect a British accent. The conversation ended with him turning on his heel and walking away in his black polished shoes while Rick was in mid-sentence. Rick immediately lit a cigarette.

"How's it going?" I asked.

"Like shit, Kincaid," Rick said. He glanced over his shoulder. The man in the blue suit was gone. "That was Jeff Holden, entertainment director of the Palace."

"What did he want?"

Rick snorted bitterly. "What he wants is for us to pack up the comedy club and get the hell out of his hotel so he can put in dollar slot machines right where we're standing," he said. "He's got surveys. He's got projections. Numbers. The other casinos are packing them in with 3-D movies and stunt shows, not comedy. Unfortunately, we've got a lease through next year that can only be ended if I sign off on it. So he's trying to make my life hell." Another snort. "Then he wants Linda's phone number."

"That Linda," I said. "Causing trouble everywhere she goes."

"She's no dummy," Rick said. "She helped me rework the schedule so I eliminated a cocktail shift. Also helped me sting a bartender who was skimming off the till. She runs this place when I'm not here. Not that I don't think she fills that uniform like a sausage casing." He blew out smoke. "She's got enough guys crazy over her to start a support group."

"Bobby Lee told me about her boyfriend," I said. "Lawless."

"Ex," Rick said. "Ex-boyfriend."

"Think he's the one who stuck Tiger Moore?" I asked.

"The cops think so," Rick said. "They were looking for him last I heard."

"You think they're right?"

"Who the hell knows?" He looked at me. "I guess you're talking about that crazy note someone slipped under Tiger's door."

"What'd the note say?"

"I didn't see it. I just heard about it from Linda. Could be Lawless. Could be some guy Jeff Holden hired, for all I know."

"Holden?" I said. The entertainment director was gone now. "What for?"

"Scare off the comics," he said. "Make 'em think there's some mad heckler out there trying to kill 'em for working the club." He flicked an ash. "He may have succeeded a little too well. I called the hospital. Tiger's taken a turn for the worse."

"You mean he might die?"

Rick nodded.

"Holden wants those slot machines in here that bad?" I said.

"Everything he wants he wants that bad." He looked at his watch. "But while this place is still open, we got more shows to do. One more tonight, if I recall."

"I'll get Bobby Lee," I said.

"Good luck."

"He did well, the first show."

Rick nodded. "He always does, the first show."

"And the second?"

"You'll see," Rick said. "He gets crazy. I gave his name to the cops, too."

"Tiger's a friend of mine," I said. "And I was in L.A. the night he was stabbed."

Rick didn't smile. "Wish I could say the same."

SIX

Dave poked his head through the curtain for the second time that night. "Five minutes, guys."

Bobby Lee Garnett and I were backstage, getting ready for round two. The Bobby Lee I had worked with the first show was not the same Bobby Lee I was working with the second show. I had dragged him away from the blackjack tables, standing next to him through three rounds of "just one more hand." He went up, he went down, he broke even and he cashed out. The gambling affected him somehow. He was sullen, moody. After he'd cashed in his chips, he walked with the air of a bitter defeated man. Uh-oh.

I was sitting in a chair, drinking more water, reading a section of discarded newspaper. Bobby Lee was pacing while he finished what must have been his fifth bourbon and water. There had been only silence between us until Dave had spoken. Then Bobby Lee said, "Hey, 'fore he comes back here, whyn't you let me close the show?"

"What?"

"Let's trade places. I'll headline and you middle."

I shook my head automatically. "No."

"Come on, man. I need the extra money. I'm down."

43

"Down?"

"I been hittin' the tables too hard," he said. "I'm busted."

"That falls into the category," I said, "of things that are not my problem."

Bobby Lee suddenly kicked a chair so hard it shot across the floor and hit the wall, bouncing off and falling on its side. "Goddammit!" he roared. "I can't get a fuckin' break in this fuckin' shithole!" He threw his empty glass at the wall and it shattered.

I looked at the broken glass and fallen chair while he stomped off in the other direction. Maybe I should get a broom. "Why don't you quit while you're ahead?" I said. "We'll do this show and—"

Suddenly I was grabbed from behind. Bobby Lee had circled behind me and turned my chair around so we were face-to-face. His eyes were watery and bloodshot, his breath foul with hard liquor. He took hold of me by my upper arms, pinning me to my chair. Back in West Texas, he must have loaded hay and worked the oil fields. He was very strong. "Loan me fifty dollars," he said. "Just until tomorrow. You'll get it all back, plus another fifty."

"No," I said. "Let go of me, Bobby Lee."

"I tell you what," he said. He went down on one knee like he was going to propose. "You play a hand. Your money. I'll tell you when to hit and when to stay. We split the winnings, and—"

"I don't gamble, Bobby Lee."

"Then let me just have twenty bucks for the slots—"

"No."

"Gawdamn you, you self-righteous son of a bitch!" And with a roar he heaved me over on my side, chair and all. The twisting action loosened his grip. The chair hit the floor while I rolled over and up onto my feet just as Bobby Lee came charging at me, his hands out in front of him like claws, his teeth bared.

Behind me was a black curtain, angled away from the stage. I stood in front of it like a matador while Bobby Lee headed at me full speed. At the last second I stepped out of the way and let him charge into it headfirst, hooking his ankle with my instep.

Behind the curtain were tables and chairs stored for use in the showroom. Bobby Lee crashed into them, his cowboy hat falling off his head, his arms slowly twisting in the black velvet until he sank to the floor, his eyes rolling like slot reels.

Dave came back through the curtain, looked at me and then at Bobby Lee. "Oh, not again." He bent to help Bobby Lee up to a sitting position, planting the cowboy hat back on top of his head.

"What do you mean, not again?"

"He and Tiger got into it two nights ago," Dave said. He walked into the dressing room. I heard water running. He came out with a damp washcloth. "Tiger said Bobby Lee tried to get some money out of him."

"I'll have to ask Bobby Lee about that."

"Won't do you any good." Dave dropped his voice into a parody of Bobby Lee's accent. "That's 'coz Bobby Lee don't remember none." He switched back to his normal voice. "The only difference is it was Tiger Moore I was picking up off the floor," Dave said. "Bobby Lee was going through his wallet."

"You mean he mugged him?"

"I had to threaten to call hotel security to get Bobby Lee to hand the cash back over," Dave said. "Those guys didn't speak to each other after that." Dave bent down and lifted Bobby Lee's cowboy hat and dropped the washcloth on his balding head, tossing the cowboy hat aside. "Dumb ass."

Bobby Lee moaned.

"Bobby Lee, can you hear me?" Dave said. "We have to do a show."

"My head hurts . . ."

"I'll get you a drink before you go on," Dave said, as if to a child. "Want another drink?"

"Jack and Coke . . ."

"Coming right up." Dave stood. "You mind keeping an eye on him? Tell him the drink's waiting for him onstage. Then he'll be sure to come out and get it. I'm going to start the show."

I nodded. "Sorry I won't be able to catch your set."

"Yeah, right." Dave left through the curtains. I heard music start up, and then Dave took the stage. Hey, how you folks doing tonight? Welcome to the Comedysino in Las Vegas.

Bobby Lee felt around blindly. "My hat . . ."

It was three feet away from him. I kicked it into his hand. He put it on his head by touch, peeling off the washcloth.

"My guitar . . ."

I looked around. It was in its case. I moved that over to him with my foot, too. Bobby Lee slowly rolled over onto his hands and knees and stood up, using the black curtain to pull himself upright. He regained his balance as if he was walking a high beam.

"When do I go on?"

"Any minute."

He lifted his head to look at the chair on its side, the shattered drink glass, and then me, lost, hurt and confused. "What'd I do?"

"You got drunk and gambled away your cash," I said. "You wanted money from me so bad you took your best shot."

He stumbled toward the bathroom and threw up. More water running. Onstage, Dave was wrapping up. Bobby Lee came out of the bathroom, the front of his shirt damp, another washcloth to his forehead. He bent down like an old man to unlatch the hasps of his case and pull out his guitar, banging it once on the floor, the strings humming discordantly. "I don't 'member."

"You blacked out." Just like during your fight with Tiger Moore. But then you wouldn't remember if you broke into his room and tried to stab him, either.

"Where . . . where's my drink?" He looked around him feebly. "I thought I asked for a drink . . ."

"There's one waiting for you out there, Bobby Lee," I said, pointing toward the stage.

He looked at the curtain part: two strips of silver gaffer's tape showed where to walk through the heavy folds. "Out there, huh?"

We both heard Dave say Bobby Lee's name and the crowd break into applause.

"Have a good show, Bobby Lee," I said.

"Thanks, man," he mumbled as he dragged his sorry ass out onstage.

Bobby Lee stumbled around onstage for fifteen minutes before he knocked his drink off the stool, dropped his guitar and then ran offstage to go vomit again. He almost knocked me down on his way to the bathroom. Dave had the sense to hit the music and bound back onstage and try to salvage the segue into my act with what material he had left over from his opening set. I'd seen three couples walk out already. Oh boy. Why had Rick kept him on all week?

Dave brought me on and after the barest courtesy applause I went into stony dead silence and proceeded to eat the big kielbasa of comedy death. When it goes right it's heaven, but when comedy goes wrong there is nothing worse. I tried every trick I knew, and came up with a few new ones. The only thing I didn't do was take material from another comedian's act. I know some great unknown comedians. I could have helped myself and no one would have been the wiser, but you have to draw the line somewhere and I don't steal. I had someone steal my act once, but that's another story.

I was in Show Business Hell for the next forty-five minutes and when I got off, it was to half as many people as I'd gone up to. I'd walked half the house. It wasn't my fault, but that didn't help. If this wasn't one of my worst nights, it was in the bottom ten. I hadn't bombed like this in a while. I'm talking years.

I got off to the sound of little more than one hand clapping and left Dave to mop up. I went backstage to get a towel to soak up the flop sweat lining my face and hands when I saw Bobby Lee Garnett had passed out, half-in and half-out of the dressing room. I stepped over him and quickly stepped out. He hadn't made it to the toilet or the sink on his last trip aboard the vomit comet. Disgusting.

I went out the artist's entrance into the casino and ran into Dave. I jerked my thumb over my shoulder. "You got a cleanup on aisle five," I said.

"Oh, no," he said. "I hate it when he does that." Dave made a face. "Thank God tonight's his last night. Ever."

I kept walking, leaving Dave to deal with the mess. If this

47

was any other bad night I would head straight for my room and the minibar, but I had a few unanswered questions about the chain of events that had brought me here. Like . . . who was the next comedian to get a shiv in the side of his neck? Me?

I reentered the club through the door by the ticket booth. Busboys were cleaning the tables, waitresses counting their tips at the bar just on the other side of the double set of swinging doors. One of them was Linda. Dolores the ticket taker said good night to Rick, who was counting out twenties from a freshly broken pack: "Forty, sixty, eighty, four hundred." He handed me my cash. "Here you go, Kincaid. Twenty twenties."

I broke the bankroll in half and put two hundred in each pocket. I had an ankle wallet in my backpack, but that was in my room. "Thanks," I said. "Got change for a twenty?"

"Sure," he said. "What do you want?"

"Two fives and a ten."

Rick broke down one of my bills. "Hitting the tables?" he asked.

"Not just yet."

"I gotta run to the office," he said, "but I'll be back to lock up. Sit down. Have a drink."

I nodded at him and found a booth along the lower level. No sense letting free alcohol go to waste. I took a seat and felt in my pocket for my drink tickets.

A white-jacketed busboy walked by with a plastic tub full of dirty glasses. I held out my drink ticket between two fingers, the two five-dollar bills folded just behind it.

"I'll get a waitress," the busboy said without slowing down.

"Nuh-uh." I moved my fingers so one five showed. He slowed, then stopped. "This is for you," I said, "if you bring me back a beer from the bar."

He took the drink ticket and the first five. "Okay."

I held out the second five. "And this is for you if Linda brings it back."

"What does Linda get?" he asked.

"One of these," I said and laid the ten on the table.

He took the second five. "Kinda beer you like?"

"Guinness. Draft. In a pint glass."

"I can't drink that shit."

"No one's asking you to." I handed him my second drink ticket. "Get yourself whatever you want."

He walked through the swinging double doors to the bar. I waited. I counted three minutes by my watch until the doors opened slowly and Linda stepped through, a pint of beer so dark I couldn't see through the glass balanced on her tray. She brought it to me with a flourish, setting down a coaster first, and then the pint.

I slipped the ten on her tray. "Care to join me?" I said.

"I don't drink with customers."

"I'm not a customer," I said. "I'm a comedian."

"I don't drink with them, either."

"Doesn't leave us a lot of options, does it?"

She looked at me, still standing, the ten on her tray.

"I get this a lot," she said. "Guys hitting on me."

"I just want talk," I said. "No action."

"I get that a lot, too."

"Rick Partino tells me you're smart, so I won't act dumb," I said. "I know I'm here because this week's headliner got stabbed in his room."

She kept standing. "Tiger Moore," she said. "How's he doing?"

I shook my head. "Not good. Now I'm trying to figure out if that attack was something against Tiger Moore, against the club or maybe just the headliner of the evening."

"What concern is it of yours?"

"I knew him."

"Friend of yours?"

I nodded.

"Don't know how you can help him either way now," she said. "I hear he got cut pretty bad."

"I'm not curious just for his sake," I said. "If I'm filling his slot, maybe that makes me a target." I shrugged. "For all I know the same psycho who tried to put a blade through Tiger's neck was in the crowd tonight, and I sure as hell hope it wasn't at the second show."

"What do you think I know about it?"

Up close she was even more beautiful than she had been from the stage. "Tiger Moore got a threatening note, maybe from a jealous ex-boyfriend of yours named Lawless," I said.

She glanced at the double doors leading to the bar and sat down, putting her cork-lined tray in front of her. The ten-spot went into a pocket. "You pick up a lot of information very fast," she said.

"Tiger show you this note?"

She nodded. "He gave it to me."

"What'd it say?"

"Just something like 'You're not funny.' "

"That's it?"

She nodded again. "I still have it."

"Why didn't you give it to the police?"

One thick, finely formed eyebrow arched perfectly. "The uniformed officer I spoke to had seen me dance topless in a show. He wanted to know more about how long it had been since I'd broken up with Lawless and if I'd started seeing anyone else."

"So you didn't tell him about the note . . ."

". . . because he never asked," she said.

"Where is it?"

"At home or in my car."

"I'd like to see it."

"I'll leave it for you at the front desk tomorrow."

"When's the last time you talked to Lawless?"

She sighed. "About an hour ago," she said. "On the phone."

"He hear about the stabbing?"

"I'll say," she said. "The police have him in custody."

"They think he's their man?"

She looked down at her tray. "I don't know," she said. "They went to pick him up after his last show at the Coliseum and he resisted arrest."

"Quite a temper to take a swing at the Las Vegas blues."

"Now you know why he's called Lawless," she said. "He's been in trouble with the police before. And the IRS. And the state highway patrol. He's got a rap sheet with all of them." She shook her head. "I couldn't take it anymore. That's why I left him. That's when he started stalking me."

"Here at the club?"

"Everywhere. Home. Work. The gym. Even out with friends. I'd look through the window of a restaurant and there he'd be. Just . . . watching me."

"There's laws against that," I said.

"That's in California," she said. "And Lawrence—that's his real name, Lawrence Porter—obviously doesn't care about laws."

"The police have him locked up for tonight, you say?"

She nodded. "Thank God."

"He ever see you talking to Tiger Moore?"

"Once," she said. "That was all it took. If he saw me talking to you right now, believe me he'd let you know he didn't like it."

"He ever threaten Tiger Moore?"

"After the show Friday night," she said. "Challenged Tiger to a fight. One of the bartenders called security."

"Last question: Lawless have any reason to be suspicious about your friendship with Tiger?"

She shook her head. "We weren't really friends. He just hung out a lot the first couple of nights and then he got that note. Tiger's a nice guy and he never tried anything, but . . . why are you smiling?"

"Something Bobby Lee said about you having to fight stares off with a stick. I guess he was right."

"Bobby Lee definitely falls into that category."

"Most comics would."

She looked at me and let a small amount of time go by. "You I wouldn't fight too hard."

My turn to let some time go by while we maintained some significant eye contact. "Thanks for playing along out there," I said, "during the first show."

"I wasn't playing." She stood up, tucking her tray smartly under one arm. "I like redheads." Then she walked away and I watched her walk. At the double doors she turned around one last time, in profile. There was no mistaking the message in her silhouette. "Enjoy your beer."

SEVEN

There was one more surprise that night.

After talking to Linda I took my pint of Guinness up to my suite and quaffed it slowly as I looked out over the nighttime Las Vegas Strip from the living room of my suite, wondering how my name would look on each of the marquees. A little after midnight I drained the last of the caramel-colored foam from my glass and stripped for bed, stuffing my clothes into a laundry bag for the hotel valet. On the road again.

I was barely dozing off when there was a knock at my door. I grabbed the courtesy robe from the bathroom. I rifled through my backpack for a can of pepper spray I carried just for surprise visits like this. A comedian carrying four hundred in cash was a ready target, not to mention I was already keeping one eye open for whoever stabbed Tiger. I could be getting an after-midnight visit from Bobby Lee or the Man in the Leather Hood.

When I looked through the peephole and saw who was standing there, I forgot all my suspicions. I unlatched the door and opened it.

"Hi there," I said.

"Sorry to get you out of bed," Linda said. She had changed from her waitressing outfit into tight-fitting faded jeans with strategically placed rips along the thighs and knees. She wore an amber Lycra halter under an open flannel shirt. She reached into the breast pocket of the shirt and slowly pulled out a folded piece of paper. "You said you wanted to see this?"

I took it from her, opening the door even farther. "Come on in."

She stepped in and I closed the door behind her. Only the bedroom light was on but the living room of the suite glowed red, blue and green from the night lights of Las Vegas. "I've never been in one of these before," she said. "Not that I haven't had plenty of offers." She moved around the room with a slow sensuous dancer's gait.

The envelope was addressed on the outside to TIGER MOORE, COMEDIAN. I opened the note inside. It was a sheet of fancy stationery, five inches square. In blocky thick letters were the words: YOU'RE NOT FUNNY.

That was it. The letters looked as though they were drawn with a Magic Marker. I couldn't get anything more from it. "The police should see this," I said.

Linda took off her flannel shirt and draped it over the back of a chair before sitting down and putting her feet up on a padded leather ottoman. "So give it to them," she said, kicking off her shoes. She put her bare feet on the soft buttery leather. "Oh, that feels good."

I put the note in the drawer of a writing desk. "Glad it was still in your car."

She shook her head slowly from side to side, letting her mouth fall open. "Home." She reached down and started to unbutton her jeans, letting me watch her.

I took a step toward her. My face was beginning to feel warm, as well as other parts of my body. My hands were in the pockets of my robe. I took them out. "You went all the way home and back just to bring me that note?"

Another slow shake of the head. "No." She stood up and dropped her jeans, stepping out of them toward me, still in her Lycra top. "I came back here for something else."

I stepped closer so she could reach the knot on the belt on my robe.

We made love by the lights of Las Vegas, using the leather couch as our bed. Red-and-green streaks washed across her face as it twisted in pleasure with her first orgasm. She might have given up dancing, but she remained as limber and strong as ever. Later, she turned herself away from me before we joined again, snapping her hips back and forth in a tangy rhythm as she looked out the window, churning us both into a frenzy. Ride 'em, cowgirl.

I dragged a blanket from the bed and we lay on the couch, warming the cool leather upholstery and each other with the heat from our bodies. We watched the lights change and flare against the window glass like flames in a fireplace.

"When you saw me standing outside your door," she asked, "were you surprised?" She had a low mellifluous voice that made a nice whisper.

"I still am," I said. "Pleasantly so."

She bunched some blankets around her shoulders and turned into me, tucking her length along mine. "When you think about it, it only makes sense," she said. "Lawless is in jail. He's been stalking me ever since we broke up. That was a month ago. Any man that even talked to me was scared off. So tonight was . . ." She made a gesture that ended in the air.

"Girl's night out?"

"Exactly." She laughed. "You're so funny."

"It's in my job description," I said.

"You'd be surprised how many comedians aren't."

"No, I wouldn't."

"Well, they're not as cute as you, that's for sure. I told you I liked redheads," she said. She sat up on one elbow, studying me. "But you're more of a strawberry blond."

"I get that a lot."

"Do you like dancers?"

"I do now," I said. "What made you give up dancing?"

"I injured my knee."

"They both work fine, far as I can tell."

She lifted one leg straight up and pointed. "See that scar? I had to have an operation."

"Does it still bother you?"

"Sometimes."

"How about now?"

"A little bit."

"Want me to kiss it and make it all better?"

"You can start there," she said, moving the blanket to the floor, "and work your way up."

I woke up at noon. By myself.

Around dawn Linda and I had worked our way from the couch to the bed, after a stop in the bathroom to test the true uses of a sunken tub with a Jacuzzi. I wasn't going to the Old Comedians' Home without some stories to trade.

I lay in bed alone, amid a tangle of covers. I got up to find my clothes cleaned and pressed and hanging from the doorknob, and a letter from Linda on the breakfast table written on hotel stationery. Thank you so much for last night. Call me. Area code 702 . . .

I showered and dressed and found Tiger's note where I'd left it. With the desert sunlight streaming through the living-room windows and over a pot of black coffee it didn't yield any more clues. YOU'RE NOT FUNNY.

I checked out of my room while I was still in it, using a computer hookup on the TV. I closed up my luggage after checking my plane ticket. I had an open return for today. Flights ran well into the evening. Plenty of time to play comedy detective before the next week's comics showed up.

I checked my bags with a bell porter, tipping heavily, then went downstairs. The Comedysino's business offices were on the ground level, next to the buffet line. As I walked by, it smelled like a good idea.

Only Dave was in the office, answering phones and opening mail. Instead of his tuxedo, this time he wore jeans and a sweatshirt that said UNLV. He hadn't shaved. "Kincaid," he said upon greeting. "You headed back to L.A.?"

"Not just yet," I said. "Thought I might hit the buffet first."

"Sure." Dave reached in a drawer and initialed a meal ticket before handing it to me. "Try the Chinese chicken salad. They make it fresh."

"Thanks," I said, pocketing the buffet pass. "Is Rick around?"

"He should be in shortly. Anything I can help you with?"

"I need the name of the police detective investigating the Tiger Moore stabbing," I said. "You meet him?"

"Yeah. I got his card here somewhere," Dave said. He searched his rather messy desk and then his wallet. "Here. Detective Charles Gregory." He handed me a business card with a gold shield printed on it. Below that was a badge number.

"Can I make a copy of this?"

"You can keep it," Dave said. "It was in case any of us thought of anything else pertaining to the case and you obviously did." He waited a beat. "You want to tell me what it is?"

"I got some evidence he might be interested in."

"Like what?"

"The note that Tiger Moore received as a threat before he was stabbed."

Dave lifted both eyebrows. "Where'd you get that? Tiger?"

"Linda."

"Linda Mallory? The waitress? The one who looks like Elizabeth Hurley?"

I nodded.

"When did she give it to you?"

"Last night."

I shouldn't have said that. "I see," Dave said. He twisted his mouth into a sardonic line. "Biff Kincaid cracks the case."

"The police might beat me to it," I said. "Still don't know who wrote this note to Tiger. How's he doing, by the way?"

"Let me page Rick and see if he knows anything," Dave said. "He's in a meeting right now with the hotel's entertainment director."

"Jeff Holden?" I asked.

"You meet him?"

"I saw him talking to Rick last night."

"The guy hates us," Dave said. "Wants to close us down so he can put in more slot machines. Rick won't let him, though. The club's too important to him."

"Why?"

"There's Comedysinos in Reno, Tahoe and Atlantic City, all doing well. The main office is in New Jersey. For some reason, they've never been able to establish a stronghold in Vegas and it bugs the hell out of them. Rick's their only representative out here and he's holding firm."

Ah, trusting youth. "Holden just hasn't found the right combination," I said. "He's tried fear and intimidation." I patted the note in my pocket. "Rick thinks he might be behind these threats and what happened to Tiger Moore. But if none of that works, Holden will try something else."

"Like what?"

I shrugged. "Maybe Rick's holding out for a piece of the action. Or maybe just a nice big check."

Dave looked at me. He hadn't lived long enough to think this way about people. "You think you know Rick that well?"

"Hey, when it comes to money I don't know anybody." I'd been sitting on his desk. I got up. "What hospital is Tiger at?"

"First Methodist."

"I'll call or come by before I hit the airport," I said. I slipped into a decent Bogart impression. "Until then I'll be working the clues."

"You gonna catch this guy, Kincaid?" Dave asked.

I pointed a finger at him like a gun and winked as I walked out the door.

Detective Charles Gregory was a six-foot-four-inch-tall black man with a heavy jaw and receding hairline, little corkscrews of gray creeping in just above his ears and into his mustache. He wore a plain blue oxford shirt with a modest silk tie and baggy khaki trousers. Not a snappy dresser, but he could go from the squad room to a crime scene and not have to stop to change. Underneath the clothes his middle-aged physique was hard and lean. He had the simple weary purposefulness I'd come across

in other policemen. Right now his steady brown eyes were looking at the note I'd just handed him.

I had come to the police station and asked for him, telling
him I had evidence in the Tiger Moore stabbing. I'd waited
twenty minutes before he'd shown up. He had a crushing grip
and wore a gun in a leather shoulder holster.

He looked up from the note. "Who gave this to you?" he
asked.

"A waitress at the Comedysino."

"I need a name."

"Linda Mallory."

"Who gave it to her?"

"Tiger Moore. How's he doing?"

"Friend of yours?"

"And comedy colleague."

"He's still unconscious," he said.

"Oh."

"Yet to tell us anything."

"What about the witness staying in the room next door?" I
said. "The one that saw the attacker."

"He went back to L.A. after giving us a description. Suspect
is six feet even, black shirt, black pants, black shoes, black
gloves and a black leather hood he wore over his head like a
ski mask."

"Now there's a fashion statement."

Gregory looked at the note again. Then he pulled out a small
plastic evidence bag and put the note into one. "I'll send this
to the crime lab," he said. "See what they come up with."

"I understand you have Lawless in custody."

"Who?"

"His real name's Lawrence Porter."

"Oh." Gordon's demeanor went sour. "Him."

"Is he under arrest for the stabbing of Tiger Moore?"

"We don't have enough evidence to charge him with that
particular crime," Gordon said. He waggled the evidence bag
and dropped it in an interoffice envelope. "But maybe we do
now." He sealed the envelope and put it in a drawer. "He's being
arraigned on charges of assaulting a police officer."

"He take a swing at one of your men?"

"No," Gordon said. "He took a swing at *me*."

"I see."

"We'll get a handwriting sample from him," Gordon said. "See if it matches these notes. If not . . ." he shrugged. "We may be dealing with two people here: one who writes notes and one who stabbed Tiger Moore."

"But the one who stabs likes to write on the wall," I said, and was instantly sorry I'd done so.

"Oh, so you saw that, huh?" Gordon gave me his dead-eye look. "That's tampering with a crime scene."

"I didn't touch anything," I said. "I just went in to look around."

He nodded once, slowly. I don't know what the hell Lawrence "Lawless" Porter was thinking throwing a fist his way. "You have any other theories, Mr. Kincaid?"

"Yes," I said. "I think whoever did this is a comedian, or has worked in the comedy business."

"Come again?"

"This note. The writing on the wall. 'Get off the stage.' 'You suck.' 'You're not funny.' Every comedian has heard those remarks at one time or another. Those are heckles."

"They're what?"

"Don't you go to comedy shows?"

He shook his head slowly from side to side. "I don't have much of a sense of humor," he said. "That's what my wife tells me."

I kept talking. "Sometimes a comedian will get someone in the audience who wants to disrupt the show, who'll start heckling him. Giving him a hard time. It's one of the things you have to learn how to deal with when you start doing stand-up."

"And how do you deal with them?"

"Me? I put 'em away in a body bag."

Another level look. No, Detective Charles Gregory did not have much of a sense of humor.

"Bad choice of words," I said. "What I mean is I shut them up by coming back at them with the most vicious insults I can think of. You don't talk to them, ask them any questions or engage them in a dialogue. You put 'em down as quick as you can. Because if one heckler gets the best of you, you instantly have five more."

"This ever go beyond a verbal exchange?" Gregory asked. "It ever get physical?"

"Sometimes."

Gregory rubbed a hand over his lower jaw. I could hear his whiskers against his palm. He hadn't shaved this morning. "You think that's what this guy is? A heckler?"

"That or another comedian."

"Why would a comedian do something like this to another comedian?" Gordon said. "Stab him in the neck."

"Maybe Lawless Porter knows."

"He isn't telling us anything."

"Maybe he'll tell me."

Lawless was led into the visitor's area in chains. Detective Charles Gregory did not take kindly to a suspect resisting arrest. A uniform cop led him over to his seat across from me and then stood watch.

I was sitting on one side of a glass partition. The visitor's area was a long room that at one time had been painted a shiny apple green. Now it was a faded jade that smelled like spit and bleach.

Bobby Lee's description of Lawless had been accurate. He was at least six feet four inches tall, with muscles that showed even under his orange prisoner's uniform. He had a deep bronze tan and sculpted handsome features with shoulder-length hair. His eyes burned with a seething mistrust of anything they looked at. Right now that was me.

We each picked up phones to talk. Lawless had to hold his with both hands cuffed together.

"Who are you?" he said.

"Biff Kincaid," I said. "I'm a comedian."

His eyes narrowed. "You work the Comedysino at the Palace?"

"Yeah."

"This about that guy that got stabbed?"

"Tiger Moore."

He shook his head, his Samson hair moving over his massive shoulders. "I don't know nothing about that," he said. His voice was surprisingly soft, like Clint Eastwood's. The effect was similarly disconcerting. "I didn't knife that guy." He leaned forward. "Because if I did, he wouldn't still be alive."

"He barely is."

Lawless shrugged.

"You don't match the description an eyewitness gave the police," I said. "He described someone smaller than you."

Lawless sat back in his chair. "Glad someone believes me."

That wasn't what I meant, but I let it pass. "I don't want to talk to you as a suspect," I said. "I want to talk to you as a witness."

Now he was puzzled. "I didn't *see* this dude get stabbed, either."

"But you were hanging around the Comedysino a lot lately, weren't you?"

"Just keeping an eye on things."

"How often were you there?"

"Wednesday through Monday."

"Let me guess," I said. "Those were the nights Linda Mallory worked."

"She's my girlfriend."

Your ex-girlfriend, I thought. "And what hours were you usually there?"

"I had shows at the Coliseum at seven and nine. That's just a block away. I was at the Comedysino by the start of the ten o'clock show."

"I wanted to talk to you about this last weekend," I said. "What happened Friday night?"

Lawless sighed. "I got there right before the start of the ten o'clock show. I see Linda, but that asshole boss of hers—the greaseball?"

"Rick Partino."

"He won't let her talk to me because he secretly wants her for himself, so all she can do is look at me. Otherwise, she'd get fired."

"She tell you this?"

"She doesn't need to," Lawless said. "I know it for a fact. I know it makes her feel safer to know that I'm there."

I'll bet. "Go on."

"So the show starts and they got that little wimp that works the door—"

"Dave Tyler."

"—he goes on and he sucks eggs raw. All I can do to sit there and listen to him without wanting to go up onstage and smack him."

"Sure."

"He's only on for five minutes. Then he brings on this cowboy guy—"

"Bobby Lee Garnett."

"—and I'd heard he was supposed to be funny. But he was drunk as hell and forgot the words to his jokes. Slurred his words. Played his guitar out of tune. Some people asked for refunds."

"What about Tiger Moore?"

Lawless snorted. "It was while Bobby Lee was onstage I see Tiger Moore come into the club, and he just walks by me like he's better than everybody or something. He hangs out by the bar entrance and waits for Linda. She comes out and they start talking. He puts his hand on her shoulder. Whispers in her ear. Linda I can see wants to get back to work. Then . . ." Lawless's face was tight. His jaw flexed. "He kissed her on the cheek. She didn't want him to but he did anyway."

"So what did you do?"

"I waited for that little asshole by the front door. He comes my way and starts to head back out to the casino—this is while that hick is still onstage—and I grab him by his arm, and say 'We need to talk.' He tells me to let go and I say 'I'll let go of you when you let go of Linda' and he wants to know who I am again and I say 'never mind who I am. What's important is what I can do to you.' And then the little punk tries to get away, so I grab him with both hands and he starts whining like a little baby and that fuck face Dave goes and calls security."

"What happened then?"

"A couple of these rent-a-cops showed up and asked me to

leave. I told them I worked over at the Coliseum and just wanted to hang out. They said okay, but stay out of here, meaning the comedy club. I said I wanted to talk to Linda and they went and got her and she got all mad at me for leaning on Tiger that way, but . . ." He shrugged. "Women don't always know what's good for them."

"You been back since?"

"No."

The uniform cop watching us tapped his watch and held up three fingers.

Lawless looked at the cop and then at me. "That it?"

"Almost," I said. "When did you hear about Tiger Moore getting stabbed?"

"Last night when the cops told me."

"Not from Linda?"

"No." He turned his head to look at me more closely. "How do you know so much about Linda?"

"I'm Tiger Moore's replacement," I said. "I flew in from L.A. yesterday."

"Yeah . . ."

"And Tiger had given Linda a note he'd gotten," I said. "Thought it was from you. Linda said it wasn't your handwriting. I got it from her and gave it to the cops. It's being sent to the lab. It could get you out of here."

Lawless wasn't interested in hearing about any note. "That all?"

"That all what?"

"That all you talk to Linda about?"

"No."

He leaned forward, his eyebrows making a V. "What else?"

"We talked about you," I said.

"And?"

"She's not in love with you anymore," I said. "I don't know that she ever was. Stalking her, following her, obsessing over her . . . it scares her. She's glad you're in jail. That makes her feel safe."

He gripped the phone in both hands so tight his knuckles started to pale. "You watch what you say to her," he whispered in his menacing feather-light voice. "Matter of fact, I don't want you talking to her anymore."

"What are you in here for?" I said. "A day? Maybe two? Then you get bail?"

"You wait until I get out," he said. "I'll see what Linda has to say about me."

I didn't want that to happen right away. I wanted to buy myself—and Linda—some more time. I had a flash of inspiration as to how to keep Lawless on ice for a while.

"Then you might be interested to hear what Linda has to say about me," I said.

There was a scraping sound as Lawless leaned forward, scooting his chair back, the phone in his hands, trying to stand up. The glass partition was scarred from other assaults. I hoped it would withstand this one. "What'd you do?" he said. "What'd you do to my Linda?"

The uniform cop stepped forward, hand on his waist. He carried a can of Mace on his belt. He unsnapped the leather top with his thumb.

I looked up at him from my chair, the phone held casually to my ear. I don't like to kiss and tell, but if it would keep him behind bars . . .

"I screwed her," I said. "Last night she came to my room and we did it. All night long."

He shot forward, his hands and head banging on the glass. It bent, but didn't give. The phone fell from his hands and I could hear him scream in rage: "Liar!"

The cop standing guard pressed a button on the wall. He was going to need backup. So far, this ought to add a good ten days to Lawless's time. I wanted to make it an even thirty.

"Oh, I'm not lying," I said through the glass. He shut up and picked up the phone to listen to me. "How else would I know about the surgery scar she has on the inside of her left knee?"

I stood up and stepped away. Lawless charged the partition like a mad buffalo, trying to get at me, his mouth open and snarling, eyes blazing, a vein throbbing across his forehead. He smashed his handcuffs against the glass partition. Once. Again.

The glass started to crack.

I glanced at the cop standing watch on Lawless's side. He was reaching for his gun now, yelling at Lawless to sit back down.

Lawless reared back like a striking animal and heaved his entire body at the glass partition and it shattered, scattering pieces across the chair I'd just been sitting in. Lawless crawled up on the table separating us on his knees, screaming, grinding broken glass into his legs as he lurched forward, blood streaming from his lacerated hands and over his steel restraints, just wanting to get at me.

I picked up the chair I'd just been sitting in. I shook the broken glass off of it and got ready to swing.

Lawless got to his feet, his chains holding him in a crouch, and bent one knee to spring himself at me through the air. I don't think even a chair was going to be much good against him. Maybe I'd overplayed my hand. Kincaid, I thought, you've done it now.

At that moment, uniformed jail guards streamed into the prisoner's side of the visiting area. They swarmed over Lawless like marauding ants, but he still stood, swinging his fists two-handed, sending one guard flying, another doubling over at the waist, and then their batons rained down on him with too many blows for him to count or resist.

I put my chair down and turned to go. Detective Gregory was in the visitor's doorway, his hands ready at his sides, watching in dismay as Lawless was dragged away, maced and subdued, still yelling.

"I knew letting you talk to him was a bad idea," he said.

"Doesn't act much like an innocent man, does he?" I said.

"He better be innocent," Gregory said. "I just got off the phone with the hospital. Tiger Moore's dead. This is a homicide case now."

EIGHT

An assault case is one thing; a murder investigation is another.

Detective Gregory had had enough of me and my clever insights into the death of Tiger Moore. He wondered aloud how much it would cost to replace the glass partition in the visitor's room at the jail as he showed me to the door. He was done with me. I'd worn out my welcome.

I caught a cab back to the Palace and without bothering anyone at the Comedysino I got my bags from the bell desk and headed for the airport. Time to get back to L.A.

I had one other person to ask about why Tiger Moore was dead, and it wasn't anyone in Las Vegas. It was a long shot, but I thought if anyone could tell me what happened, it would be Louie Baxter, the comic who had brought Tiger Moore around to the Comedy Store many months ago.

I caught a flight from Vegas to L.A. at three in the afternoon. I made it home to Beachwood Canyon before rush hour. I unpacked, checked my messages and called the Comedy Store. I was booked every night through the weekend, starting tonight at nine-forty-five in the Original Room.

My next call was to the number for Louie Baxter I'd gotten from the Comedy Store. Disconnected. He'd moved again. Not surprising. You get a hit sitcom, the first thing that changes is your address.

I walked down to the bookstore on Franklin Avenue just below the Canyon and bought the trade papers. Every Tuesday one of them—either *Variety* or the *Hollywood Reporter*—published the names of all broadcast and cable TV series currently in production and who produces them.

I found it in the *Reporter*: *Baxter's Place* was produced by Mission Control Productions in association with Gottschalk Entertainment. Gottschalk Entertainment was the offices of Max Gottschalk, Louie's manager. Back at home, I thumbed through an industry guide I had and found phone numbers for both offices. I tried Mission Control Productions first. I'd seen their logo at the end of what episodes of *Baxter's Place* I'd caught on TV. It was archival film of an Apollo LEM touching down.

I dialed.

"Mission Control."

"Louie Baxter's office, please."

"One moment."

Hold hold hold . . .

"This is Erica."

"I'd like to speak to Louie Baxter, please."

"He's in a script meeting at the moment. May I take a message?"

"Tell him Biff Kincaid called." I left my number.

"Will he know what this is regarding?"

"Not yet he won't," I said.

She didn't know what to say to that. "I'll be sure to let him know you called."

"That should do it."

I hung up. Just for grins, I called over to Max Gottschalk's office.

"Gottschalk Entertainment."

"May I speak to Louie Baxter, please?"

"He's in a producer's meeting right now," the female voice said. "May I take a message?"

I thought so. They didn't want to say he was in, they didn't want to say he was out. "Biff Kincaid," I said.

"Pardon me?"

"That's the message." I said. "I'm Biff Kincaid and I called."

I hung up and I waited. Something else was up and no one wanted to say.

Hmmmm . . .

I walked back down to the bookstore on Franklin. I was looking for a different kind of entertainment publication this trip and they didn't sell them. The neighborhood supermarket did, though, and they were just a little farther east. They had all three tabloids I was looking for, right by the checkout stand. The *Enquirer*. The *Globe*. The *Star*.

I took them back home and leafed through them, learning more than I wanted to know about public people's private lives. I found Louie's name and face in a cover article entitled "Backstage Battles of TV's Funniest Families!"

Small words in big type explained how several sitcoms were beset by sniping and jealousy among the cast:

> And on the set of *Baxter's Place*, one of the top-rated new series of last season renewed for fall, several coworkers are complaining to producers about how Louie Baxter has gone from a grateful unknown stand-up comedian getting his big break to a swaggering star who demands script changes for scenes he's not even in, limos to travel the fifty feet from his trailer to the set, and bodyguards who harass and intimidate fans.
>
> "He claims to have gone clean and sober after his second rehab," says one insider, "but he's spending a lot of time in his dressing room. If anyone new shows up on the set, he has private detectives check them out."
>
> Baxter is so paranoid about security that for the first show taping of the second season everyone had to wear a special color-coded pass. The girlfriend of one of the writers stuck her pass in her purse and before she knew it, Louie's burly bodyguards had hustled her out into

the parking lot and were threatening to toss her off the lot before she could explain herself.

The writer stormed off the set and had to be coaxed back with a personal apology from Louie.

And on the set of *Low Lifes*, the fur flew when . . .

So Louie Baxter was rumored to be back on the snort and the sauce. Second rehab? He was a party animal when I worked with him, and now with fame and fortune he had unlimited access to Hollywood's twenty-four-hour circus. No wonder he was in two different meetings in two different offices at the same time. If I called his house, I'm sure he'd be there, too, just unable to come to the phone. Perhaps he was trying to throw someone off. Or trying to lure them in.

I wondered if he had gotten any notes similar to that left for Tiger Moore. I wondered if he knew Tiger Moore was dead.

I didn't have to wait long to find out. My phone rang. "Hello?"

"Biff Kincaid?"

"Yeah."

"What are you doing calling Louie Baxter?"

The voice was deep but soft, just loud enough to get the message across.

"I'm a comedian," I said. "I want to talk to him—"

"About what?"

"Can I finish my sentence?"

The slightest of pauses. "Sure."

"I wanted to talk to him about a mutual friend."

"Who?"

"Tiger Moore."

"I know Tiger."

"And who are you?"

"A friend of Louie's."

"So am I," I said. "But I don't call people back and ask their business with him."

"Quit complaining," the voice on the phone said. "Some phone calls don't get returned. What's going on with Tiger?"

"He's dead."

Silence. I could hear a hand being put over the receiver. Words were spoken. I couldn't make out what and to whom. Then the hand was taken away and the phone traveled to another hand.

"Kincaid?" A different voice. High and froggy and familiar.

"Hi, Louie," I said.

"What—what happened to Tiger?"

"He's dead," I said. "Someone broke into his room at the Palace in Las Vegas and stabbed him to death."

"What's the name of the room up there?"

"The Comedysino."

Long silence. "Was he playing the Comedysino?"

"Yeah."

"The cops catch whoever did it?"

"Not yet."

"How long ago this happen?"

"He got stabbed Sunday night sometime after midnight," I said. "I flew in and did the show Monday. He died this morning around noon."

"Jesus," Louie breathed.

"There's more," I said. "I don't know if you want me to say everything I have to say over a cordless phone when someone could listen in."

Appealing to his paranoia worked. "Where are you?" he asked.

"Home," I said. "Beachwood Canyon."

"Can you come to the studio?"

"Sure."

"Let me leave a pass for you at the gate. When can you be here?"

"Fifteen minutes."

"Okay," Louie Baxter said. "Fifteen minutes. I may still be in rehearsal, but you can hang and relax and we'll talk when I'm done."

"See you then."

I hung up.

NINE

Baxter's Place was taped out at the Radford Studios, in Studio City, or Sitcom City as it was known among comedians. It housed a large concentration of soundstages ready to accommodate live audiences for tapings. It was close to where I lived in Beachwood Canyon: just a short hop on the Hollywood Freeway to Laurel Canyon, a quick right and you were there. From the outside, it's a gated compound with guards. Inside, the atmosphere is that of a college campus—people on bicycles, pedestrian traffic, battery-powered carts—except all the lecture halls looked like airplane hangars. Sometimes the doors were left open and passersby could look in and see where TV was made. Not always a pretty sight.

I drove my RX-7 up to the gate and gave the guard my name. I got a little yellow pass to wear on my dashboard and some quick directions to the soundstage where *Baxter's Place* was being shot. I parked close to the entrance, so I wouldn't lose my car. I hadn't been there enough times to know my way around. I wandered among the tall, wide windowless buildings and acted like I belonged there. Who knows? One of these days there might be a Biff Kincaid show, if the gods of luck and laughter were kind enough.

The soundstage wasn't hard to find. On the outside of the giant walls was painted the show's logo. At the one labeled *Baxter's Place* I found a side door with a bored security guard acting as host.

He nodded at me. "You got a pass?"

"On my car."

"That's a lot pass."

"What other kind of pass do I need?"

"You need a stage pass."

The guard was tall and weedy with big-lidded blue eyes and a droopy black mustache. He didn't look like much but he carried a gun and it didn't seem too heavy for him. He had been leaning on his hands. Now he wasn't.

"How do I get a stage pass?"

"Your name on the list?"

"What list?"

"The visitor's list."

"My name's Biff Kincaid," I said. "Louie Baxter asked me to come see him. He didn't say anything about lists or passes."

He unhooked the mike on his walkie-talkie. "Mobile four to base."

A reply came back: "Base copy." I recognized that voice. It was the same soft deep voice I'd spoken to on the phone before Louie had been allowed to talk.

"Have a visitor."

"Name?"

"Biff Kincaid."

"Visual."

The guard clicked off the mike. "Would you step over here, please?" He used the mike to point to an X taped on to the asphalt.

"Sure," I said. I stepped over the X.

"Face the wall please."

"Okay." I felt like I was getting my driver's license renewed. I heard the slight hum of an electric motor and looked up. A security camera was angling itself to look down at me from about ten feet up. When it reached me I waved.

The walkie-talkie crackled. "Got him."

A moment's pause. I stood looking at the camera and the guard stood looking at me. A good time to make a joke. "One to beam up, Mister Scott," I said in my best Captain Kirk voice.

The guard didn't smile. "Everybody says that."

I switched to Bones McCoy: "Dammit, Jim, scrambling a man's molecules across the universe, it's not natural!"

Nothing.

"I kent dew much moore, Captain," I said in my best Scottish burr. "She's abooot ta blow!"

That cracked him up.

"Gotcha," I said.

"Stop," he said, shaking his head. "I got a job to do."

"I'm a comedian," I said. "I gotta try."

The voice on the walkie-talkie crackled. "Clear."

The guard's smile vanished. He reached for the stage door and opened it for me. "You know where to go?"

"No."

"Straight through, past the set, to the production office."

That made no sense to me. I nodded as if it did and stepped in.

The door closed behind me. I blinked, adjusting my eyes to the darkness. There wasn't much to see, but after a few seconds I realized that was because I'd come in the same way the audience members would and my view was blocked by bleachers set up to house them.

I walked around the elevated rows of seats to find the set, sitting in a pool of unfocused light that threw the jovial surroundings into deep shadows. There were three regular sets: Baxter's Place, the bar that Louie's character owned and operated; his basement apartment below the bar he shared with several bottles of supplies that fueled some late-night comic scenes; and the pizza parlor next door where the characters crowded around a table at the end or beginning of every episode for a slice and a smile.

The stage was completely empty except for a burly set worker wearing pants too baggy for him and a T-shirt too tight, wandering through, checking props. He looked up at me through horn-rimmed glasses. "Help you?" he said, not liking the sound of either word.

"I'm looking for the production office."

He lifted a hand and pointed once in reply and then went back to what he was doing.

"Thanks," I said, and headed in the direction he pointed.

The end of the soundstage led to a built-in hallway that housed dressing rooms, wardrobe and makeup. In the middle was a door left propped open that adjoined another building. I walked through, simply because it was normally lit and I heard a muffled sound of dialogue and then laughter punctuated by a few handclaps. A table reading of that week's script. I stepped toward the sound.

"Kincaid."

It was the whispery voice from the phone. I turned around, looking back toward the soundstage. The fluorescent-lit hallway contrasted poorly with the darkened set. I didn't see anyone, just the faint orange glow from the set and the deep shadows surrounding the bleachers.

One of the shadows moved and broke away from the darkness. "Here I am," it said, and stepped into the light.

He was about five-seven, shorter than I was, with a close-cropped fringe of black hair on the sides of his head. He was losing his hair on the front and top—hell, he'd lost it. He wasn't much past thirty, either, judging by the light sun wrinkles around his eyes and mouth. He had a heavy day's growth of black beard and curly chest hair that poked out the top of a black T-shirt under a denim jacket that bore the logo of *Baxter's Place* on one pocket and the name DIRK on the other. He wore tight jeans and laced steel-toed boots. Combat clothes. He had brown eyes and a round face with a Roman nose. He looked fashionably lethal. He moved with smooth springy steps, like a greyhound.

He had something in his hand: a squawking metal-detector bar, about a foot long. He motioned with his palms. "Get your hands over your head," he said. "I have to search you."

I complied. He ran the metal detector over my body, stopping at a pocket when it sang. I pulled out my keys. After that I was clean.

He stepped back and holstered the metal detector on a loop on his belt. "You're okay," he said.

"Let me guess," I said. "You're Louie's bodyguard."

"Dirk," he said. He nodded toward the continuing talk and laughs. "They're rehearsing right now. Louie asked if you wouldn't mind waiting in his dressing room."

"No."

"This way, then." He made an after-you kind of arm gesture and I walked ahead of him toward a wing that led away from the rehearsal hall. The wing led to another hall that was lined with doors, each marked with a cast member's name. I found the one labeled with Louie's name and put my hand on the knob.

Dirk stopped me. "That's not it," he said. "That's a decoy."

I walked farther down the hall and at the end was a door marked PAINT. I stopped outside it while Dirk unlocked it.

He did a quick sweep of the room while I stood in the doorway. It was about the size of a one-bedroom apartment, with a couch, some chairs, a TV, a VCR, a treadmill, a stereo, a small refrigerator, a phone, a computer, a coffee table piled with scripts, a closet and bathroom with a shower.

Dirk stepped lightly behind me and closed the door. "The trailer's being rigged with a new security system," Dirk said. "This is just temporary. Have a seat."

I parked on the couch while Dirk unhooked the metal detector from his belt and put it in the closet. Then he stripped off his denim jacket to show a nine-millimeter pistol in a shoulder holster. "You a cop?" I asked.

"Ex-LAPD." He opened the refrigerator and got out two bottles of mineral water. He handed me one as he sat down. "Now I'm private security."

"How long you been with Louie?" I asked.

"About three weeks," he said.

"And what prompted your mutual association?"

"He called me. I used to bodyguard another of his manager's clients." He grinned.

"What's funny?"

"Usually I'm the one asking the questions."

"Bad habit of mine," I said.

"Louie said you were like this," Dirk said.

"What else he tell you?"

"Not much," he said. "Said you weren't an easy guy to get to know. Funny comic, but something of a lone wolf." He got up from his chair and went over to the computer. He waggled the mouse and the screen came on. "So I had to check you out on my own."

I didn't say anything.

"Brian Francis Kincaid," he read off the screen. "Twenty-two sixty-eight Beachwood Plaza, apartment #12. Drives a red Mazda RX-7." He read me my license plate number, driver's license number and I stopped him at four digits into my social security number.

"So you ran a credit check," I said. "I haven't found those to be very accurate."

"I didn't stop there," he said. He left the computer and came back and sat back down in front of me. His movements were quick and lithe, his manner beguiling, his voice remaining soft. I didn't feel I was dealing with a stupid or unstable man. He did what a bodyguard was supposed to do; he made you feel safe. "I ran your bank account for wire transfers or checks from the tabloids. Looked at your phone bill. I've got the numbers of all the gossip stringers in town. You were clean."

I nodded, satisfied. So that's what this was about.

"Then I called my old cop buddies," Dirk said.

I waited.

"You killed a man," he said.

"Once," I said. "I'd like to keep it at that."

"What'd he do," Dirk asked, "to need killing?"

"I don't think he needed it," I said. "It was him or me. He had a pistol and I had a shotgun. End of life."

"How'd it happen?"

"Long story."

Dirk waited.

"He was a bodyguard," I said, "for a comedian who stole my act."

Dirk tilted his head like a dog who'd heard a curious sound.

"There more?" he asked.

"Yeah. I don't like people stealing my act."

"What happened to the comedian?"

"He's dead, too."

Dirk waited. I drank my water.

"I've killed people," Dirk said.

"Not like in the movies, is it?"

"No." He paused. "Looks good on the résumé, though."

His delivery was completely deadpan. I looked at him and laughed once in the back of my throat. "That's harsh."

He grinned. "Cop humor," he said.

I snorted again, repeating the joke. "Looks good on the résumé."

"Finally," Dirk said. "I made someone around here laugh."

Just then Louie Baxter came through the doorway, and it wasn't an easy fit. Louie was big, 225 pounds and six feet two inches of him. He was solid like a fullback, and to accentuate the image of an athlete gone to seed he wore a football jersey over a T-shirt and baggy jeans and beat-up sneakers. He had unruly brown hair that corkscrewed out from his head, small green eyes and a fleshy face that looked like it had gone a few rounds with a barstool. Louie's nose was slightly flat, his mouth wide and half-open and one and a half chins. He was a comedian in the mold of Jackie Gleason and Sam Kinison, big and heavy and full of too much energy to sit still for very long.

"Kincaid!" he said. He came over to me and lifted me up off the couch with a crushing bear hug. Big and heavy can also mean big and strong. He smelled of sweat, cigars and cinnamon rolls. "Great to see you, man."

When he let me go I remained standing. "Good to see you, too, Louie. You're doing well."

"Hah!" He slammed his dressing-room door shut on the sight of the other cast members heading for their dressing rooms. "Dealing with a bunch of Harvard kids writin' the show, Kincaid. They all worked on—what's 'at fucking college newspaper of theirs?"

"The *Lampoon*," I said.

"Yeah. What the hell's a lampoon anyway? Some kind of duck?"

"I think it's a form of satire."

He went for the refrigerator and rifled through the contents, pulling out a big bottle of Perrier. I guess work was over for the day. "Yeah, well, these fuckin' overeducated assholes think they know everything, but they don't know funny. What I need are some comics, you know?" He gestured with the bottle to see if I wanted another one.

I declined. He popped the screw top, took a gulp and kept talking. He was making fifty thousand a week and drank imported mineral water like it was Budweiser. "I tried to get Billy Ray in here. You know Billy, right?"

I nodded. "Billy's funny."

"Yeah, Billy's hysterical. Anyway, I can't get even him in a punch-up session. The producers say it's because Billy's not in the union. But you know why? Really?"

"Why?"

"He's too old." Louie gulped half of his bottle of water. "He's forty. My new executive producer had a seminar at UCLA for budding TV writers. Bragged about how no one on his staff was over thirty. Bragged about it." He gestured with his Perrier so hard foam sloshed over the top and onto the carpet. He was working himself up. "These fuckin' kids ain't been on the road, they ain't been in the clubs, they don't know life! Here, they're writing a show about a guy who's middle-aged, owns a bar and lives with his two brothers in the basement and they got me making jokes about the Ivy League and the Internet. I don't know any of that shit."

I noticed Dirk had become completely still, moving only to watch Louie. He had become a part of the chair he was sitting in.

"And the same EP got his frickin' job by pitchin' the network on how he was gonna boost the ratings another ten points by giving me a brother on the show! You watch the show?"

"Sure," I said, politely lying. I'd seen it only a few times on the road.

"All last year, twenty-six shows, I got a mom, I got a dad, no brother. This year, boom! I got a younger brother. Shows up on my doorstep, tells me he wants to be a comedian. They say it'll add a family dimension to the show. They ain't foolin' me. They got this kid from open-mike night at the Laugh Factory."

"He's a comic?" I said.

"That's a matter of opinion," Louie said. "He's twenty-two years old and a certified personal trainer. All he'd done was under-fives on soaps. The first week's script has him walking out of the shower with a towel wrapped around his waist. The kid has no timing, no delivery, no material . . . just a set of abs like a Polish accordion."

Louie finished his Perrier and found another, popping the top off, pausing before drinking, still standing up. He used to drink beer that way, and around the same time of day. Just as suddenly as his tirade had begun, it was over. "So," he said, "what happened to Tiger?"

I repeated what I'd told him over the phone as preamble. Then I told him what else I'd found out. "Tiger had gotten a note," I said.

Dirk spoke for the first time in five minutes. "What'd it say?"

" 'You're not funny,' " I said, "in capital letters." I looked at Louie. "I snuck into the room where he was stabbed and on the wall was another message: 'Get off the stage, you suck.' "

"Jesus," Louie said. Louie and Dirk exchanged a meaningful look.

"Go on," Dirk said.

"I met with the police detective investigating the assault— well, now it's a homicide," I said. "They thought it might be the jealous boyfriend of one of the waitresses Tiger was sweet on. The boyfriend's been stalking her since they broke up. He's in custody. He says he doesn't know anything about what happened to Tiger. When the cops tried to take him in he resisted arrest, so he's on ice for a while."

"Were there any witnesses to the attack of Tiger Moore?" Dirk asked.

"One," I said. "The man staying in the room next door to Tiger's. He ran out into the hallway when he heard the commotion and then saw the attacker flee down the hallway."

"He get a look at him?"

I nodded. "He was dressed entirely in black with a black hood or mask on to hide his features."

"A ski mask?"

"The eyewitness said it might have been made of leather."

"You get this eyewitness's name?"

I shook my head. "The police questioned him."

Dirk nodded. He would look into it. "They have any other suspects?"

"The police? No. I do."

Dirk leaned forward. "Tell me."

I told him about Bobby Lee Garnett and the Palace's interest in shutting down the Comedysino. Dirk listened. He was good at that. "Who was the detective you spoke to at the Las Vegas Police Department?"

I pulled out Charles Gregory's card. "Here."

Dirk took it and looked it over.

"Don't know if he's too keen an answering any more questions," I said, "especially if you say you know me."

"We have something else besides questions," Dirk said. He handed the card back to me. "We have a note of our own to show him."

I looked from him to Louie to back again. "What kind of a note?"

Dirk got up and walked over to the closet. He reached up to the top shelf and pulled down a shoe box. He opened the shoe box and pulled out a plastic bag. Already protecting the evidence. He walked over to me and showed me the note. Inside the plastic bag, the note was open so I could see what it said.

It was the same vellum paper, the same handwriting, the same everything. Only the message was different, written in blocky characters in permanent marker, like the author was making diagrams instead of letters.

STOP, it read. YOU'RE KILLING ME.

TEN

"When did you get this?" I asked.

Louie said, "I got back here—in my dressing room—after last Friday night's taping. It was about one in the morning. You know, tape day: you go until it's done." He pointed at the note as if it might still bite him. "It was left on top of the TV, propped up like a place marker at a fancy dinner."

"Who could have come in and left it there?" I asked. "Anyone?"

"Kincaid, I lock my dressing room when no one's here."

"Uh-huh." I turned it over in my hand. "This the first one you got?"

Dirk shook his head. "No. It's the second."

"Where's the first one?"

"I got it at home," Dirk said.

"What did it say?"

" 'Who told you to become a comedian?' " Dirk said, as if reading off a cue card. "Same paper. Same style handwriting. Or printing, if you want to call it that. Left taped to the bathroom mirror after tape day, two weeks ago."

"Door locked then, too?"

Dirk and Louie both nodded. "I dusted the whole place for prints both times," Dirk said. "Nothing."

"Think it's an inside job?"

"I did until I heard what you had to say," Dirk said. "Now I don't know what to think."

I handed the note in the evidence bag back to Dirk. "Louie, how long you known Tiger Moore?"

"Long time," Louie said. "We started out together."

"Where?"

"Chicago," he said. "Almost fifteen years ago. Hadn't seen him much lately, though."

"I heard you brought him around to the Store."

"Yeah, he came here to the set a couple of times. I had a spot that night at the Store. Thought I'd try to get him in, so I talked him up to the talent booker. He got some weekend spots there. Maybe played La Jolla. Hadn't heard much from him since, and that was a year ago." He shook his head. "Still can't believe he's dead. You know him?"

"Sure," I said. "We did a few gigs together. Good guy."

"Yeah. Funny guy."

"You know anyone bore him a grudge?"

"Not enough to kill him."

"What about you?" I said. "Make any enemies lately?"

"Now *that* list is getting longer every day," Louie said. "I fired a couple of writers. One of the cast members got replaced this season. I dumped my old manager. Now I got the tabloids on my ass and I'm suing them . . ." He shook his head. "I thought making it big was supposed to be a lot more fun."

"How about mutual enemies?" I said. "Someone who had it in for both you and Tiger?"

Louie blinked. "I'd have to think about that."

There was something there, something Dirk didn't see and wasn't meant to. Dirk was looking at me. If Louie didn't want Dirk to know, maybe I could get Louie to tell me in private.

I played along in front of the bodyguard. "While you're thinking," I said, "see if there's anyone else that might fit the pattern."

"What do you mean?"

84

"Anyone else that might be the target of these notes."

"Okay." Louie nodded. "But we gotta keep this quiet, Kincaid. I got some KGB action going on around here."

"It's my turn to ask you what you mean," I said.

"We got a spy," Louie said. "In-house."

"Someone's selling information to the tabloids," Dirk said. "They're saying that Louie's gone paranoid because he's drinking and doing drugs. As you just saw, that's not it all. He's been clean and sober for three months."

I looked at Louie and he wanted to look away. Something else there. Again.

Dirk said, "I instituted some extra security measures when this first note showed up. Now it's in the press this week. That information can only be coming from someone closely associated with the show." Dirk ran a hand over his bald head. "I'm trying to find out who that is. At first, I thought it was the same person who had left the note. You know: trying to drum up business. But now . . ." He spread his hands.

Louie looked at Dirk's watch. "Kincaid, you got plans for tonight?"

"I'm doing a spot at the Store at nine-forty-five."

"The Store? Great!" He turned to Dirk. "Let's go out to eat at the Palm and then hit the Store. I'll go on after Biff and then we'll head out to the Malibu house."

Dirk looked less than thrilled. "We got a rehearsal tomorrow morning at eight," he said.

"Hey, what are you worried about?" Louie got up and started putting on a jacket. "Dinner and a show. If it gets too late, we'll stay at the Westwood apartment. I got you and Biff looking after me tonight. How can I get into trouble?"

The Palm is in Beverly Hills on Santa Monica Boulevard, a classy steak house that only recently began to offer menus to its patrons. The regulars were honored with caricatures of themselves on the walls, often marking a favorite booth or table. Louie hadn't made the wall yet, so he always asked for the booth with Sam Kinison's face painted on the inside wall. The maître d' hugged Louie when he came in and when the menus arrived Louie waved them away. We ordered dinner salads, creamed spinach, a plate of onion rings and Louie had steak while Dirk and I had seafood.

"You eaten here before, Kincaid?" Louie asked, his eyes searching the room for other celebrities.

"Not nearly often enough."

"I love this place," Louie said. His eyes found me. "You know why?"

I shook my head. "Why?"

"No losers."

I had a Cajun blackened swordfish filet that almost covered my plate and Dirk had a lobster that looked like something from *20,000 Leagues Under the Sea.* We all drank iced tea. Louie got up to table-hop with producers, agents and managers he knew. I noticed every time he got to his feet Dirk watched him the entire time he was absent from the table.

The check came in a leather wallet and Louie paid it with a gold card, tacking on a fifty-dollar cash tip peeled off from a wad in his pocket.

"I gotta pee," Louie said, getting up for the last time.

"Me too," Dirk said automatically.

"Come on . . ." Louie said.

"No, I really gotta pee," Dirk said.

"I can't even go to the *bathroom* by myself?" Louie said, and the two of them headed off.

I wondered if Dirk was hired just to protect Louie from himself. I sat alone until the check came back with the tip still folded inside the leather wallet.

"Hi there."

I looked up into the face of a beautiful young woman of about twenty-five, with shimmering blond hair that fell down her shoulders in waves, wearing a short black dress that didn't cover a lot of tan skin. She had a full, toothy smile and dancing green eyes. A beauty.

"Hi," I said.

"Can I have a seat?"

"Sure," I said. "Until my friends come back. I think we're about to leave."

She slid into the booth like it was tailored for her. "You mean Louie Baxter?"

"Yeah," I said. "Him."

She had a drink with her. She set it on the table and took the straw in her mouth without using her hands, looking up to make sure I was watching her act sexy. "How's Louie doing these days?" she asked.

"Good," I said. "Louie's good."

"How do you know him?"

"Fellow comedian."

She used one hand to stir her drink slowly. "He keeping his nose clean?"

I smiled at her.

She batted her eyelashes. "What's so funny?"

"What's funny is you think I'm so stupid," I said.

She stopped stirring.

"I don't know who you string for," I said. "Which tabloid, I mean." I pointed out the window. "That Buick has been parked in the same valet zone since we sat down." I looked back at her. "Don't think I didn't notice you at the bar when I walked in. You pulled a cell phone out to make a call as soon as you saw Louie. When we walk out of here, we're going to get hit by paparazzi."

She leaned forward. She had dropped the mask of the flirtatious vixen. Now she was all business. Her eyes glittered like polished gems. "How would you like to make a thousand dollars a day for a ten-minute phone call to me?"

"By what? Selling out a friend?" I shook my head. "I'm a comic. I need money, I hit the road."

She had a card hidden somewhere on her and she laid it on the table. I picked it up. "You can call me at that number, anytime, day or night—"

"Hello, Sheryl," Dirk said. "Can you say 'busted'?"

She looked up at Dirk, like a vampire looking at a hammer and stake. "Time for me to go back to the bar, huh?"

"I trust you made no progress with our friend here."

She flicked her eyes at me. "Just introducing myself."

"Yeah, well, introductions are over, sweetheart. Go root through a movie star's garbage."

Sheryl scooted out of the booth and stood up next to Dirk. She was just a shade taller than he was. "See you on TV, Dirk."

"Tell the shutterbugs out front I'll be ready for them."

Sheryl walked away on black high heels. I watched her go. "Now that's trouble," I said.

"If she ever gets near Louie, it sure is. She's just his type." Dirk glanced over his shoulder where Louie was pumping the hand of a silk suit and tie. "What did she want?"

"Information."

"What'd you tell her?"

"Nothing."

"Yeah, she didn't look too happy." He looked down at me, still standing. "Your price too high?"

"Never set one."

"Most comics who come to see Louie want to sell him a script or get a part on the show."

I shook my head. "Not me."

"Not interested in TV?"

"Sure. But only if I can still be funny."

Another glance back at Louie. He was at another table, putting on an impromptu performance for the foursome there, staggering around like Frankenstein's monster. "You seen the show?"

"*Baxter's Place*? Yeah. Couple times."

"And?"

"It's not as funny as Louie's act."

Dirk grinned. "You sound like him."

"It's true."

"Hey, guys, ready to go to the Store?" Louie bounded back to our table. He was still wearing the same football jersey he had on at rehearsal. He was pumped up from his latest round of glad-handing. "Jesus, I just met the heads of development for two movie studios and another network," he said without waiting for a reply. "They all love me on the show."

"We got some paparazzi waiting for us out front," Dirk said.

"I'll be sure to put on my happy face."

"We want to make it quick," Dirk said. He tilted his head in my direction. He was referencing something they had talked about on the way to the bathroom.

"Okay. Uh. Biff?" He sat down in the booth next to me when he said my name. I had to scoot over.

"Yeah, Lou?"

"I need you to do me one giant huge favor," he said. He lowered his voice to let me know this was on the QT.

"What is it?"

He pulled an orange stub from his pocket. "I need you to get my car from valet parking so we can all make a clean getaway."

I looked at the ticket and then at him. "I don't follow you." I did, but I didn't like getting other people's cars for them.

"Get the car and give the dude who brings it this." Louie wrapped a twenty around the claim check. "We'll be watching through the window. Get in the backseat and we'll come out. Now, no matter what those assholes say, don't give them a picture."

"I doubt they'd run a picture of me."

"They will if I'm trying to pull you off a guy." He smiled wryly. "Come on, Kincaid. I hear you don't run from fights."

"It's a genetic Irish trait," I said. "Can't be helped."

He held out the claim check and the money. "Please?"

"Just this once, Lou," I said. "And just for you."

He clapped me on the shoulder. "I owe you one."

"You remember that when I collect."

He got up to let me out. Dirk was smiling at me. "Good man," Dirk said.

I didn't smile back. I had the feeling this was his idea. I headed for the door. I saw Sheryl sitting at the bar. She winked at me. I held her card out and waggled it between my fingers, then looked back at Dirk. He wasn't smiling anymore. Good. Teach him to make me an errand boy.

I walked out front and handed over the claim check and the twenty. The valet made a show of running for Louie's car, a silver Lexus sedan. As soon as I stepped outside I saw two photographers emerge from the Buick across the street. They ran through traffic, their hands on cameras with lenses the size of dinner plates. They had flashes that looked like motorcycle headlights.

They stood out in the gutter, waiting for the car to come around. One of them was short and portly, wearing a coat and tie, and another was tall and skinny, wearing a white T under a flannel shirt and his salt-and-pepper hair in a buzz cut. The short and portly one had a goatee and light brown hair cut full, and wore prescription sunglasses, the shades tinted light so he could wear them at night and still see.

"Hey, chief," Buzz Cut said. "Where's Louie?"

"Louie who?" I said.

"Louie your cokehead buddy," said Night Shades.

"I don't know anything, guys," I said. "I'm just the schmuck who has to stand out here and talk to you assholes."

They laughed at that but stopped when the Lexus came screeching up, the front fender nearly knocking Buzz Cut in the knee. "Hey, watch it, shithead!" he yelled at the valet.

The valet was wearing a white shirt, red vest and black pants. He had jet-black hair and a Latin complexion. He wasn't even as tall as Buzz Cut. "Joo watch where you stand, pastard."

"Fuck you, wetback," Night Shades said in response.

"You try that again I'll pull you out of that car and stomp your ass into the ground," Buzz Cut spit at the valet.

"I ready for joo hite now," the valet said, taking a step forward.

I heard the door to the restaurant open. I turned around. Dirk and Louie came trotting out. Buzz Cut and Night Shades went into combat stance, firing off flash after flash while yelling behind their viewfinders.

"Louie! Got any blow?"

"Louie! What about that stripper you screwed in rehab?"

"Louie! You gonna fire any more writers?"

"Louie! How about a toot?"

Louie's face was grim as he walked around behind the car and got in the passenger seat.

I felt Dirk's arm at my elbow. "Backseat, Biff," he said.

I dived into the backseat, turning around to see that Louie

90

had his head down as Night Shades' flash went off again and again, pressed up against the passenger-side window. It was like there was lightning inside the car.

The valet tried to block Buzz Cut's shots and Buzz Cut blinded him with his flash and then shoved him back against a parking sign, crouching down to take aim at Louie through the open driver door. Dirk stepped in his way and Buzz Cut shoved him aside.

What Dirk did next, he did very fast.

Buzz Cut's move against Dirk turned into a kind of an orchestrated fall, with Dirk stepping aside and lightly pushing sideways on Buzz Cut's shoving arm so he lost his balance and stumbled backwards against the curb, landing hard on his tailbone. Dirk had hardly moved and Buzz Cut was now sitting on his ass.

As Dirk tried to get in the car, Night Shades rushed around to hit Dirk from behind. Dirk closed the door and turned and when the photographer lunged at him, Dirk simply wasn't there. He dropped down and to the side, lifting up as Night Shades went over him to land on the sidewalk. Shades lifted his head once and fell back, moaning. Buzz Cut had yet to get back on his feet. The valet had regained his vision, enough to start kicking Buzz Cut's camera against a wall until the glass parts shattered.

Dirk opened the driver's side door and got in, hitting the gas. We peeled out onto Santa Monica Boulevard.

"To the Comedy Store," Dirk said.

ELEVEN

My spot at the Comedy Store was at nine-forty-five, and the schedule was running behind, so it looked like I wouldn't get on until a little after ten. Louie called the night manager of the Store on the way over to see if he could go on after me. We arrived at nine-thirty-parking in the back and going in through the kitchen. Louie spent ten minutes greeting every waitress and bartender with handshakes and hugs, ordering a round of Perriers for Dirk and me.

This is what I didn't like about spending time with famous people. You become invisible, a hanger-on, a part of the entourage. You become the guy who gets the car or holds the table or reads a script or gives someone a ride to the airport. I knew some comics who made that situation work for themselves very well. I never saw the benefit of concentrating on anyone's career but your own. If I wanted to do that, I would have become an agent or a manager.

I watched Dirk watching Louie. Every time Louie greeted an old friend, Dirk watched the handshakes and the hugs to see if anyone was passing him a bindle, a joint or a pill. It was Louie's management who had hired Dirk, and I figured it was Dirk's job to see that Louie stayed out of trouble and showed up at the set on time.

I'd had enough of watching other people do things. I heard laughter through the swinging kitchen doors, from an audience that was waiting for me. I gave Dirk a wordless nod and walked toward the Original Room.

I went into the Original Room to watch the other comedian wrap up. There were about fifty people in the audience. Joan Felton was on stage, and she was closing with a series of singing impressions to music on tape. She was killing.

I took a moment to read the crowd, see where the different pockets of people were and when and how they laughed. Almost subconsciously I took a breath in and let it out, feeling more relaxed and comfortable than I had all day. I was taking a break from the intrigue and mysteries of the last twenty-four hours and now going to get a chance to cut loose. Offstage was where I found falseness, pretense and subterfuge; truth and beauty were behind the mike and in front of the lights.

Joan ended—as she had ended her act for the last ten years—with a takeoff on Madonna singing commercial jingles and the audience just about fell out of their chairs. She wrapped it up with a thank you good night and let the applause spill around her, then turned to the piano player and asked, "Who's next?"

"Biff Kincaid," came the reply.

"Oh, my, you folks are in for a treat." Joan shielded her eyes from the lights, trying to find me in the darkness. "You there, handsome?"

"Right here, gorgeous," I called back.

We'd done the road a few times together and always had fun. Joan was five feet five inches tall and small-boned with long black hair and a voice like a cartoon rabbit, and she was a great drinking companion, did well onstage and once asked the night manager of the motel we were staying in for an extra key to my room. What the hell, we were still friends the next day.

She grinned. "Well, this next guy I've had the good fortune to work and sleep with on the road . . ." Laughs from the crowd.

"No, seriously he is one of the funniest guys I know here at the Store, and so please welcome, Biff Kincaid."

The piano player hit a few bars of a song and I walked up and Joan and I hugged onstage. I hadn't seen her in a while. After we broke from the hug she kissed me on the mouth and the audience went "woo!" and clapped some more.

"Thanks, Joanie," I said, reaching for a napkin to wipe the lipstick off my mouth. "Hi, folks."

I launched into my opening bits and took it from there, throwing in a few new lines I was working on and improvising here and there. I was loose, relaxed and comfortable. I let myself play a little jazz microphone, letting the lines and the laughs fall where they might.

The blue neon star to stage left went on to let me know I'd been on long enough and I wrapped it up just in time to a hefty slice of applause and when I turned to the piano player and asked who was up next, he responded with one word: "Louie."

"Ladies and gentlemen, this next comedian I worked with on the road a long time ago, and I knew he was going to make it big and I wasn't wrong," I said. There a was a small buzz in the back of the room. I could see Louie's shadow looming in the hallway. He was still chatting, high-fiving, schmoozing, his attention moving from one person to the next. The world was one big Hollywood restaurant to Louie. "He's now the star of the biggest breakout sitcom on network television this year, and he's about to turn the Comedy Store into *Baxter's Place*." As soon as I said that I heard a sharp intake of breath from several audience members and several more turned to crane their necks and catch a glimpse of him in the back of the room. I'd forgotten just how famous Louie had become in the last year. "Please welcome, Louie Baxter!"

Louie charged through the crowd like his number was being called out onto the football field and when he reached the stage he grabbed me in a bear hug and lifted me up off the ground. He hadn't been that glad to see me when he first saw me. "Biff Kincaid!" he yelled to the audience as he held me up. "Biff Kincaid!" he yelled again. Then he let me go and kissed me on one cheek and I stepped off the stage, making my way to the back of the room. The applause was multiplied by the magical factor of fame, punctuated by whoops of appreciation. Nothing makes a crowd more excited than seeing someone they've seen on television; everyone loves celebrities, even in L.A., where they're supposed to be used to them.

"How the hell are ya, Hollywood?" Louie called out. He was carrying a bottle of Perrier, a big one he'd had someone sneak in from the Pink Dot down the street, and he swigged it like a forty-ouncer of malt liquor. The crowd responded with another round of applause.

To his credit, Louie didn't waste time chatting with the crowd or letting the surprise of his appearance soak in. He took the mike out of the stand, set the Perrier down on the front table, and said to the couple sitting there, "Mind if I drink with ya?"

They shook their heads no. "Good," Louie said, "cause this is as close as I come to drinkin' these days. Quit drinkin' folks, quit drinkin'. Why? Cause the last time I got drunk I woke up in someone else's house with my car parked sideways in the driveway."

Laugh.

He continued from there. Nightmare stories of bingeing that led up to a routine about going into rehab. He cracked the crowd up with stories of his roommate, group therapy and the chores he had to do. A true comedian, no aspect of the experience had been wasted on him.

I watched him from the back of the room. I felt a small shadowy presence at my side and realized Dirk was standing next to me. The back wall was lined with comics, wanting to look upon the latest example of breakthrough success. There was an underlying sense of competition: he might have a TV show, but can he still hold a crowd? I'd seen plenty of TV and movie stars come in after a year's absence from the stage and get a standing ovation when they came on, but not when they left.

I'd also seen plenty of famous comics come back, bump an act like he had, and do the better part of an hour while every other comedian on the bill to follow could do nothing but wait. To his credit, Louie delivered a solid fifteen minutes, got the light and brought on the next act, whom he apologized to for taking his time and making him wait but he just wanted to come back to the Comedy Store where it all began for him "because I'd missed coming here and performing for you wonderful people. Keep watching the show! Now here's Steve Alves!"

He shook Steve's hand and got off, joining me and Dirk at the back of the room. The Perrier bottle was empty and Louie was sweating. "Well, think I still got my stage chops, Kincaid?"

"Still got 'em, Lou."

He turned to Dirk. "Hey, you know who's here?"

Dirk shook his head.

"One of the guys I ran into at the Palm . . ." Louie started to snap his fingers. "Can't remember his name. He's that agent that handles screenwriters over at William Morris. He said he'd look at your script." He turned to me. "You know Dirk's a writer?"

"No," I said. "He never said anything to me about it."

"Aspiring," Dirk said. The mention of his ambition had made him slightly uncomfortable. It was obviously something he had said to Louie in confidence.

"So where's your latest script?"

"In the car," Dirk said.

"Well, go get it, and let's walk it over." Louie pointed somewhere in the dark. "I'll hand it to him."

Dirk hesitated. "You going to be okay?"

"Hey, hey, hey . . ." Louie spread his arms. "I got a roomful of people watching me," he said. "Kincaid can keep an eye out for trouble while you're gone."

Dirk fished the keys out of his jacket pocket and clenched them thoughtfully. "I'll be right back." He ducked out the rear exit.

Instantly, Louie turned to me. "You got any coke?"

"Louie . . ."

"That's right, you're clean." He turned and walked away from me like I was a bad accident. He went through the connecting door to the Main Room before I knew what was happening. On the way he passed a waitress and lifted a bottle of beer from her tray and dropped a ten in its place. He upended it and didn't stop drinking as he walked through the door.

The door led to three places: the Main Room, where other

acts were playing tonight; the men's bathroom, with several stalls he could hide out in; and to a side exit to the kitchen hallway, where he could easily duck out the back or head upstairs to the offices. I could either follow him or try to cut him off at the pass. I hesitated, and that was a mistake. One of the doormen came through—after Louie had disappeared—carrying a chair in each arm and the leg of one got caught on the doorway and, as I tried to get through, he dropped the chairs and extricated first one chair leg and then the other. When I got into the Main Room, Louie was not there. He could have gone backstage. I checked the men's room first. No Louie.

I went backstage at the Main Room. Still no Louie. The Comedy Store is a labyrinth of warrens and passages, with hideouts and secret places it took me years to map out and would take me half an hour to check them all. Staircases led up to the offices and the offices led to rooms and the rooms led to another staircase, both inside and out.

I'd lost him.

I went back down to the Original Room and found Dirk standing in the middle of the hallway, asking comics as they walked by: "You seen Louie? Louie Baxter?" He had a script in one hand and panic on his face.

He didn't stop panicking when he saw me. "Kincaid, where's Louie?"

"I don't know," I said. "He gave me the slip."

"Goddammit!" Dirk allowed himself one word of anger and then had himself back under control. "We have to find him."

"I figured that."

"I don't know this place that well, though. How many exits are there?"

"Too many to count," I said. "This is the Comedy Store. If he wants to, he can stay hidden. He can leave and no one will know."

"What is this, the Magic Castle?"

"Close."

Dirk turned, looking at the headshots of all the comedians on the walls, as if looking for a clue. "I have to find him."

"Okay."

"Will you help me?"

"As much as I can."

"Good." He looked down at the script in his hand as if he'd forgotten it was there, and marched to a trash can and threw it in.

"You might need that later," I said.

"There's no agent here from William Morris," Dirk said tightly. "There never was."

We didn't find him that night. Dirk and I searched the Store until it closed up at 2:00 A.M. Louie was long gone. One comic had seen him get in a car out front—a beat-up Ford—and drive off, east down Sunset. No description of the driver. No license number. He had vanished into the Hollywood night.

At three in the morning, Dirk and I were cruising Sunset, driving aimlessly in Louie's Lexus.

"You can just take me home," I said, after an hour of silence.

"Okay," Dirk said.

He drove me up to Beachwood Canyon and let me off at the corner to my street. I opened the car door and hesitated. "What happens now?"

"I'll keep looking for him," Dirk said. "If I haven't found him by six . . ." He looked at his watch. "In three hours, I'll call his manager and tell him Louie won't be showing up for work today."

"He done this before?"

"Not on my watch." He hesitated. "That's how I got this job. The last bodyguard let him out of his sight for a minute and he was gone."

"Where do you think he is?"

"Louie or the bodyguard?"

"Louie."

"Someplace next to a pile of coke and a case of booze," Dirk said. "The bodyguard has probably been feeding stories to the tabloids." His face was illuminated by the amber glow from the

Lexus's instrument panel. "Even if we found him now and poured a vat of coffee down his throat, he wouldn't be any good to anyone." He shook his head. "He's going to lose the show over this."

"It's not your fault."

Dirk smiled bitterly. "It'll be my fault, believe me. I'm paid to accept responsibility for the star's behavior."

"He's an addict, Dirk," I said. "He'll get coke any way he can."

"That's what I don't understand," Dirk said. "It's more important to him than money, than the show, than comedy, than his family . . ."

Silence.

"So what's your script about?" I asked.

Dirk made a face. "Something that happened when I was a cop."

I nodded. I didn't ask to read it. He didn't offer. The exchange would do neither of us any good.

"Well, see you, Kincaid."

"See you, Dirk."

We shook and I got out, walking up the block to where my apartment complex sat at the end of a cul-de-sac. It was a twelve-unit building, nice and cozy. There were a few ways up to my apartment. One of them was around by the garage, where my car was normally parked. It was then I remembered I'd left my car out at Radford Studios, and would have to take a cab out tomorrow to pick it up and drive home.

The other way to my apartment was up a stone staircase between my building and the house next door. The house next door was fronted by a lawn thick with plants and trees, and a tall streetlight stood at the line of demarcation, bathing the foot of the staircase in a soft glow.

There was someone sitting there.

All I could see were a pair of sneakers under baggy jeans. Between the feet was an open bottle of champagne and an open square of wax paper, dusted with white powder. A second later I recognized Louie's figure, hunched over, his elbows on his knees, his head down.

I stopped at the foot of my own staircase. "Lou?"

He slowly raised his head. He looked ten years older since I'd last seen him. His eyes were reddened with drink and smoke and coke and God knows what else. His face sagged at the edges with the effects of an all-night binge. He opened his mouth and worked it carefully, as if his hands were slippery on the controls.

"Kincaid," he said.

"Let's go inside, Louie," I said. "You can lie down on my couch."

His eyes closed for a second then opened again. His mouth worked some more. "I know who he is, Kincaid."

"Who?"

"This heckler guy. The one who's been passing me notes. The one who killed Tiger Moore."

"Who is he, Louie?"

He was too drunk to completely hear my question, too coked to entirely answer. "But it can't be him," he said. His lips were numb. He sounded as though he'd gone to see the dentist and gotten a shot of Novocain. "It can't be who I'm thinking of."

"Who are you talking about, Louie?"

Louie looked up at me through his inner haze and tried to smile. "A dead man, Kincaid. A dead man who crawled out of his grave."

TWELVE

I got Louie up and into my apartment and sat him on the couch. I kept the lights low. It was still night outside. I kept the music off and told Louie to keep his voice down. My neighbors weren't in the nightclub end of show business and had previously complained about after-hours noise. I had made a deal with them: I kept it quiet at night, they made as little noise as possible in the morning.

Louie sat on my futon couch and I sat in my TV chair. He was out of champagne and out of cocaine, but I had a Guinness in the fridge and gave it to him. I stuck with water. Too close to coffee time and there was no guarantee I was going to get any sleep that night.

I sat and listened while Louie told his tale.

It happened two years ago. On the road.

There were three of them: Louie, Tiger Moore and an opening act named Chad—Chad Karp. They were booked for a string of three one-nighters in northern Nevada, out on the long lonely stretch of I-80 that ran across so much empty barren landscape it was like driving across the moon. There were towns that dotted the highway, hundreds of miles apart, lonely isolated places where a comedy show once a month would pack the house. Towns with names like Farway. Talmadge. Alandale.

Tiger and Louie had driven in from Vegas, two buddies booked together for a few nights on the road. Louie was not quite the TV sensation he was to become two years later. He was six months away from his big break. Tiger, Louie and Chad all met up in Farway. They were to do one night there, a Thursday. The Friday night was in Talmadge. Saturday night's show was in Alandale.

They were all to get paid in Alandale. Two hundred a night for Louie. One twenty-five for Tiger. Seventy-five for the opener and emcee, Chad. Times three shows among them they were going to end up with more than a thousand bucks. Cash.

There were at least a hundred miles of driving between each gig. Chad had taken the bus in from somewhere else. Seattle, Louie thought. Maybe Portland. He couldn't remember. Louie was well onto establishing his world-class consumption of pot, booze and what little cocaine he could get his hands on. Tiger drove. It was his car. Chad sat in the backseat.

The shows did not go well. The audiences were plentiful, and even Louie's act—a crowd pleaser filled with props and stunts that had big-city humor and Chicago references as punch lines— often went over the heads that wore the cowboy hats that filled the chairs. This was after Tiger had done no better, often touching on many of the same subjects that Louie would talk about. They were good friends, but a bad match.

And the new guy, Chad . . . Chad was doing the worst of all. Chad would get heckled.

Chad Karp was new to the comedy game. His look was young, his act green. He was a little on the small side, about five-eight, with a lean musculature and small eyes over a big nose and limp black hair. His teeth stuck out in front and his ears swung out from the side of his head like the open doors of a Volkswagen. He had a high nasal voice and a honking laugh that sounded like a goose flying south for the winter. He had acne. His Adam's apple bobbed when he talked. He didn't have enough material to do well on an open-mike night, much less hit the road as an opener.

When he stood onstage the first night in Farway and stuttered his way through his collegiate humor, the audience grew bored, then restless, then rowdy. They started to yell things back at him. Get off the stage. You suck. You're not funny. Bring on the strippers. Next.

Tiger had to follow Chad, and fared a little better, but by the time Louie got onstage chaos reigned. Customers began uncovering pool tables, most patrons were in full chatter, and some wise guy plugged the jukebox back in and started playing it during Louie's act. In one night their week had gone from a scenic tour of northern Nevada to a hell gig. Louie and Tiger had played hell gigs before. Chad hadn't.

Back at the hotel that night, Chad had asked Louie and Tiger how they thought he did. They tried to be encouraging. Don't let them get to you, Tiger said. Yeah, Louie told him. Just do your act. They went over some of his material and punched it up a little, but it was weak to begin with. Chad said he was trained as a Shakespearean actor, but his heart was in stand-up. Well, Louie told him, this ain't Shakespeare, kid.

It was a two-hour drive to Talmadge, over a barren windswept landscape. While getting gas, Tiger and Louie exchanged whispered warnings: *This kid doesn't have it. Who sent him? Should we call the booker? How's he going to do tonight?*

They did not have long to wait. The show in Talmadge went better. This time, when he was heckled, Chad Karp responded with good-natured insults that had the recipients standing up and taking a bow. As Chad was emcee, he was on and off the stage all night, even closing the show. Tiger managed to get through his set OK, and Louie's wild prop act kept the crowd laughing. The show ended with Chad onstage, calling one heckler a "drunk redneck" and the man got up onstage with two shots of tequila and he and Chad toasted each other.

Not bad, they thought as the three of them drank at the bar afterward. Some of the audience members came up and made sure Chad knew it was all in fun. He shook their hands. They had one more night to go, and that was at the Payroll Saloon in Alandale.

They had no indication of what was to come.

The Payroll Saloon was a working man's bar, full of oil workers and cowboys and miners all wearing their best-pressed hats. It was just off the highway, more than one hundred miles from Talmadge, on the eastern side of the state, toward the Utah border. The three of them walked in just an hour before show time, no chance to find their lodgings and freshen up. On the way there, the heat in Tiger's car had gone out. It was late February. There was snow on the ground in the parking lot. They were cold, tired and hungry when they walked in. Saturday night in Alandale, Nevada, was already in full swing.

They asked the bartender, a woman of about fifty missing some front teeth, for the manager. The manager came out and bought all three of them a welcoming round. *I heard you did a good job in Talmadge last night,* he said. *Tonight's going to be a little different.*

How so? Louie asked.

You got to understand, the manager told them, *that these are just good ol' boys out to have a good time. Blow off a little steam. They don't mean no harm. They're not used to comedians. They yell out something to you, just keep doing your act. I'll be here in case of any trouble.*

Tiger and Louie looked at each other. *What kind of trouble?* Louie asked.

A pause. The saloon manager in Alandale was a former oil worker himself. He had thick stout arms and a permanently hard gut even though he was at least fifty years old, his handsome face puffed with drink and ruddy from the sun. He had a thick-combed blond mustache and lumberjack beard shot through with gray. He wore a red flannel shirt and work boots stained from the oil fields. His name was Parkins.

Fights, Parkins said. *There have been some fights here.*

Fights . . . with the comedians? Chad asked.

Parkins nodded. *Some of these good ol' boys come onstage,*

they hear something they don't like. They don't know it's all part of the show.

Maybe we'll skip it. Chad said. His face had gone pale.

Your decision, Parkins said. *I'm to pay you for the run.* He handed them the keys to their motel rooms.

He pointed to a small platform set in the middle of the dance floor, chairs and tables on both sides, like a theater in the round. *There's the stage*, he said. *Good luck.*

There was a call for a fresh keg, and Parkins went to go replace it. The three of them were left standing in the middle of the Payroll, hundreds of miles from home. There were posters on the wall of women in bikinis holding automatic weapons. There was a dart board with a hunting knife in it. Heads of deer and bear were stuffed and mounted on the walls. They were a long way from the familiar urban environs of comedy clubs, of busy streets and nightclubs in shopping malls. This was way out in the sticks.

The show that night was chaos.

On Saturday nights the Payroll Saloon had two-for-one drink specials, waitresses in high-heeled boots and halter tops, blaring country music and tables full of rowdy off-work roughnecks and cowboys who treated the comedians as a series of moving targets. Chad Karp was heckled as soon as he got onstage. He began to respond with taunts of his own. He accused one pair of cowboy hats sitting stage side of being gay lovers, and began an improvised routine about what really went on out in the oil fields, complete with physical postures and sound effects depicting them having sex with each other.

The previous night in Talmadge the bit had killed, with one group high-fiving each other and taking bows, blowing exaggerated kisses at the stage.

Tonight, however, it silenced the crowd. Louie heard the wooden honking sound of a chair going back. One patron got up and stood in front of the stage, his hands at his' sides as if he had a pair of six-guns strapped there, talking to Chad in a low even tone. Chad responded by telling him to sit down and shut the fuck up.

The man jabbed a threatening finger at Chad and said he

would see him after the show. Then he walked back into the crowd to more applause than Chad had gotten when he took the stage. Chad gave the finger to his back. Others started to boo.

This was getting out of hand, and the show had barely begun. Louie and Tiger were sitting at a small table against a side wall. Louie saw what was happening and got a flashlight from behind the bar and tried to signal Chad to get off, but before he could catch Chad's eye a half-empty beer can came sailing out of the crowd. It narrowly missed Chad's head to crack against an amplifier. Instantly, Chad reached down and threw it back. Beer corkscrewed out the top and onto the crowd.

This time the can found a mark on the right cheekbone of one of the few women in the establishment, a veteran waitress with rouged skin and blond curls. She was holding a tray high as she crossed an open space on what was normally a dance floor but was now set up with square cocktail tables. On the tray were two full beer pitchers and half a dozen frosted glass mugs. The blow to her face was just below her right eye. When the edge of the beer can struck her, she was not seriously injured but stunned enough to jerk her head back with a "huh" sound, lose her balance and fall to the floor.

The tray went down with her. The pitchers and mugs, both made of glass, shattered when they hit the floor, the pitchers exploding like melons, the mugs breaking into shards that flew like shrapnel up off the floor, with most of the clear sharp fragments bouncing harmlessly off the waitress's person as they hit her hair and clothes. It was only one short jagged piece from a broken mug handle that drilled into the fleshy part of her chin just underneath her jaw, lodging so painfully she cried out again, the sound cut off as she touched the wound with her fingers and found the glass sliver still there, and resuming her wails when she pulled her fingers away and saw what was on them.

Blood.

Sissy! someone nearby yelled. *Her name is Sissy*, Louie thought dully as she was helped to her feet, sobbing, wet with beer, and she made her way limping to the back office for first aid, helped along by an abundance of strong arms and sturdy backs.

As she left, the eyes of the audience went from the scene of the accident to the stage platform, where Chad Karp stood frozen in the meek spotlight from just overhead. It had all happened so fast he hadn't had time to react. Now, with all attention in the room focused on him, he tried to think of something to say.

I didn't mean to hurt anyone. . . . he said. *She's going to be all right, isn't she?*

The sound system went out with a squeal of feedback, as an unseen hand turned the speaker volume first up, then down, then off. The little red-and-green glowing lights over the amplifier faded out like dying fireflies.

Chad's eyes went to Louie and Tiger. Tiger was edging toward an exit. *Never mind getting paid,* Louie whispered to him. *Never mind the show. Let's get in the car and get out of here.*

Louie looked at Chad still onstage. Chad looked back at him and understood. Time to go. He put the mike in the stand and stepped down off the stage.

Or tried to. A table was suddenly shoved against the edge of the stage and Chad couldn't step down. He stepped back and tried to get off another way and another table was slid into place, blocking his way.

The smoky neon-lit air was filled with the sounds of chairs scraping backwards and tables moving forward as everyone got to their feet. Chad was blocked in on the stage from all sides. There was nowhere for him to go. He was hemmed in by tables, all pressed against the stage, no bigger than a bathroom stall. Behind that was a phalanx of cowboy hats and flannel shirts, silently closing ranks.

Louie and Tiger were being ignored. Their exit was still clear. They could leave anytime they wanted to.

Chad looked over the heads of the crowd, slowly shuffling forward, to make eye contact with Louie and Tiger.

Guys? he asked. *Help.*

Then Chad panicked. He jumped up on one of the tables, not built to support human weight, and almost immediately lost his balance and pitched forward into the ready arms of what had once been an audience and was now something more closely resembling a lynch mob.

A roar went up from the crowd and as Chad struggled to his feet, fists beat down on him like a swarm of bees and Louie saw him get struck on the ear, in the eye and in the nose before disappearing in a sea of backs.

Louie and Tiger waded in through the crowd, shoving their way toward Chad. *Stop!* Louie was yelling. *Let him go!*

A gunshot cracked through the air and all fell silent. There was a brief scuffle and then Louie heard a voice say: *Let 'em through.*

The crowd parted and Louie saw in horror that Chad was on his hands and knees on the floor, blood leaking from his nose, one eye swollen almost completely shut. The man that had stood in front of the stage and threatened him had taken his own belt off and was now using it as a dog collar around Chad's throat. Chad's face was turning red. His captor held Chad in place with one hand. In his other he held a gun. It was pointed at Chad's head.

You're killing him, Louie said.

The man with the belt was wearing a black pearl-buttoned Western shirt with white piping. His cowboy hat had been knocked off in the fight, revealing a balding head of black hair over a knobby scalp. He had a thick broken nose and small beady eyes. His teeth were stained and crooked and his mouth was an angry thin line, now twisted in a snarl. He was strong, with powerful shoulders and arms like cables.

Ya'll comedians come here and start talkin' trash like he done, ya'll got to pay the price, he said.

Onlookers agreed: *Tell 'em, Del. Set it straight.*

Just let him go, Louie said, *and we'll be on our way.*

We don't want any trouble, Tiger said.

Del tightened the belt leather around Chad's neck a notch, so Chad had to raise up off the floor like a raring animal to keep from choking.

Pete? Del called. *Hoyle? Let's show our vis'tors how we do the two-step here in Alandale.*

Two of Del's drinking buddies moved in, one on each side, and stepped a single boot on each of Chad's hands, pinning them to the floor. Chad's arms were stretched tight as Del pulled upward. Chad gave a strangled scream. He was choking.

I'll make a deal with ya'll, Del said. *What we're gonna do to him can either be spread three ways, or it can just be his to bear.*

Louie felt the crowd behind him, closing in, cutting off his exit. Bodies jostled behind him, letting him know they were there.

Ya'll are either with him, Del said, *or against him.*

Chad looked up through his one good eye, pleading silently with his fellow comedians.

Silence. Louie and Tiger looked at each other, then at the hundred or so sullen angry faces surrounding them. Fear twisted in Louie's gut like a stabbed snake.

Take him, Louie said. And stepped back.

With a roar, the crowd rushed forward, shoving Louie and Tiger aside in their eagerness to get their hands on Chad. Chad was lifted up on his back by the hands of the crowd like a victorious football player, but with the belt still pulled tight around his neck so that the last Louie and Tiger saw of him was his face, jerked upside down, his eyes looking at them with horror at their betrayal as he was carried off.

Even inverted, Louie could read Chad's lips. Even through the howls, he could hear his last words.

I'll get you for this, Chad screamed at them. *I'll make you pay.*

Then he was gone, carried out of the club and into the dark Nevada night, buoyed by bloodlust ready to bay at the moon.

Louie hesitated in his story. "We never saw him again," he said. "I always thought they killed him."

"And now?" I asked.

"Now I wish they had."

THIRTEEN

"What happened after Chad Karp was taken away?" I asked.

"We left out the back way," Louie said. "We found our car and took off down the road. Didn't stop until after we crossed the state line and hit Salt Lake City, two hundred miles later."

"Did you phone a report in to the police or the highway patrol?"

"No."

"Why not?"

"We were followed for fifty miles to make sure we didn't. Some cowboys in a pickup. We slowed down once to use a pay phone and they rammed us from behind."

"Did you ever see Chad Karp again?"

"No."

"Did you ever hear what happened to him?"

"No."

"Did you ever ask?"

"No."

"Not the booker? The club owner? Anyone?"

"No." Louie was slumped over on my couch, his head in his hands, almost level with his knees. The empty can of Guinness was on the floor between his feet. He had been talking for two hours. It was dawn outside.

"Who was the booker on that gig?"

"Mark Roper," Louie said numbly. "Out of his club in Salt Lake City. I can't remember the name of it."

"Mister Silly's," I said. "I played there once."

"Yeah. Mister Silly's."

"Is it still there?"

"I don't know," Louie said. "When we got to Salt Lake City we didn't call him or stop by the club or anything. This was just before dawn. We got gas and food and I had Tiger drop me off at the airport. My next gig was in Phoenix. I don't remember where he was going."

"Did Tiger ever make any inquiries?" I asked.

"Not that I know of." Louie straightened up, leaning back against the couch. He looked like hell on a plate with a side order of fries. "We never talked about it again."

"Never?"

"I thought they killed him."

"All the more reason to report it."

"But we were there. We didn't do anything. Doesn't that make us accessories or something?"

"I'm not a lawyer."

Louie shook his head. "Tiger and I went our separate ways after we got to Salt Lake City. Six weeks later I got the *Tonight Show*, and Max Gottschalk signed me. Things started to happen for me in Hollywood. I didn't see or speak to Tiger until about a year ago, when I signed my deal for the show. He came to the set during my first season and asked if I could get him a show-case at the Store. I did, and after a few tries he got made a regular. I didn't hear from or about him again. Until . . . this."

I got up and made coffee. I heard birds chirping outside in the blue morning light. It had been a while since I'd pulled an all-nighter.

I came back in the living room carrying two steaming mugs. Louie waved his away. The guy would do coke and booze all night, but didn't want any caffeine in his system. Go figure.

I sipped. "So, you think this is him? Chad Karp? He's the guy who killed Tiger and left notes for you?"

"I don't know," Louie said, staring off into space. "It could be. If it is, then he's going to want to kill me the same as he killed Tiger. For revenge." He looked up at me. "You gotta help me, Kincaid. I don't know what to do. I got the show now. My dad's going to retire, and he just lost his business. I can't . . ."

His eyes glistened with tears. I wasn't moved. One of the aftereffects of cocaine abuse is depression. Right now his heart was a deep black pit lined with cold mossy stones that no daylight could warm. Today, he wouldn't be any good to anybody who wanted him to be funny.

"You need some rest," I said. "I'll call Dirk. He can come pick you up."

"I heard about you, Kincaid."

"Heard what?"

"A booker doesn't pay you, you find him. A comic's in trouble, you help him. Someone starts a fight, you finish it."

"My partner's a talking chimp," I said. "We live on a houseboat. Together we're detectives, this fall on ABC."

"You know what I mean. You look into problems. Find things out. A lot of people owe you."

"Strictly amateur," I said. "Mostly luck."

He turned to me as if I'd said something else. "I'll give you money, Kincaid. I'll cover all of your expenses. Just see if you can get anywhere with this, find out if it is Chad Karp come back to haunt me."

"Maybe what you need is a private detective," I said. "Or the police."

"And tell them what? I let some other comic get beaten half to death? Then I might be the one going to jail." He wiped the moisture off his face. "I hear you're as good as any gumshoe, Kincaid," Louie said. "You won't stop until you get some answers. All I'm saying is I'll foot the bill." He reached into his pocket and pulled out a bankroll, dropping it on the table like a bundle of dried leaves. "There's five thousand. Cash. Let me know when it's gone or just keep the change."

I picked up the money, and then the phone to dial Dirk's cell phone number. "On one condition."

"What's that?"

The line began to ring softly in my ear. "I'll let you know."

Louie fell asleep before Dirk came to pick him up at my apartment a little after eight in the morning. "I'm going to try to take him over to the set," Dirk said. He looked like he'd slept in a bus station. "See if maybe we can get a half day out of him. Gottschalk's going to meet me there."

I played dumb. "Who?"

"Max *Gottschalk*," Dirk said reproachfully, as if I should already know. "Louie's manager."

"Ah."

"He wants to talk to you."

"Who?"

"Max Gottschalk. I thought every comedian knew who he was."

Of course I knew who Max Gottschalk was. Max Gottschalk was more than a manager. He was a career-maker. He was big-time.

"About what?"

"He didn't tell me."

"Okay."

Dirk reached under Louie's shoulders and hefted his sleeping bulk. "Help me get him out to the car, will you?"

An hour later I was lying on my couch where Louie had spent most of the morning, catching up on my sleep when the phone rang.

"Yeah."

"Biff Kincaid?"

"Yeah."

"Max Gottschalk."

"Yeah."

Pause. Max Gottschalk was used to people sitting up a little straighter when they talked to him. Especially comedians.

"I'm Louie Baxter's manager."

"I know."

"Dirk Pastor gave me your home number."

"Is that Dirk's last name," I said. "Pastor?"

He ignored that statement. "We need to talk."

"Okay," I said. "Talk."

"In private."

"I'm alone."

"In person."

"You mean like I have to get up and off my couch?"

"I don't think you realize who you're talking to," Gottschalk said, dropping his voice half a key to make him sound more sinister.

"I don't think you realize you woke me up," I said, and hung up on him.

I put the cordless phone back on the floor next to the couch and closed my eyes. Managers. I'd had three of them. They took fifteen percent, and knew everybody in show business until the day they signed you.

I was just putting a toe back on Cloud One in Dreamland when the phone rang again. This time I wasn't going to be nice.

"What," I said.

"Biff, it's Andrew Carruthers."

At that I opened my eyes. "Drew?" I said. "Drew Blue in a wooden shoe?"

He couldn't help but chuckle. "You don't know how long it's been since anyone called me that."

"Hey, when you managed the Santa Barbara Comedy Club for five years that's all I heard anyone call you." I sat up on my couch. "And you booked me in there often enough."

"Well, you killed every time," he said. "Had to bump you up to headliner because I couldn't get anyone who wanted to follow you."

"How've you been? Last time I was in Santa Barbara you had moved on."

"That's right, I went to New York for about a year. Time to get out of the nightclub end of the comedy business," he said. "Sounds like I woke you up."

"Well, that's not the first time that's happened."

"Yeah, but alone?"

We both had a light laugh at that one. "I'm not quite as wild as I used to be," I said.

"I know some ladies up in Santa Barbara that'll be sorry to hear that," he said.

"So what are you up to these days?" I rubbed my face with one hand. I could blow off sleep for an old friend, especially one who had booked me at least a dozen times over the last five years.

"Well, I just moved back from New York a few months ago."

"So you're back in Santa Barbara?"

"No," Drew said. "I'm in L.A."

"Great! What are you doing?"

"I'm working for Max Gottschalk."

The pieces fell into place. "Uh-huh."

"I met him in New York at Catch A Rising Star," he said. "I was working as a talent booker for Jane Calley's syndicated TV talk show."

"I know Jane," I said. "She's funny."

"Yeah, good comic," he said ruefully. "But try telling her producers that."

"I tried catching her show on the road," I said. "But I couldn't find it on the schedule."

"She only sold to fifty markets," Drew said. "And then some of them started dropping her even before the initial thirteen-week commitments were up, after that . . . last I heard, though, she was writing for Letterman, so she got a good gig out of it."

"So how did you meet Max Gottschalk?"

"I booked Louie for Jane's show to plug *Baxter's Place*," he said. "And Gottschalk came along for the ride. He'd heard about me from the club in Santa Barbara. When Louie stayed up all night and missed the taping, I had to scramble to get another act. Max liked the way I hustled comics and handled crises, and gave me his card. When the show was canceled I was at loose ends so I called him in L.A. and he started freelancing some stuff to me when he had clients in town because he doesn't have a New York office and then three months ago he asked me to come to L.A. and work for him."

"Huh," I said.

"He's got a lot of clients on the air right now and looking to expand his producing responsibilities as well as his roster of talent," Drew said. "Man can't be everywhere at once."

"Uh-huh." I think I could see where Drew was going. I smelled schmooze on his breath.

"So when Max came storming out of his office five minutes ago with his face turning different shades of purple and told me that some dime-a-dozen comic that he had never heard of had hung up on him after smarting off every time he asked a question, I almost didn't have to ask for a name."

At that I laughed. "He woke me up," I said.

"Max isn't used to being hung up on," Drew said. "Doesn't happen to him a lot anymore."

"I'm a pain in the ass," I said. "What can I say?"

"Sooooo . . . I offered to call you back and see if I could get you to come down here and meet with him this afternoon."

"About what?"

"About Louie," Drew said. "He didn't show up for work today."

"That's not my fault."

"No," he said quickly. "And I know that."

"So why should I come down and meet with a millionaire that thinks every comic in town—even dime-a-dozen names he's never heard of—is at his beck and call?"

There was a pause.

"Well . . ."

Another pause.

"It would make me look good to my boss," Drew said.

"That's a good reason," I said. "What time?"

"Three o'clock good for you?"

"Sure," I said. "Where?"

"Fifty-six seventy Wilshire Boulevard," he said. "Between Masselin and Hauser. Used to be the E! building."

"I'll find it."

"See you then and there, Biff," Drew said. "Thanks again."

"Always good to talk to you, Drew."

I hung up, rolled off the couch and onto the floor and staggered over to the wall, where I unplugged the phone, then fell into bed and went to sleep.

I dreamed of Chad Karp, chained to a tree, a winged gargoyle tearing at the young comic's face until he screamed.

Max Gottschalk's offices were on the top floor of the 5670 Wilshire building, and that's a long way up in a very fast elevator. The penthouse floor housed his production and management company, and the reception area was lined with a dozen poster-sized photos of his very famous clients, all of whom had sitcoms on TV that lasted well into syndication heaven. He was a rich man off of other people's talents.

I gave my name to the extremely cute receptionist with straight blond hair and warm brown liquid eyes and a stud in her tongue. Before I sat down the door opened and my old friend Andrew Carruthers came out to greet me.

We shook hands and hugged and shook again. Drew was my height and lean and strong. I'd seen him throw a few drunks out of the Santa Barbara Comedy Club with his own two hands. Last time I saw him he wore polo shirts and khakis with sandals. Now he was in a dark blue double-breasted suit with a green silk tie and white button-down shirt and polished black shoes. Two years ago, he was going prematurely gray but now his hair was completely white, by destiny or design, I couldn't tell. He had worn it at surfer length at the club in Santa Barbara but since going to New York he'd cut it off and spiked his hair up with gel.

"This your new power look?" I said, stepping back to admire his fine duds. "What the up-and-coming comedy manager is wearing?"

"The TV producers I worked with in New York took me shopping," he said, striking a model's pose. "You can't get decent clothes in L.A."

"You don't *need* decent clothes in L.A., Drew."

He patted my stomach. "Looks like you're still hitting the gym," he said.

"Yeah, but some days it hits back," I said. "You're looking trim." I saw a red mark on his right jaw. "Hey what's this? Don't tell me they use you as a bouncer here too?"

He touched the bruise as if it was a shaving cut. "No, it's from my Krav Magra class," he said. "Israeli secret service method of self-defense. They throw you around a bit." He smiled. "Go ahead, hit me. I'll take you down."

We started shadow boxing and trading dialogue from the Rocky movies. It was an old routine that no one had ever found amusing except us.

The receptionist interrupted our horseplay. "Andy, Max is ready for you."

I dropped my fists. "Andy?"

"Yeah, they already had a Drew working here."

"So? You can be Drew Two."

He led me toward the offices. "It's what Max started calling me."

"Didn't you correct him?"

He winced. "I tried."

He held the door open for me and we walked into a bullpen of cubicles. At the end of an aisle a pair of wooden double doors barricaded what must have been Max Gottschalk's office. The doors were closed. We walked through, Drew nodding his way among the cubicle workers and peering into the half-open doors of the offices of the other managers-in-training such as himself.

A young man of about twenty-five with a completely shaven head and two earrings in one ear was seated just outside Gottschalk's office. He was wearing one of those phone mouthpiece things that made him look like he worked for the space program.

"Steve," Drew asked, "is Max off the phone yet?"

Steve glanced at his phone, reading it like a sonar monitor. "He's still talking to London. He did have two calls waiting but he must have taken those. I'll bring you in as soon as he's off— oh, he's off right now."

"I'll take him in," Drew said, and led me through the double doors. He opened them to reveal Max Gottschalk's office. It was as big as my entire apartment in square footage, with light beige carpet and plush leather-and-wood decor, like a British men's club. The centerpiece was a massive black wooden desk polished to a mirror shine and empty except for a legal pad, a pen and another phone headset like the one Steve was wearing. The entire back wall was made of window glass, showing a westward view of Los Angeles and since today was a clear day

I could see all the way to the ocean. I felt like I was in God's waiting room.

"Have a seat," Drew said, pointing to a padded leather chair. "He'll be right out."

I looked around as Drew left. "You leaving?" I asked.

"Max wants to talk to you in private," Drew said, his manner suddenly hushed and formal, a local cleric in the presence of a cardinal. "Stop by my office on the way out and I'll walk you to your car."

As Drew closed the doors behind me, I sank into a soft burgundy chair and waited for someone named Jeeves to present me with brandy and cigars. I heard a faint flush of water and a door next to a paneled bookcase opened up and out stepped Max Gottschalk. He walked around to sit behind his desk, not looking at me until he was in position.

He was about five-six, slightly tubby around the waist, wearing a monogrammed white dress shirt with a tie that should have been hanging down the street at the county museum. He had a trimmed black beard and a mane of coifed silvery hair that framed his small eyes and expressionless liver-colored mouth. He looked like a soap opera villain. I had heard about him. When he came to watch comics he stayed for just a few minutes and never laughed. The man had made a career out of being impassive.

He sat in his high-backed black leather swivel chair, the arms adorned with buttons and studs. If this was God's waiting room, I felt like I was talking to His lawyer.

"I have a problem," Max Gottschalk said. He steepled his fingers and looked out his picture windows.

I waited. He had yet to make eye contact with me.

He swiveled slowly around to lock his gray eyes onto mine for full dramatic effect. "I said, I have a problem."

"I heard you the first time."

"I just got off the phone with the head of West Coast Entertainment for what's currently the number-two-rated broadcast network in the United States," he said. "They are within five prime-time ratings points of taking the lead for this quarter from the number-one-rated network, and they think the show that could put them over the top is *Baxter's Place*."

"Okay."

"So when the star of that show arrives at work looking like he's just hitchhiked his way back from Mardi Gras, then as that star's manager as well as executive producer of that same show responsible for production overages, which are now most certainly going to occur, I have a problem."

He gave me his best boardroom tractor-beam look. I think I was supposed to start sniveling.

"And when I have a problem," he said, "you have a problem."

"Oh, yeah?" I said. "How's that?"

"I don't need any of Louie's old comedy buddies coming around to party it up with him on a weeknight hoping they can get a staff writing job, a guest part on the show, or a chance to drive his new Lexus," he said. "Andy told me you guys go way back, and you were made blood brothers from the hell gigs you did together, but when I get a phone call from the head of—"

"Oh, knock it off," I said.

His gray eyes flickered momentarily and his mouth remained open half a second before he closed it. I'd gone off prompter.

"You can spare me the vice principal's speech," I said. "I didn't take Louie out last night and get him all cranked up. He did that on his own. You should know that; you're the one who hired Dirk to be his guard dog. Louie gave him the slip at the Comedy Store and took off with parties unknown. He showed up at my place about three in the morning. By then he was too wired to sleep so I let him talk it off. But if you're looking for a stray dog to kick around this morning because your client can't keep his hands off the nose candy, you picked the wrong guy."

I stood. "Yeah, you got a problem. But so does Louie. He has a manager who cares more about what the network board of directors thinks than about his own client."

I turned to go. When I tried the double doors I found they wouldn't open.

"There's a magnetic lock on those doors," Max Gottschalk said behind me, "which I control from my desk."

I turned around. "You got something else to say?" I said. "Or did you want to hear more of my charming repartee?"

"Have a seat," he said. He gestured. It was an effort. So was the next word he said. "Please."

I dropped myself back in his chair. He was big on long silences, drenched in power and meaning.

"I wish to apologize," he said.

I looked at him. I got a good tractor-beam look myself.

"I did not misread the situation," he said. "Louie's inability to work on the set today was drug-related."

I shrugged.

"But perhaps I misread you."

I nodded only once.

"I asked you here to show you something," he said. "On tape."

He opened a drawer and pulled out a remote control. He pressed a button, and panels on the bookcase next to the bathroom started to move, revealing a large TV/VCR combo.

Gottschalk pressed a button and the TV came on, catching a daytime talk show in the middle of a segment. It wasn't the tape. It was what was on broadcast television this time of day. The sound was off.

"I taped this story off a satellite feed two hours ago," he said. "It will be broadcast around the country in syndication tonight." He glanced at his watch. "It's probably just starting to hit the East Coast markets. No one else in this office has seen this."

He hit another button and the talk show disappeared and the anchor for a tabloid TV news show came on the screen. I couldn't name the talking head, but the show's logo was in the lower right hand corner: "Page One."

Before the volume kicked in, I saw Louie's unsmiling face in a box suspended over the anchor's shoulder. Below that was the banner: BAXTER'S BINGE. Uh-oh.

"—our *Page One* reporter, Sheryl Franklin, was at the scene where Louie Baxter started his binge of booze and brawling."

Cut to Sheryl. She looked even more stunning than when I'd seen her last night at the Palm. She had changed from her short black dress into a more elegant business suit, and as she did her opening on-camera host wrap in front of the Palm Restaurant on Santa Monica Boulevard, she evinced the moral tone of a bank loan officer turning down an application to buy some low-income housing.

"Thanks, Ted." She made a gesture over her shoulder. "Hollywood's heavy hitters come to finish up a day of deal-making here at the world-famous Palm restaurant. It's also where Louie Baxter began his night of excess that would end in production being shut down for the day on the hit sitcom *Baxter's Place*. It started with a slugfest between Baxter's bodyguard and some local paparazzi and *Page One* has it all on tape."

Cut to a grainy slo-mo video of Dirk's encounter with the photographers last night. There was no sound. There had been a third photographer that night, one with a video camera. By the angle and distance, I could tell he was inside the same Buick the other two paparazzi had come from. Interesting idea: two shutterbugs moved in for the stills, while a third one stayed behind for the video. The photogs I'd nicknamed Buzz Cut and Night Shades moved against Dirk and even at reduced speed Dirk's moves were subtle and graceful as he sidestepped their rush against the car and turned their own clumsy energies against them, sending both men sprawling on the sidewalk. I could see Louie's face in a three-quarter profile in the front seat. I was hidden in the shadows of the backseat, visible only as a black shape.

Sheryl narrated the action: "It was after having a lavish dinner with an old comedian buddy from his hard-partying stand-up days that Louie Baxter encountered a pair of paparazzi outside the Palm. When the camera lenses got a little too close, Louie ordered his burly bodyguard to clear the way."

Cut to the Comedy Store. File footage taken from the sidewalk in front of the Sunset Strip location.

Sheryl's voice continued: "Then it was on to the Comedy Store, where Louie Baxter entertained a packed house with stories of his newfound sobriety."

"Huh," I said to myself.

The tape froze.

"What?" Max Gottschalk said.

"It wasn't packed."

Gottschalk shook his head. "This girl. Sheryl Franklin. I remember when she was doing bit parts on the beach-and-bikini shows and banging the producers for extra lines."

I motioned. "Let's see the rest of it."

The tape restarted. The story cut to footage of Louie onstage in the Original Room at the Store. Someone had come into the audience and sat with a hidden video camera in their hat or lap, on the front row, a strict no-no at the Comedy Store. The audio was so bad, subtitles were supplied: *I quit drinkin' folks, quit drinkin'. Why? Cause the last time I got drunk I woke up in someone else's house with my car parked sideways in the driveway.*

Sheryl's voice-over narration returned: "Louie isn't just telling jokes, he's telling the truth." On the tinny laugh, the screen cut to footage of a white Trans Am overturned in the garden of a Malibu estate. "This was the scene three months ago when Louie Baxter was arrested for reckless driving after his high-priced sports car went spinning out of control in the oh-so-chi-chi neighborhood of Malibu, California."

The screen was filled with a shot of Louie leaving court, accompanied by a lawyer and Max Gottschalk, his head down, ducking reporters' questions.

"It was in front of a judge that Louie was given a court-ordered rehab stay here at the New Light Center in the Pacific Palisades."

A shot of a simple Mediterranean building set against an idyllic garden setting.

"But Louie has been the subject of rumors that he had relapsed, using drugs and alcohol again since the taping of the second-season opener of *Baxter's Place*." Cut to behind-the-scenes footage of Louie rehearsing on the set of his show. "There was tension on the set over the writing of the show, which Baxter was unhappy with. His manager even hired personal security to make sure no one has the chance to pass him any drugs or bottles of booze."

Back to the grainy video of him performing at the Comedy

Store. "Was this just the start of another wild night for Louie Baxter? He was allegedly seen later in the evening asking fellow comedians where he could get drugs and driving off in search of them.

"This morning, production was shut down on *Baxter's Place* and—according to a spokesperson for the production company— it's because Louie Baxter has the flu."

Cut to Sheryl standing just outside the Radford Studios gate, talking to the camera, pouring irony over her words like warm maple syrup.

"But if he has the flu, he has yet to see a doctor, and neither has anyone else who came into contact with him today. It's possible that this is just the latest hangover for Louie and his increasingly troubled show. Ted?"

Back to Ted in the studio; "Thank you, Sheryl. Who knows what's next for party boy, Louie Baxter? Up next on *Page One*, did the Russians capture a UFO during World War II?"

Max Gottschalk clicked the tape to a halt and turned the TV off. Little motors moved the wood panels back into place and the bookcase reassembled itself. I looked at him, outlined against the skyline of L.A.

"You do have a problem," I said.

Gottschalk nodded. "The network has only ordered half of the second season of *Baxter's Place* at the moment. Thirteen episodes. The next show order is made in six weeks."

"I see."

"Do you have any idea what started this?" Gottschalk said. "What got him going? Was it a woman? Is he unhappy with something with the show?"

"There's this new kid that they hired to play his younger brother," I said.

Max Gottschalk nodded. "Larkin Thomas."

"Louie says he's an open-miker."

"The first show with him in it tested through the roof with a focus group of women eighteen to thirty-four, so the network loves him. Louie and I have talked about this, and I have that situation under control. Could it be anything else?"

"You don't know about the notes?" I asked.

He shook his head. "I know Dirk's asked for extra security on the set," Gottschalk said, "but I thought that was to keep out drug dealers. What notes?"

"Louie got two notes backstage at the *Baxter's Place* sound-stage within the last two weeks," I said. "Both of them similar in wording, identical in their source. I sought Louie out yesterday because I had seen a similar note up in Las Vegas just a few days ago. I was replacing a comedian Louie knew who'd been threatened in exactly the same way."

"Who's that?"

"Tiger Moore."

Gottschalk nodded. "I've met Tiger. Tiger's been in this office. Where is he now?"

"He's dead."

Gottschalk jerked in his chair as if someone had run a current through the seat. It was the first spontaneous move I'd seen him make since I'd met him. "He's what?"

"Someone broke into his hotel room in Las Vegas and stabbed him to death."

Gottschalk sat back in his seat, leaning his head against the back, shaking it from side to side in a motion of denial, saying no to the heavenly fates. "Oh my God."

I told him about hooking up with Louie when I got back to L.A., and the threatening notes to both Louie and Tiger.

"What do these notes say? 'I'm going to kill you' or what?"

"They're of a specific tone," I said. "Like something a heckler would say. 'Get off the stage.' 'You suck.' 'You're not funny.' One message was written on the wall over the bed where Tiger was stabbed."

"And does Louie have any idea who might be behind this?" Gottschalk asked.

I nodded. I told him the story of Chad Karp. Max Gottschalk listened with a rapt expression.

"Louie never mentioned this to me," he said, with a tone of betrayal. "Is there anything else?"

"Not that I know of."

"Of course," Gottschalk said. "This is just what he told you." He smoothed his beard with his hands, his eyes widening and head cocking in a gesture of well-what-have-we-here. "I . . . I . . . I don't know what to do."

"Louie asked me to look into this," I said. "He gave me some money and I'm going to hit the road tomorrow and see what else I can find out."

"Shouldn't we tell the police?"

"The police in Las Vegas already know," I said. "I was going to bring them up to speed on what's happening with Louie."

"What about hiring a private investigator?"

"You've already got one of those in Dirk Pastor," I said.

Gottschalk snorted. "The man can't outsmart the tabloid press," he said. "You think he can catch a killer?"

I shrugged. "His job is to look after Louie."

"He can't seem to do that too well either."

Silence. Perhaps Dirk Pastor's long-range employment possibilities were limited.

"How much money did Louie give you?"

"Five thousand dollars," I said. "Cash."

"That include any kind of a fee?"

"I'm not charging one," I said. "Expenses only. Louie's idea. His offer. He knew I was going to keep after this anyway, but he also knows I'd have to cancel my spots at the Store."

Gottschalk looked puzzled. "How much do those pay?"

"It's not a matter of getting paid," I said. "It's a matter of getting to do them at all." If he didn't understand, I wasn't going to explain it to him.

Gottschalk opened a drawer and pulled out a small leather folder. He opened it up. I saw it was a large wallet. In it was a pad of green-colored checks, some credit cards and a pocketful of cash. He reached into the pocket and patiently counted out some deceased chief executives. When he was finished he put the wallet away and slid the small stack toward me with his fingertips.

"Here's another five thousand," he said.

"I don't need it."

129

"Take it anyway," he said. "Travel first-class or put it in a mutual fund. I don't care. All I ask is you let me know what you find out."

"That may be nothing."

"Then keep it anyway." He allowed himself a small smile.

I reached forward and picked up the money. "This doesn't mean I work for you," I said.

"I know your first obligation is to Louie."

"No, I'm not working for him, either." I put Gottschalk's five grand next to Louie's, inside my expanding billfold. I was getting quite a stake for not doing much so far.

"When this is over," Gottschalk said, "we can talk about some other things."

"Like what?"

"I'd like to see your act."

"Most nights I'm at the Comedy Store."

This time he allowed himself a fraction of a smile. "Do you know how many comedians spend years of their lives trying to get my attention?"

"That's their problem," I said. "Drew knows my act very well."

"Drew? She's our in-house legal counsel. You know her?"

"I mean the other Drew. Drew Carruthers. You call him Andy. He's seen me a dozen times. See? I saved you a trip."

He shook his head, amused in spite of himself. "Here I am offering a chance to showcase for my office, and you act like I want you to pick up my laundry."

"I'm sure we'd get around to that," I said. "Right after I detailed your car."

"I'm responsible for over a billion dollars' worth of programming on the air for four networks and in international movie box office receipts," he said. "When I pick up the phone and make a call, that's what's on the line."

"Sorry to interrupt again," I said. "But the people responsible for those movies and TV shows are not in this room. Those are the writers and performers you found in the comedy clubs over the last twenty years. I saw the pictures in the lobby, and I know who you rep. A blind man could see those people were gifted.

You just packaged them right. So before you break your arm patting yourself on the back, remember you're not the one who made them funny."

The smile increased. "When I scheduled this meeting, I didn't know I'd be getting a lecture."

I shrugged. "I didn't know you needed one."

"You have a tendency to speak your mind, Mr. Kincaid."

"Especially onstage," I said. "And using a microphone."

I stood.

"Are we done?" he said.

"I am." I nodded at the double doors of his office. "You going to let me walk out of here or do I get to look for an ax and chop my way out?"

He pressed a button underneath his desk and I heard the magnetic seal that held the doors together open with a *chunk.*

He wanted to keep up the verbal chess game we had going. It was appealing to his ego. He wanted to convince me how important he was. It was a disease of the successful.

"You'll find, Mr. Kincaid, as you continue in your career that this business is not about who you can make laugh or for how long or why. It's not about jokes or stage presence or any kind of magic you can make with an audience. I used to think so. Now I know the truth. It's all about money. Anything anyone does on- or offstage is just to move a piece of it closer to them."

He leaned back in his chair like he'd just put my king in check.

"I'll be sure to tell that to Chad Karp," I said, "next time I see him."

Then I left.

FOURTEEN

"Biff, what did you *say* to him?"

Drew was walking me to my car. The receptionist with a stud in her tongue had winked at me on the way out. So had Max's secretary. Steve.

"I told him it wasn't my fault that Louie had gotten himself trashed last night," I said. Our conversation echoed in the subterranean parking garage. True to Hollywood etiquette, we'd stayed silent as we shared an elevator down with other people from his office. "Your boss was looking to pin the blame on the comic and I wasn't going to let him."

"Yeah? Anything else?"

"He showed me this story that's going to be on a tabloid show called *Page One*," I said. "Sheryl Franklin's the reporter. Look for it tonight."

"Is it bad?"

"For Louie's reputation? It starts at bad. Then it goes downhill from there."

Drew didn't look happy. "What *else*?"

"I told him Louie was unhappy with this new kid they got on the show, Larkin Thomas," I said. "But Gottschalk said he had that all under control."

At that, Drew's lips pressed together and he looked straight ahead.

"You figure into that plan, don't you?" I said.

"Can't talk about it right now," Drew said. "But something's in the works."

"Okay, so I spill my guts for your boss, but you can't give me a clue."

"We're making a formal announcement tomorrow," Drew said. "I'll make sure you're informed."

I smiled. "See, now you've really made it," I said. "You've got the industry poker face down."

Drew cracked a grin in spite of himself. "That's Max," he said. "He loves corporate cloak-and-dagger. I mean, look, he has me bring you into the office but he won't let me sit in on the meeting. Nobody has more than two pieces of the puzzle."

We were at my car. "Is this guy really who you want to be with?" I said. "I didn't get the idea that he knows comedy or even what's funny."

"His numbers are what make him right," Drew said. "He knows a lot of people on the film and TV side, and I mean a lot. He could get you a six-figure development deal at a network by picking up the phone."

"So I could sit on my ass for a year while a couple of writers try to figure out if I should be a cop with a talking dog or a bumbling dad with a loving wife?" I said. "No thanks. I don't want my act to end up as punch lines in a sitcom pilot that never sees the light of day."

Drew laughed. "Same old Kincaid," he said. "Never gave a damn about anybody's opinion but his own."

"The only thing I give a damn about right now is who killed Tiger Moore," I said. "Everyone else seems to be more concerned about five ratings points than one dead comic."

That night at the Comedy Store I saw I was being followed.

A gold-colored Mercedes picked me up as I left Beachwood Canyon. It stayed with me as I zigzagged across Franklin to the residential part of Hollywood Boulevard and then down to Sunset. As I pulled into the Comedy Store it cruised by once, then circled. By that time I'd parked and staked out the Original Room in time to see Sheryl Franklin valet-park the gold Mercedes across the street at the House of Blues. Ah-hah.

She was wearing a two-piece outfit this time, a mint green halter top and a microskirt with white high heels, all designed to show her tan flat stomach and tan long legs as she ran across Sunset, dodging traffic. She looked like a flight attendant on Aerobics Airlines.

I sat in the back of the Original Room and waited as she studied the lineup and bought a ticket, taking a seat toward the back. When the waitress came around she ordered a glass of red wine and asked where I could be found and by the time the waitress pointed to my seat I was no longer there. I ducked into the bar and got a bottle of beer. I came into the Original Room through another entrance and took the seat next to Sheryl before she knew I was looking for her.

"Looking for me?" I said.

She turned and saw me, her bright blue eyes registering delighted surprise. She leaned in and gave me a one-arm hug and a light kiss on the cheek. "Biff! Hello! So good to see you again!"

"I saw your report on *Page One*," I said.

She expertly ran a hand through her flowing blond hair. "What did you think?" she asked, batting her eyelashes at me. She had a great smile. "How did I look on TV?"

"Let's cut the shit," I said. "I know you're not here to see me go on."

"Remember that video we had of Louie's act that you saw in my story?" she said. "We had you on tape too. I thought you were very funny."

"If you checked into my background," I said, "you'll see I'm not fond of having my act recorded without my permission."

She reached into her purse. "That's why I brought you the tape," she said. She handed me a small black rectangle with a metal casing. A Hi-8 tape.

I looked at it.

"It's all there," she said. "You, Louie and the guy after. I can't remember his name."

I nodded and pocketed the tape.

"Don't I even get a thank-you?" she said.

"It's something you shouldn't have done in the first place."

"I just can't help being a bad girl sometimes."

I smiled and shook my head. "You never stop, do you?"

"I call it power flirting," she said, moving sensuously in her seat. "I've done well with it over the years. Made all the easier when the subject is someone you'd look twice at anyway."

I didn't have anything to say to that. I put my bottle of beer to my lips and shrugged with my eyebrows and looked at whoever was onstage. "What are you working on now?" I asked.

"You."

"And what do I know?"

"Why Louie Baxter fell off the wagon with a *thud* heard around Hollywood."

"What's the latest from the set of *Baxter's Place*?" I asked.

"Louie stayed home to sleep it off. The cast and crew are going to have to work overtime to get an episode wrapped by Friday. The script's been rewritten so Louie has a lot less to do." She sipped her wine. She was not smiling. "Not a good sign. You know the cute kid who plays his younger brother? Larkin Thomas? He did a spread in *GQ* that hits the stands next week. He's getting a ton of fan mail and he hasn't even been on the air yet. The writers are pushing to make him as big as Louie in the show. And he has something Louie will never have."

"What's that?"

"Fuckability."

"Who told you this?"

"Who do you think? Larkin Thomas. He told me everything." She leaned in so close I could feel her wine-scented breath on my face like flower petals. "Except for the fuckability. I know that when I see it. Don't you know? Funny men with handsome square jaws are all the rage."

"You seen this kid's act?" I said. "You sure he's funny?"

Her eyes scanned my face and focused on my mouth. "Max Gottschalk thinks so. He just signed Larkin Thomas as a new client."

"Is that so?" That must have been the big news Drew couldn't tell me in the parking garage. I let her keep her face close. "So is that your lead tomorrow?" I said. "Louie Baxter may be out of a job?"

She shook her head silently, a smile playing at the corners of her lips. "No. Too early for that."

"So what's going up on the satellite feed tomorrow?"

She sat back. "That Louie Baxter's being stalked by a mysterious fan who's left three notes on the set."

"Three?"

She smiled and nodded and sipped her wine. "You know about the first two, don't you? Well, there was a third one today."

"What'd it say?"

"That's unknown. The note was delivered to Louie unopened, and Louie was, you know, home with the flu."

"You know, I'm getting the idea where you get your information."

She put a finger to her lips, and then to mine. "A good reporter never reveals her sources."

"Someone close to Louie," I guessed. "Very close."

"Now-now-now, Biff. You must always think the best of your fellow man."

"Thanks for the warning," I said. It was almost time for me to go on. "Do me a favor, though. Leave my name out of your future stories."

She pouted. "Don't you want to be on TV?"

"Not on your show."

"But this is going to be big," she said. "Everyone will want to know about the Heckler."

"Who?"

"You like that?" She winked at me and shifted in her seat. "I made that up myself. Like Son of Sam or the Night Stalker. It's catchy." She giggled, then lowered her voice to sound like she was doing a voice-over for one of her stories. " 'The Heckler. When will he strike again?' "

I left the Store that night and decided to hit the other clubs. There was someone else I wanted to talk to. Larkin Thomas.

I drove east on Sunset and tried the Laugh Factory first, since that was where Louie said Larkin had done the open mike night. He wasn't there and he hadn't been in. I cruised down to Melrose and walked into the Improv. As I scanned the restaurant outside the showroom I realized I didn't know what Larkin Thomas looked like. I checked the schedule. Larkin Thomas had been on an hour ago. A ten-minute showcase. Max Gottschalk must have phoned it in.

The emcee was Bobby Hall, a comic I knew from around town and I snagged him in the hallway outside the showroom. He took me back out to the restaurant and pointed out a figure sitting at the bar: blue jeans rolled up at the cuffs, black boots, and the kind of white-ribbed tank top commonly referred to as a wife-beater. The straps were stretched over the muscles of his shoulders and back. He was drinking a beer so light and clear I could see through it from where I was standing. No one was talking to him and there was an empty barstool on either side. The comedy circle is a tight one. He hadn't broken in yet.

I asked Bobby how he'd done onstage. Bobby took one thumb and pointed it down. I told Bobby to let me know if he needed an extra comic on the show and went to meet Larkin Thomas.

I took the stool on the left and nodded at the bartender. We shook hands and he greeted me by name. Larkin turned to look. The bartender asked me to name my poison and I ordered a Guinness.

"You sure you want to sit there, friend?" Larkin said by way of greeting.

"Let me know if there's some reason I shouldn't," I said.

"You a comic?"

I nodded.

"At this club?"

I nodded again.

He leaned back on his barstool and looked at the schedule. As he held on to the bar I could see the muscles move under his skin. "What time you on?"

"I'm not on the schedule," I said. "The emcee knows I'm here in case of any fallouts."

He turned back to his beer. I had the feeling it wasn't his

first. He had full black hair, slick with gel, a Roman nose and hooded blue eyes. A good-looking kid. "Too bad you weren't here an hour ago," he said. "Could have had my spot."

"I don't bump other comics," I said.

He snorted. "Who says I'm a comic?" He nodded at the stool where I was sitting. "You're the first one who's wanted to sit there all night."

"Why do you think that is?"

"Because Louie Baxter put the word out on me," he said. He gestured with his beer mug. "None of these assholes will give me the time of day."

"Louie's scared," I said.

"Of what?" Larkin said. "Of me? I know I can't carry a show all by myself. I know I'm the straight man who feeds him all the setup lines. Jesus, he complains to writers on the set if my dialogue is too funny. Every scene they got me in a T-shirt or a wife-beater if I'm wearing anything at all. I was a personal trainer for three years. I know what's going on."

"That's not what he's scared of," I said.

"Oh." He looked at me. "You mean the death threats."

I nodded. "They're more than threats at this point."

"What do you mean?"

"There's a comedian named Tiger Moore," I said. "Friend of Louie's. Got the same threats up in Vegas, and they didn't turn out to be empty."

"What happened to him?"

"He's dead."

Larkin was quiet for a while. "They have any idea who did it?"

"The police? No. I think it's the same person who's after Louie. And I came out here tonight to see if you had any ideas on the subject."

He recoiled as if I'd read him his first Miranda right. "Me? No! I never heard of this Tiger Moore and I barely knew who Louie was until my agent called me in for the audition."

"Anyone else?" I said. "Someone who got fired recently, might have felt burned on a business deal . . ."

Larkin shook his head. "Can't think of anyone. Sure as hell

wasn't me. Jesus, who the hell can get past Baldy the Guard Dog to say two words to Louie? That bodyguard sticks to Louie like he's the freakin' president of the United States or something."

My Guinness had settled and I started drinking it. I nodded toward the showroom. "So how'd it go in there?"

He sank his head until it connected with the bar surface. "I suck," he said. "I stink. I'm not ready for this."

"No," I said. "You're not."

He lifted his head and looked at me. "All I hear from everyone else is how I'll get better."

"That'll only happen if you stick with it," I said. "And you'll only stick with it if you love it. Do you love it?"

He shook his head. "No."

I waited.

"I stand up there and I feel like my heart is going to come out of my chest. My hands feel like ice. I can't think of anything to say. Sweat comes pouring off my forehead . . . I . . ." He turned to me, smiling for the first time. "I'm not funny. I'm not a funny guy. I don't have that good of a sense of humor. My new manager says that stand-up is a great way to get exposure and he's right, but it's just been torture. I dread going onstage, I feel miserable after and everyone thinks I suck."

"Then you should quit," I said.

"I want to." He sighed, and half an inch seemed to go out of his muscles. "Acting's so much better. I've got my lines written for me, I know where to go, what to do . . . I feel I can color in a character, you know? Give him dimension. That's fun. That's . . . relaxing, even."

"Then stick with that," I said. "But stand-up's too tough a game to play for anything but keeps."

"Yeah." He thought it over a little bit and seemed to sit up straighter. "I just can't do it anymore. I don't want to. Not right now. Is that a good enough reason?"

"That's an excellent reason," I said. "You ever want to come back it'll always be here."

"Okay." He looked around him. "Well, no reason to stick around here and feel the warmth, is there?"

"No."

He drained his beer and threw some money down. He got up and put on a black leather jacket. He'd been sitting on it. "Thanks," he said to me. "What's your name again?"

"Biff Kincaid."

We shook. I handed him my business card. "You hear anything you think I should know about Louie, call me."

He tucked the card away. "Louie doesn't talk to me unless the cameras are rolling," he said. "But nice meeting you."

"Drive safe."

I watched him go, walking out of the Improv with all the bounce and juice a twenty-two-year-old should have. I heard a motorcycle engine roar to life and speed down Melrose.

Bobby Hall came over. "What'd you say to him?"

I smiled. "To get the hell out of here and make room for the real comics."

Hall laughed. "Kincaid, you crack me up." He looked at the schedule. "And speaking of room . . ."

"Yeah?"

"I think Frank Waller is a no-show. You want to do some time?"

"Absolutely."

Tuesday I drove to the airport with one packed suitcase and the ten grand cash in my pocket. I hadn't called ahead to make reservations. With ten G's to burn, I was going to improvise.

I kept checking my rearview mirror to see if I was being followed. I wasn't looking for Sheryl Franklin's gold Mercedes. She was out taping a segment for air that day. This would be a different car.

I spotted it as I cruised past the oil wells on South La Cienega: a blue Toyota MR2. A little too conspicuous for a follow car but a good performance match for my ticket-red RX-7. The windows were tinted so I couldn't see in. It had to be someone from the *Page One* staff. They were going to stay on me. That's the only way they could own the Louie Baxter story. My first priority should have been to shake whoever was on my tail. I didn't mind. It was just Sheryl letting me know she cared.

I got to the airport and parked in the lot, taking the shuttle to Terminal One at LAX. There I studied the monitor listing departing flights and bought two tickets, one to San Francisco and one to Las Vegas. I'd picked two flights departing within an hour of each other from gates set side by side. I went through airport security carrying only the one bag, bought a newspaper and sat down, waiting for my tail to break cover.

I spotted him by a coffee cart, a twenty-five-year-old sandy-haired guy about an inch taller than me with his haircut styled to stick straight up, fashionably faded jeans and a bowling shirt. I shook my head. They hadn't chosen a professional, just an eager beaver production assistant who had never followed anyone in his life.

He made a phone call and then sat down in the waiting area two seats over and across from me, pretending to read a magazine. I got out my San Francisco ticket and looked it over, making sure he could see the flight number written on the outside. Then I went up to the San Francisco gate and checked the time. I called the Comedy Store from a pay phone and canceled my shows for the week. I sat back down and waited until he got up to go and purchase a ticket for the same flight at the gate, and then while he was distracted I got my boarding pass for Vegas. I sat back down in my old seat. He wandered off to make another phone call. He thought he had me. He had so much to learn before he was to become a Jedi like his father.

The flight to San Francisco was called thirty minutes before the flight to Vegas. I got in line, hanging around with the other passengers, and when it started to board I made sure my shadow was in line behind me, then made a show of getting paged. I went to the phone, checked my messages at home and got back in line. The guy sent to tail me was now twenty people ahead of me. He kept turning around to look at me by pretending to scratch his ear.

I saw him get on board and then ducked out of line, walking over to the flight to Las Vegas. In my window seat I looked out and watched the flight to San Francisco taxi and take off. Bye bye. Say hi to Sheryl for me.

I was on my own.

I landed in Las Vegas and rented a car. I drove straight to the Palace, valet-parked and walked through the lobby and into the offices of the Comedysino. Dave Parker was on the phones, his glasses pushed up on his cherubic face, his curly black hair dangling over his forehead. He was taking a reservation for that evening's show.

"Yes, ma'am," he said. "You need to check in at the door by seven-thirty." Pause. "We'll see you then."

He hung up. "Kincaid!" he said, standing up to shake my hand. I took it automatically, even knowing what I was going to say to him. He was wearing jeans that looked too new and a T-shirt that didn't hide the jiggle of his torso. "Rick didn't tell me you were coming into town."

"Rick doesn't know I'm here," I said.

"You got another gig?" he asked, sitting back down.

"Yeah," I said. "I'm working the unsolved murder of Tiger Moore."

That was an unusual thing for me to say. Dave nodded after a few seconds. "I haven't heard anything. You?"

"I was on my way to see the Las Vegas police. I thought I'd stop by here first."

"Why? The Vegas cops call you back in?"

"They didn't," I said. "I've got some information for them."

"Oh? Like what?"

"That's where you come in," I said.

Dave sat up a little straighter in his chair. "Really?"

"I've still got to fill in a few blanks," I said.

"Such as?"

"Why did you leave that note backstage for Tiger?" I said.

Dave blinked, took hold of the arms of his chair like he was thinking of making a run for it, decided against it, sat back, took off his glasses, cleaned them and put them back on. "Biff," he said, "I have no idea what you're talking about."

143

"Tiger's killer didn't leave that note," I said. "He wrote it, but he gave it to you. You probably didn't even know what it said. You left it backstage for Tiger to find." I paused. "Why?"

He spread his hands. "Biff, why are you accusing me of this?"

"It's the only possible answer, Dave," I said. "No one could have gotten backstage at those particular times except for you and Bobby Lee Garnett. Bobby Lee's a worthless falling-down drunk, which worked in your favor. You just waited until he was passed out and slipped the note into place."

Dave had a light film of sweat across his pale forehead. He was looking up at me through his glasses, trying to stretch his mouth into something like a smile. It was the same smile he probably gave the schoolyard bully after his books had been knocked out of his arms and kicked down the hallway, before he got stuffed into a locker.

"Tiger's dead now," I said. "There've been three notes left for his friend Louie Baxter in L.A. I don't think you had anything to do with those but I think they're from the same person who left the notes up here. What I want to know is who is it?"

Dave moved uncomfortably in his seat, as if a hole had been cut in the bottom and he was being probed internally. He used his fingers to wipe at his face. They came away slick and trembling. "I don't know."

"How'd he contact you the first time?" I asked.

"An envelope came for me," he said. He looked around to make sure no one else could possibly hear his confession.

"Like the one you delivered?"

He nodded. "By overnight delivery."

"What was in it? The first note?"

"No note. Just five hundred dollars."

"Cash?"

He nodded. "I was looking around for Rick, wondering what to do with the money or what it was for. Then the phone rang. It was . . . him."

"Who's 'him'?"

"I don't know."

"Where was he calling from?"

"I don't know."

"When was this? Do you know that?"

"A week ago. Right after Tiger had started his week here."

"What did he say?"

Dave licked his lips, trying to bring blood back into them. "He said, 'Did you get my present?' I asked who are you, what do you want . . . He wouldn't answer. He just said 'Would you like another five hundred?' And I didn't say anything so he told me there was another envelope delivered to the front desk with my name on it. Then he hung up. I got up, I went to the front desk, and sure enough there was another delivery there for me. I opened it up and found another five hundred cash with an envelope inside, addressed to Tiger. While I was standing there the front desk got a call for me. I took it. It was him again. I started to ask him something and he cut me off. It was like he was there, in the lobby watching me. I looked around to see if I could spot him on a pay phone, but it was too crowded.

" 'Deliver it tonight,' he said. 'He's not to know where it came from or how it got there.'

" 'I'm not doing this,' I said, 'unless I know what I'm delivering. What's inside?'

" 'A message,' he said.

" 'What's it say?'

" 'Hello.'

"Then he hung up."

Dave didn't say anything else right away, so I prompted him. "So you delivered the note that night."

Dave nodded. "While Tiger was onstage. I didn't know what it said until he showed it to me—you know that, 'get off, you suck' stuff. I didn't know if it was a joke or not, but I saw Tiger's reaction and I had the feeling it wasn't.

"Then Tiger got attacked and I knew it had something to do with that note and whoever had sent it. Right after Rick had told me what happened to Tiger I knew the police were on their way and I was figuring out what I was going to tell them when a second envelope came to the front desk, addressed to me. No note this time. Just a picture of me saying good-bye to my mom as I went off to work. That morning."

"She in town visiting?"

Dave lowered his eyes. "I live with my mom. She's not in the best of health and I'm the only child. Nobody here knows my situation. But *he* knew. And he wanted *me* to know that he knew. I called my mom to make sure she was all right, and she'd gotten a note, slipped in the mail slot, addressed to me. I asked her to open it up and read it to me over the phone. It consisted of one word: 'Don't.' "

I nodded. "Short but sweet."

"So you can't tell the police I did this, Kincaid." Dave was pleading from his chair. "There can be no way for him to know I told you. He'd come after my mom and me. I can't let anything happen to her. She's old and sick." His voice started to break. His eyes glistened with tears. "If anything happened to me there's no one else to take care of her. She'd end up in a state home or something."

"I won't tell the police," I said. "At least not right now."

"Thanks, Kincaid." He sniffed and wiped his face.

"You save the courier pouches the money came in?"

"You mean as evidence?"

"Yeah."

"No."

I looked at him and thought: I had guessed correctly. He had been the source of the note delivered to Tiger Moore. But who was delivering them down in L.A. to Louie Baxter?

"What did he sound like?" I said. "The guy on the phone."

"I don't know."

"What do you mean? You said you—"

"He used one of those buzzer things people who've had throat cancer use," Dave said. "Made him sound like a robot. I don't know what his real voice sounds like." He shivered, even though the room was normal temperature. "Watch out for this guy, Kincaid. He's clever, and he's dangerous. Let me know when he's dead or in jail."

Detective Charles Gregory was in a bad mood. I didn't know how good a mood he was in before until I met with him now. I showed up at the front desk at the station house and asked to see him. He came out wearing his badge on his belt and gun on his shoulder, right next to a large chip he'd placed there.

"You ever think of making an appointment?" he said by way of greeting. "I guess comedians show up whenever they feel like it."

"I was in the neighborhood," I said. "I thought I'd drop in."

He held the gate open for me and nodded me through to the desk sergeant on duty. "What is it now?" he asked.

"I have some information I thought you might find useful."

He sat behind his desk. I took the empty chair.

"All right," he said. "Spill it."

"There's another comedian getting notes down in L.A.," I said. "Louie Baxter."

He wrote that down. "Should I know that name?"

"He's got a sitcom on TV."

"I'll ask my wife," Gregory said. "She watches TV. I don't."

"No?"

"No, I read these things called books. Police officers do that sometimes."

"Maybe I came at a bad time."

"How would you know?" he said. "You didn't bother to ask."

I scooted my chair back. "I'll tell you the rest of what I've learned later," I said, getting up. "Maybe I'll write you a letter."

"Sit down, Kincaid."

I sat.

Gregory toyed with his pen and looked up at the fluorescent lights before fixing his large brown eyes on me. "You remember that guy we had in custody? Lawless?"

"Sure."

"Yeah, that's right, he tore up the visitor's room for you. I forgot." He handed me an eight-by-ten. "You remember her?"

The strikingly beautiful face looked out from a publicity photo. The gravity-defying figure was sewn into a costume that left too little to the imagination. I didn't have to use mine. I'd seen it all.

I looked up. "Linda Mallory," I said. "The waitress at the Comedysino. Lawless's ex-girlfriend."

Gregory nodded. "Lawless made bail last night," he said.

"Oh, no."

"He went to Linda's apartment. Rick Partino was there. Lawless killed them both."

I felt as if someone had dropped an anvil on my chest. I could move my arms and legs, but I didn't know what to do with them. My head seemed to be made of iron shavings. Gregory waited me out.

"I was just at the Comedysino," I said. "Dave—the guy answering the phones—didn't say anything about it."

"He doesn't know yet," Gregory said. "Call came in from Linda's roommate two hours ago. Another detective caught the squeal. I just came from the crime scene. You know what they were doing in her apartment, alone, together, late at night? Working out a vacation and paid holiday schedule for all the waitresses. Then Lawless came in and killed them both. Beat 'em to death with his bare hands."

I picked up the picture of Linda again. "Rick trusted her," I said. "She was smart."

"Yeah."

Silence in our conversation. I could hear phones ringing and keyboards clacking, the endless rank-and-file processing of crime.

"Where's Lawless?" I asked.

"In jail. Again. Sobbing. Saying he loved her. He can't live with the guilt. Wants us to give him the death penalty."

"Think he'll get it?"

"I hope so."

"If he does," I said, "I'd like to be there when he's executed."

"I'll save you a seat for the show."

Nothing more to say. Not right then. I'd tell him about Louie and Chad Karp and everything else a few minutes later. Not just yet.

"I apologize for my bad mood," Gregory said.

FIFTEEN

Before I left, I told Gregory about Louie Baxter and the notes that had been left for him and what had happened two years ago with another comedian named Chad Karp. I gave the detective Max Gottschalk's business phone number and advised him to watch *Page One* that night. He said he'd have someone at the station house tape it. When he was home, he liked peace and quiet and didn't like the TV on except during the NBA playoffs.

I didn't tell him about Dave delivering the note to Tiger. It doesn't sound like it would have done him any good anyway. I didn't tell him that I was going around and seeing what else I could find out. I did, however, tell him I'd spent the night with Linda.

"You tell Lawless that?" Gregory asked. "Is that why he smashed the glass in the visitor's room to get at you?"

"Yeah," I said.

"I thought so," he said. "Why'd you do that if you knew he was so jealous?"

"I wanted him on the inside a little longer," I said. "I figured if I got him riled up he'd cause trouble and stay behind bars a little longer."

"Didn't work out quite that way."

"I guess not."

"You might even say that idea backfired," Gregory said. "The judge he saw the next day said the incident was an unnecessary use of force and refused to increase Lawless's bail. Wanted to know why the prisoner had been antagonized by a visitor he'd never met before."

Meaning me. "And now Linda's dead," I said.

"He might have done the same thing anyway," Gregory said.

"I'll try to believe that," I said. "Who made his bail, anyway?"

"His bosses over in the show he was dancing in. Said the show wasn't the same without him."

I was going to make a smart remark about how I hoped they felt as guilty as I did, but I realized that that really wasn't possible so I kept quiet.

"How'd this happen?" Gregory asked. "You and Linda?"

"We talked earlier that night at the club," I said. "She came up to my room and brought me the note I later turned over to you."

"What time was this?"

"A little after midnight."

"She just came to your room?"

"Yeah."

"And stayed."

"When I got up in the morning, she was gone."

"Ever talk to her again?"

"No."

Silence.

"I can't help but feel partly responsible for her death," I said.

"There's no way to tell," Gregory said. "There's only what's been done and what the system can do about punishing those who committed the crime. There's no bringing her back. There's no lessening of her pain. You can't communicate with her. It's done."

"You think Lawless will face capital punishment?" I asked.

"My honest opinion is I think he'll commit suicide in prison," Gregory said.

"I hope so," I said.

"You're new to this," Gregory said. "You'll learn not to hope."

I left Las Vegas later that same day. I didn't want to spend the night there. It was night when the plane lifted off for Salt

Lake City and the Vegas strip glittered below me like the path to Oz.

I felt guilty and Gregory hadn't tried to talk me out of it. Maybe if I hadn't provoked Lawless, she'd still be alive. But if the ghost of Chad Karp had never shown up to play his deadly games, there'd be no maybe about it.

Louie Baxter thought Karp was out for revenge. Well, whaddaya know? Now, so was I.

I got to Salt Lake City and into an airport hotel in time for the evening news. I surfed the local cable until I found what I was looking for: the daily broadcast of *Page One*.

Sheryl Franklin's story was in the second segment. Ted the anchor led into it: "Louie Baxter, comedy's biggest reigning party animal, was back on the set of his still-a-hit sitcom *Baxter's Place* today after missing an entire day due to what his manager calls the flu, but the rumor mills call it a big fall off the sobriety wagon."

So kind, so tender in its approach. *Page One* was a friend to the celebrity in need.

"Sheryl Franklin has the story."

The screen cut to eerily tinted backstage footage of Louie on *Baxter's Place*, slowed down and with slasher movie music underneath. Sheryl's voice was heard narrating: "Is a mad stalker hunting Louie Baxter on the set of his own TV show? And is this the reason he allegedly went on a drinking and drugging binge that left him unable to work Tuesday?"

Cut to a man in shadow, his face unrecognizable and his voice distorted so he sounded like Satan. Subtitles were used so he could be understood. "Louie definitely feels someone is after him."

Sheryl: "This is a close friend of Louie's, who saw him just hours after Louie Baxter dispatched his bodyguard to beat up paparazzi trying to get a picture outside the world famous Palm Restaurant. We had that story for you first here on *Page One*."

Once again, I saw the footage of Dirk Pastor in action, gracefully arcing the photographers into their own destruction.

Back to the mystery witness in shadow: "Louie told me he had a stalker who was leaving notes for him that sounded like something a heckler would say: 'Get off. You stink.' That kind of thing."

Uh-oh, I thought. Who is *this* guy? Maybe he was the drug dealer Louie ran off with that night, the driver of the Mercedes.

Mystery man: "He said he wasn't sure who it was, but it could be someone who wanted revenge on him for something from Louie's past."

Cut to Sheryl, standing in front of the studio where *Baxter's Place* was taped. She was wearing the two-piece outfit I'd seen her in last night at the Comedy Store.

"On the set of *Baxter's Place,* security is tighter than ever. But still, this mad Heckler seems to get through. Yesterday another note was left for Louie Baxter. Its contents are as yet unknown, but it has rattled an already unstable star. So far, the Heckler's attacks have all been on paper, but they've left their mark on Louie's psyche. Louie Baxter was back on the set today, learning his lines and desperately trying to make up for the time that was lost by his fall from grace. Scripts have had to be rewritten to cover for this absence—and the possibility of other delays by the frightened comedian unless this crazed stalker is stopped. The Heckler's presence has already hit Louie where it hurts the most—in the funny bone. Ted?"

Back to Ted, the platinum-haired anchor: "Thank you, Sheryl. Coming up next—was George Washington, the father of our country, America's first pothead? The answer when *Page One* returns."

Theme music to commercial. I turned off the television. Yikes. Sheryl Franklin had pointed a finger at whoever had left the notes, had given him a name, and was trying to flush him out in the open. I don't think she really knew what she was doing. She might draw the Heckler's attention to herself.

I got out the local phone book and looked under nightclubs for Mister Silly's Comedy Club. I'd only played there once and it had been a few years ago. I hadn't killed and I hadn't fallen in love. It was a week that fell in between great and terrible and I hadn't thought about it much since it happened.

It was a Tuesday and I couldn't remember if they were open or not on Tuesdays. I dialed the number. A male voice answered with a tape recording that said tonight's show was an open-mike night, with anyone welcome to perform. Sign-up was at seven o'clock in front of the club. Then it gave the address. When the voice started pitching the show that week I hung up.

I looked at the clock radio in my room. Six-fifteen.

I got directions at the front desk. Mister Silly's was less than five miles away. A seven o'clock sign-up for an open-mike night was unheard of in L.A. There were open-mikers that stood outside the Laugh Factory at six in the morning for fourteen hours to get three minutes of stage time, but that was on the Sunset Strip in Hollywood. I guess the supply was a little sparser here in Utah, or perhaps it was the demand.

There was a nip in the air as I got out of my rental car and walked to the front door of Mister Silly's. It was a converted disco den that had opened during the height of the comedy boom and had stayed open until the Next Big Thing came along.

It was six-forty-five. There were a dozen open-mikers clustered out in front, most of them younger than me. One guy was in a full clown outfit, complete with floppy feet and red nose and white-face makeup. When someone said something funny, he reached in his pocket and honked a horn.

I skirted the group and gently tried the front doors with one hand. Locked. The front windows showed the headshots of who was playing this coming week. The opening act was someone named Tim Apple. Big fat guy with a face-splitting grin. Slight fuzzy duplication on the photograph and clumsy lettering on his name made me think he was a local.

The middle act was Jenni Markham, Comedy Mom. A housewife comic: big 'do, large square-framed glasses, middle-aged, perky smile. Two headshots. One was a close-up, and then, set at a wacky angle, a full body shot showing her wearing a cleaning outfit with a microphone plugged into a vacuum cleaner, kid's toys scattered around, her hair frazzled. Cute.

The headliner was Bobby Lee Garnett, the Comedy Cowboy.

I'll be God-damned, I said to myself as I studied the same headshot I'd seen posted outside the Comedysino in Vegas. The hat parked back on the balding head, the straw in the teeth. Boy howdy.

I looked at the sign advertising show times and prices. Wednesday through Saturday. Bobby Lee wasn't due in for another twenty-four hours. I wondered where he was holed up now.

I looked around the gathered performers for a face to match Tim Apple's headshot. I spotted it talking to the clown. I approached and looked at him over the clown's shoulder until he looked back.

"Are you Tim Apple?" I asked. "The emcee?"

"Yeah."

I introduced myself and made a flattering comment about how he had lost weight since the headshot had been taken. "I'm in town just for the night," I said, "and I came down here looking for some stage time."

"They should have the sign-up sheet out here by seven," he said, looking around. "Don't know where Bonnie is with it . . ." He looked back at me. "Bonnie's the assistant night manager."

"I've played here before."

"Oh! Well, then, maybe you already know Bonnie."

"It was a few years ago," I said. "I can't even remember where the condo is the comedians stay at."

"I do," Tim said. "Just came from cleaning it up."

I pointed at Bobby Lee's headshot. "I know that guy," I said. "Is he in town yet?"

Tim rolled his eyes up in the back of his head. "Yes."

"Is he at the condo?"

"He showed up about three this morning, pounding on the front door," Tim said. "Took an all-night bus in from God knows where and walked here from the station in his cowboy boots 'cause he couldn't afford a cab. Smuggled a bottle of Jack Daniel's in his suitcase and opened it up and started a one-man party. At three in the morning. He finally passed out about noon."

"I just wanted to ask him where I could find Mark Roper," I said. "Or maybe you know."

"The booker?" Tim frowned. "I couldn't tell you. He's got some one-nighters and some other clubs in the West, so he's always on the move. Again, you might want to talk to Bonnie. She's a little more up on the business workings of the club." Tim spread his hands and affected a mock-Spanish accent. "I jess de emcee."

"Mind if I drop by the condo to talk to Bobby Lee?"

"Be my guest," Tim said, "but judging from the way he's sawing logs, he's not going to be upright anytime soon."

"Is the front door open?"

Tim stepped forward to tell me in a confidential tone of voice that the key was inside a hollow stone frog by the front porch. He gave me directions and I thanked him. I got back in my rental car and within fifteen minutes I was at a complex of a dozen duplexes, with one address on the street level and another for the second story. The comic's condo was on the ground floor. The condo above had a sign in the window that read FOR SALE OR LEASE. Big surprise. Once comedians move in, there goes the neighborhood.

I found the key inside the frog and opened the flimsy lock on the front door, which was about as sturdy as wet plywood. A good kick would have served just as well. Inside, on top of a pile of freshly laundered linen pockmarked with some very stubborn stains, I saw a well-photocopied note that outlined the rules and regs for comedians ("no illicit drug buying, taking or selling; no prostitutes, out-call escort services or strippers; no urinating on the public grounds of the condo complex"). Jenni Markham, Comedy Mom, was going to have a wonderful time.

The living room was essentially bare, except for some carpet that had been worn almost into a fuzzy green mat. The place smelled of old laundry and new garbage. There was a coffee table that would last all day at a yard sale and some rubbery dishes in the sink. I couldn't tell if they were clean or dirty. On the counter was the bottle of Jack, with about two fingers of amber liquid sitting at the bottom. Bobby Lee had put in a full shift. It was all they could do to keep up with him at the distillery.

I heard a sound behind me like a diesel engine going uphill. It stopped. I stepped out into the living room and stilled my breath, listening. It came again, from an open darkened bedroom doorway. I stepped toward it and turned on the bedroom light, a single yellow overhead bulb that cast a feeble glow around the room. There was a dresser from an earlier decade, an open closet with one bare wire hanger where Bobby Lee had thrown his luggage, and Bobby Lee himself, sprawled out on the bare mattress of a double bed. He'd used some folded linens as a pillow. He was fully dressed, in a different pair of jeans, boots and Western shirt than when I'd last seen him. These weren't his stage clothes. On the floor was a denim coat that had a fake sheepskin lining.

He had one arm flung up over his head and out of his half-open mouth came the diesel-engine sound, interspersed with equal bouts of silence.

I leaned over the end and pinched him on the fleshy part of his upper arm, beneath his bicep. "Wake up, Bobby Lee."

He snorted and stirred. I twisted the flesh in my fingers and he waved at me with his arm. I stepped back and his arm hit the mattress and he started the diesel snore again.

This wasn't working. I went into the kitchen and found a plastic mixing bowl that didn't seem to have been used lately. The water out of the tap was clear and cold and I filled the bowl with it, walked back in the bedroom, and threw it on Bobby Lee like his mustache was on fire.

His whole body jerked like a defibrillated corpse but it washed the glue out of his eyes. He blinked and tried to sit up, but he had a rather heavy hangover sitting on his head.

"Where am I?" he spluttered. *Whur em Ah?*

"You're in the comedian's condo for Mister Silly's Comedy Club in Salt Lake City," I said.

His eyes lolled around in his head like eight balls after a slow break until he closed them again. "And who're you?"

"It's Biff Kincaid," I said. "We've already met, Bobby Lee."

He heaved his feet over the side of the bed and planted them on the floor, leaning so far forward so his head hung between his knees. He smelled like booze and a bad bus ride. "Vegas," he said. "Just a couple days ago."

"That's me."

"What're you doing in Mormon town?" *Yew.*

"I'm looking for someone," I said. "I thought you might know where he is."

He lifted his head. He seemed to have aged five years since I'd last seen him. There were tobacco-juice stains on his lips and the front of his shirt. In the corner was a lone suitcase with a Greyhound tag still on it. "You see a bottle around somewheres?"

"There's one in the kitchen," I said.

"There anything in it?"

I went and got the bottle of whiskey and a clean glass. "You want any ice?" I called.

"Ice and Coke," he called back. It sounded like it hurt him to raise his voice above a whisper.

I found three ice cubes and half a can of cola gone flat in the refrigerator and poured it in with a finger of the whiskey. I swirled the glass a few times and brought it back into the bedroom.

Bobby Lee reached for the drink but I held it back.

"Come on, man, I'm hurtin' here," Bobby Lee said.

"I'm looking for Mark Roper," I said.

"Gimme that damn drink and I'll tell you where he is," he said.

I handed it over and Bobby Lee gulped it so fast, some spilled over the sides of his mouth. He stopped to breathe and I repeated I was looking for Mark Roper.

"Portland," he said and went back to scuba practice.

"Portland, Oregon?"

"Yeah," Bobby Lee cocked his head at me. "There's a Portland somewheres else, ain't there?"

"Maine."

"Yeah, well, he ain't in Maine." He drained the rest of the glass. It was like a tonic. Shoulders back, chin up. "That it for the Jack?"

"No refills for now," I said. "When's the last time you talked to Mark Roper?"

"Hell, I don't know. When I took this shit gig, I guess."

"When was that?"

"A month or two." He started to suck on the ice. "You're a nosy sumbitch, you know that?"

"Where can I find him?" I said. "You have a phone number?"

"He works out of a club there called . . . called . . ." He pressed the dewing glass against his forehead. "Man, you sure there ain't no more in that bottle?"

I held out my hand for the glass and made a fresh drink of whiskey and stale soda. I brought the bottle back with me so he could see it was empty and tossed it at his feet. "This is all the party left in the house," I said, handing the glass over. "Now what club does Mark Roper work out of?"

He took his time with this one, drinking it in sips, not gulps. "I'm tryin' to remember," he said. "You can always leave a message for him there and mail and stuff. Haggerty's . . . Hilarities . . . naw . . . Haskell's! Named after that Eddie Haskell guy on *Leave It to Beaver*."

"I know Haskell's," I said. "I played there a few years ago, but Roper wasn't affiliated with it then."

"Hell, I think he's the manager or assistant manager or something. You know him?"

"He booked me for the week at Haskell's," I said. "I never met him."

"He's a big sumbitch," Bobby Lee said. "Big like a football player. Shaggy hair, like he's in a rock band from England or something. Big mustache, beard, glasses. Can hardly see his face."

"Thanks," I said, and turned to go.

"Hey," Bobby Lee said, "I got a question for you."

"Okay."

He picked up the empty bottle of Jack Daniel's. "How do I git another one-a these in Mormon town?"

"You'll find a way, Bobby Lee."

The next day was Wednesday. I pointed my rental car west along I-80 that afternoon into Nevada. Buildings and people dropped away, and within a few hours I was driving across a barren landscape with few exits. Those I saw were marked with signs that read NO SERVICES. Keep drivin', mister.

I saw few cars, either behind me or coming the opposite way. The sky was open horizon to horizon, with low rocky hills in the distance. I could see ahead for miles, the land so flat the road before me shimmered like a mirror. My rental car had a radio and when I hit the scan button it just kept endlessly looping. There was no signal for it to lock on to. When I needed to pee I just pulled over to the side of the road. No one passed. Once I shut off the car's engine and listened to the wind.

It took me almost three hours to reach the town of Alandale. When I pulled in it was after dark, taking an exit off the freeway and driving less than half a mile. The sign at the city limits listed the population at five hundred. There were bullet holes in it.

I slowed my car and drove down the main street. There were maybe a dozen businesses, all supplying basic tools of rural survival. Nothing extraneous. Nothing superfluous. Everything was closed. No one was out. There was one stoplight. It blinked red.

I made the trip through the business section of Alandale in less than a minute, then turned around and drove through it again. I didn't see a single person. There was a motel at the roadside where I'd made the exit, but none in town. There were side streets that branched off into lightless residential areas, but in a small town I'd learned patrolling houses in a strange car is a good way to get someone to draw a bead on you.

I followed the main road farther out, to where it was just unlit asphalt. Louie's directions were blurred by the years, but I found the dirt road he had spoken of that led to the Payroll Saloon. I took it slowly, looking for ruts and rocks, my headlights the only light except for the stars.

There was little scrub and no trees. The land was flat. No houses. I could see lighted oil-well-drilling rigs in the distance. I was out there in the wide open. If anyone approached me I'd see them coming, but where would I go?

I drove for close to a mile. The Payroll Saloon should have been there, looming out of the black emptiness. Maybe I'd gotten Louie's directions wrong. I found a dirt patch to turn around in and as I was maneuvering my rental car the headlights caught something. I stopped and reversed direction, focusing my high beams on what lay ahead.

I'd found the Payroll Saloon. What was left of it.

All I saw was the charred foundation, with a few jagged tim-
bers sticking out of the ground like stalagmites. I put the car in
park and got out, walking closer. The Payroll hadn't been a big
place, but there was precious little left of it now. The embers
had died long ago, the flames voracious in their appetite. The
remains lay before me like a blackened graveyard.

It had burned to the ground.

I got back in my car and headed back onto the dirt road. My
tires hit something that stuck up from the dirt and clanged
against the muffler. I turned around again, casting light on what
I'd just run over.

This time I didn't get out of the car. I didn't want to. I could
see perfectly well from where I sat.

It was the wooden sign that had been posted by the side of
the road, marking the place where the Payroll had been open.
It consisted of a white post with a single arm extended, an inverted L-shape with two metal rings. The sign itself, with the
words *Payroll Saloon* written with an old-time flourish reminis-
cent of the days of the Wild West, had been spared by the fire.
Instead, someone had taken a red paint brush and in large block
letters written a message for all to see, letting them know who
had been there and why.

NOW THAT'S FUNNY!

The hair on the back of my neck started to prickle. The Heckler had been here before me.

I drove back toward the freeway and found the lone motel in
town. It had a dirt parking lot, a sign that read MOTEL and just
below that VACANCY in neon letters. The light was still on in
the office. I parked and walked in.

The office was the front part of someone's own home, sec-
tioned off by a half-closed door. I jangled a small cowbell when
I entered, so I waited patiently by the counter while a small
stout woman with unnaturally black and bountiful hair came
through the half-closed door, leaving behind the glow of a television set tuned to a laugh track.

"Like a room for the night?" she asked. She wore large, thick glasses and carefully applied bright red lipstick and blue eye shadow. She had on a sweatshirt that read UTAH JAZZ and jeans stretched tight over her thick lower body. Her voice was high and nasal, her tone friendly.

"Please," I said.

"Just one of you?"

I nodded. She slid me a room card and I began to fill it out, pausing to hand her my credit card. She wanted to know how long I planned to say.

"Hard to say," I said. "At least through tomorrow."

"Just visiting?"

I didn't mind the questions. I could respond with a few of my own. "I'm looking for someone," I said.

"Oh? Who?" she asked, opening a drawer and fishing out a key. She handed it to me. "I know just about everyone around here."

"Gentleman by the name of Parkins," I said. "Used to run the Payroll Saloon before it burned down."

Her head jerked back as if she had been slapped. Her eyes were wide and frightened. Her red lips drew into a thin line. "How do you know about the Payroll?"

"I was just out there," I said. "I saw it. What's left of it."

"Ned!" she called to the back, her voice hard and high. "Come out here!"

I looked over her shoulder to see if her husband or father was going to come out with a shotgun. I started doing some fast explaining. "I don't mean to cause any trouble," I said to her. "I'm just here trying to find out what happened—"

Ned came out of the back room. Ned was a German shepherd the size of a Harley. I could see muscles move under his thick coat of black-and-brown fur as he walked on all fours. His ears were up and his eyes were locked on me. He trotted to the counter, stood up on his hind legs and put his paws on the counter. He parted black ragged lips to show large stained teeth and started to growl.

"You better get out of here," the woman behind the counter said. "Give me my room key back. I ain't rentin' to you."

"I didn't see another motel," I said.

"There ain't one for sixty miles," she said. "Get in your car and head back where you came from."

I backed out the door. Ned's eyes followed me all the way. When the door closed behind me he vaulted the counter, put his front paws on the glass so I could see how tall he was, and started to bark like there'd been a prison break.

I got in my car and drove off.

I spent the night in my backseat, and I wish I could say it was for the first time. It's a long lonely road for a comedian, but I'm not as young as I used to be so rather than risk the three-hour drive on no sleep back to Salt Lake City I went a half hour down the freeway and pulled over at a rest stop to doze until dawn. I'd counted five cars in the last thirty miles. With no more than a cold concrete washroom and a pay phone for my comfort I bunked in my clothes, listening to the Nevada wind outside make whistles out of the window cracks, drifting off to sleep to do some California dreaming.

What woke me was the sound of other cars.

Trucks, actually. Pickups. Three of them.

There were maybe half a dozen men crammed into the cabs who got out, and as I sat up, blinking in the glare of their headlights, I saw that they had guns in their hands and hard business on their minds.

I scrambled over the partition into the front seat and as I was fumbling my keys out of my pocket I saw one down-jacketed gloved figure breathing steam step forward in all his backlit glory and lay a baseball bat against my windshield. It cracked and held but my vision was ruined and as I cranked the engine I heard twin shotgun blasts and felt the back end of the car sag as my two rear tires were shot out.

I would have made a run for it anyway, as the motor caught and revved, but the baseball bat smashed into the windshield again and this time the safety glass burst and scattered all over me like a bucket of sharp crystals. I closed my eyes and threw my hands up to protect my face and I felt hands and arms reach through and drag me out from behind the wheel and over the hood of my rental car, bits of glass slicing through my clothes, until I was held kneeling on the asphalt in front of the radiator grill. Cold wind whipped through my hair as I looked up and saw a tall figure in a down vest with a red flannel shirt step forward. He still had the baseball bat in his hand. A hunting cap with earflaps was on his head, the flaps buttoned under his chin. He had gray-stained work gloves on the hands that held the bat and scuffed brown boots. I couldn't see his face.

He reached out with the hitting end of the baseball bat and lifted my chin up with it.

"Who are you?" he said in a soft deep drawl.

"My name's Kincaid," I said. "I'm a comedian."

Immediately, I realized that was a foolish and dangerous thing to say.

"Comedian, huh?"

I nodded. He took the bat away from my face, moved it in front of me like a magic wand and then as the other men held me he jabbed me in the stomach with it. I let out a sound and tried to double over in pain, but couldn't.

"What you want around here?" he asked.

"I'm looking for a man named Parkins," I said, my midsection hurting with the effort. "He used to run the Payroll Saloon."

"Jim Parkins is dead," the man with the baseball bat said.

"Sorry to hear that," I said.

The man with the baseball bat started to walk around me, his boots crunching on the pavement. The others in the group made room for him. I watched him go out of my sight, walking behind me, hefting the bat. "Parkins died inside the Payroll Saloon when it was burnt to the ground," he said. "Chained to the stage, along with two other men."

"Who left them there?" I asked.

The baseball bat landed with a *whump* in the small of my back, just on top of my right kidney. Now that hurt.

"He didn't give us his fuckin' name!" he yelled. "All he did was chain us together and pour gas all over the place!" *Whump.* He hit my other kidney. I yelled in agony. "He wore a mask

163

and he never said a fuckin' word!" The bat landed three times again, this time on my legs and ankles. By the time he was through with me, I'd be lucky if I could walk.

One of the other men spoke up, "Jesus Christ, Del, don't cripple him."

"Shut up!" Del yelled.

Del. I remembered that name from Louie's story. Del was the one who had taken Chad Karp off into the night.

I didn't have time to think about it much more because Del's bat landed on the back of my head like he was hitting a runner home from second base. My vision exploded and my head hung forward as I tried to clear the stars out of my eyes before they went nova.

I heard Del quickly walk around in front of me and the bat land hollowly on the ground as Del dropped it to kneel. I found the strength to lift my head as he unsnapped his hunting cap and took it off.

The left half of Del's face was nothing but red angry scar tissue, like his skin was made of wax and someone had taken a soldering iron to it. His skin looked as though it had melted and run before setting. The scar tissue covered the corner of one eye and part of his mouth. He looked half-human, half–something else.

"When the Payroll started to burn, he disappeared. It was just me, Parkins and Clayton, my best friend. We were left chained together around a post. The flames got closer and hotter. I heard Parkins scream. His legs caught on fire. I smelled his flesh burn. His clothes, too. Clayton passed out from the smoke. I knew I was gonna be the last to go." He started to take his gloves off. "But I had a knife in my boot, and I managed to shake it loose. It fell where I could reach it. I did what I had to do."

He held up his hands. Both right and left thumbs ended in ragged, fleshy nubs.

"I cut my thumbs off and slipped the cuffs. I stumbled outside while the others burned up."

He put his gloves back on. "Burns don't hurt so bad at the

time when you get 'em. It's later, in the hospital, when they have to pick the dead skin off, that's when it feels like they're going at your face with a wire brush." He reached into a sheath on his belt and pulled out a game skinning knife, one with a blade at least three inches long and as wide as a banana leaf. It was mounted in a pistol grip for Del's thumbless hands. It had been sharpened to a deadly gleam and used on far bigger prey than me. He turned the blade in the headlights so I could see the tip was serrated on one side. "So I'm gonna ask you something once, then I'm gonna ask you again, and if you can still talk through what's left of your face I'm gonna ask you a third time. If all three answers are the same, then I'll know you're telling the truth: who was he? Who's the man that done this to me?"

"Another comedian," I said. "A man you dragged offstage at the Payroll two years ago. His name was Chad Karp."

He reached out and clenched a hand in my hair to hold my head upright. "See, now that don't count, because we killed that comedian feller. Killed him slow, just like the work order said. So you better start thinkin' of another name." He slipped the point of the knife slowly into my right nostril. "Say good-bye to your nose, handsome."

The night was pierced with the sound of a siren's wail. Del froze and looked around. I kept my eyes on him. I could feel the edge of the knife start to cut into the skin on the inside of my nose. I was keeping very still.

"What the hell—?" Del said. "How did she—?"

He didn't have to wait long. A station wagon remodeled into a patrol car slid to a halt on the asphalt of the rest stop so hard it raised dust. Red-and-blue lights flashed over the scene. A door slammed and I heard a woman's voice bark out, "Hold it right there, Delbert Lacey!"

The knife in my nose disappeared back into Del's belt, leaving a warm slice just above my upper lip. He stood, nudging the bat aside with his foot. "Let him up, fellas," he said.

I was helped to my feet. The pain in my legs and head had receded to a dull throb and I stood like a marionette at rest. If

I was let go I would have sunk to the ground. My nose was bleeding and the first drop reached my mouth. My only salvation was in the hope that the woman I heard was wearing a badge.

She was. She stepped into view, a shining sheriff's star pinned to the dark blue down vest she was wearing against the cold over a brown law uniform. A pretty face, carrying some extra weight. Blond hair pulled back in a bun under a trooper hat. A small jagged scar under the chin. I wanted to kiss her.

"You all right, mister?" she asked.

I nodded and sniffed some blood back up my nose. "I'll live."

"You need to go to the hospital?"

I managed to stand on my own two feet, brushing off the hostile hands that held me. "Nothing's broken." I looked at Del, who was standing back, looking at me like a snake with his rattle cut off. "Not for lack of trying. How'd you find me?"

"Alice Turpin at the motel called to let me know there was a stranger in town asking questions about Jeff Parkins." She turned to Del. "You're still on probation, Del. This isn't going to look good to the judge."

"Aw come on, Sissy." Del's entire manner had changed, from dominating bully to pleading screwup. "Gimme a break."

"I'm through throwing breaks your way, Del Lacey." She took me under one arm and led me toward the patrol car. "Let's go, mister. I'll send a tow truck for your vehicle."

"It's a rental," I said.

She held the door open for me. Del and the others started to get back in their pickups. While the sheriff was busy getting in her side of the car, Del picked up his baseball bat and pointed it at me and glowered with his scarred face. "There's gonna be another time, comedy man."

We looked at each other until the sheriff drove me out on to the highway and back toward town.

SIXTEEN

On the drive back into town I told the sheriff about my evening so far, including my encounter with the Alandale, Nevada, welcoming committee and its charismatic chairman. "You know this Delbert character from before?" I said.

The sheriff's eyes were unreadable in the dashboard glow as we sped along the Nevada highway in the dark. "You could say that," she said. "He's my ex-husband. Still got his last name. Sheriff Lacey. Though most everyone around here calls me Sissy."

"You use that name when you worked at the Payroll Saloon?"

She looked over at me. "Who are you, mister? What are you doing here in Alandale asking questions?"

"I didn't know there was a fire until earlier today," I said. "I was looking for Parkins, the owner."

"He's dead," the sheriff said. "Burned to death in the fire."

I nodded. "Del told me."

"Some creep kidnapped Jim Parkins, Del and Clayton Hollister and tied 'em up in the Saloon and then he torched it." She looked at me again. "You got any idea why?"

"Maybe."

She slowed. We were approaching a lone building by the side

of the highway a few miles away from Alandale with a sign out front that simply said "SHERIFF." "How about you tell me once we get inside."

The interior of the sheriff's office was not much bigger than a gas station. There were half a dozen holding cells, four cruisers parked outside including the one Sissy Lacey drove in, and a police scanner that stayed quiet.

The clock on the wall said it was three-thirty in the morning. No sleep tonight. Sissy cleaned up the cut on my nose, checked my bruises and then made coffee. After she handed me a steaming blue metal mug that was comfortingly hot in my hands, she said, "You never told me who you were."

"My name's Kincaid," I said. "Biff Kincaid. I'm a stand-up comedian from Los Angeles."

She took a moment to listen and then nodded. "Comedian, huh? We don't get too many comedians around here. Why'd you make the trip all the way from L.A.?"

"Long story."

"We got time and we ain't going anywhere."

"This goes back a couple of years," I said, "to a comedy show you had at the Payroll."

"Uh-huh."

"You remember?"

" 'Course I remember. I was there." She pointed to the scar on her chin. "That's how I got this."

"I heard a comedian threw a beer can from the stage and it hit a waitress in the face," I said. "She went down on the floor, the glasses she was carrying on her tray broke and a piece cut her open. Her name was Sissy, too. That you?"

She nodded. "Jim Parkins—my boss—took me to Doc Harper's to patch me up. Believe me, if Jim had been there he would have put a stop to what happened. So would I. I was training to be a deputy then. I heard about it the next morning."

"Your former husband and his buddies rushed the stage and took hold of the comedian who threw the beer can."

"Del and I had just gotten divorced," she said. "He was in the Payroll every night making sure I wasn't stepping out on him. I guess these days they'd call it stalking. I never was able to get the straight story of exactly what happened next."

"The comedian who threw the beer can was named Chad Karp," I said. "Del and his friends held him down while Del offered the other two comedians on the bill a choice: They could stay and share in his punishment or hit the road. They left, leaving the poor opening act to fend for himself against an angry mob led by Del."

"I knew Karp's name," she said. "I'm the one that found him the next morning." She set her coffee mug down and looked at a piece of the wall of the station house as if it held a window to another time. "They . . . Del . . . tied him to the back of his pickup truck and dragged him along a dirt road. I grew up in the South. The Klan used to do that to people."

"Jesus," I whispered.

"When they was through dragging him, they tied him to a wooden post out yonder in the hills. Del . . . he used to do construction . . . he had a portable butane torch with him and he used it to heat a knife and he . . . went to work on Chad. Torturing him."

I was silent. I'd seen the look in Del's eyes. Like a coyote looking at a cat.

"Sometimes he used the knife, sometimes he used the torch, but he went for the most sensitive parts. His fingers. His privates. His . . . face."

I closed my eyes. The pictures I was imagining wouldn't go away. Chad Karp chained to a post, screaming *No . . . please . . . stop . . .* until he was unable to form words anymore. Just bubbling moans.

"Del was drunk out of his mind when he called me up at home and told me where to look for the body. When I found Chad, it was just after daybreak. The ants had gotten to him and the birds were waiting their turn. He looked like something out of a horror movie. Blood had run from the top of his head all the way down his face. Del had . . . Del had scalped him. His face looked like charred meat. His hands were no better. It . . . ." She closed her eyes. "It was awful." She opened her eyes again.

"I called Doc Harper and he came out to help me cut him down."

"Where was the sheriff?"

"He had been there already," Sissy said ruefully. "He was Clayton Hollister. Del's best friend. I ran against him last election and got him voted out of office." She looked into her coffee cup. "He died in the fire, too."

"Chad's assault have anything to do with you unseating him?"

"With Clayton Hollister and Del Lacey running around here, this was like Dodge City in the old days. When it got out what they had done to Chad Karp, folks had had enough. Now at least the sheriff's office is on the right side of the law." She tilted her head at me. "You'd come up here two years ago Clayton would have worn this uniform and watched while Del went to work on you in one a' them holding cells over there. Happened many a time."

"So there might be a few people out there who would want revenge on Del Lacey and Clayton Hollister?"

She nodded. "But not Jim Parkins. He was a good man. He banned Del from the Payroll Saloon after that night until Clayton let him slide two months on his protection money." She grinned. "Jim let me have a look at his books during the election campaign last year. I was going to have Clayton prosecuted but someone went and burned him up last month."

"Anyone ever press charges against Del for what happened to Chad Karp?"

She shook her head. "No."

I sat up a little straighter. "I don't understand that. You had a body, you had witnesses . . . why couldn't the FBI or the state police make a case for murder?"

"The only witnesses we had would swear Del was somewhere else. They all swore the show went fine. They didn't know how one of the comedians ended up chained to a post."

"But you had a body."

"No, we didn't."

"Why?"

"Because Chad Karp wasn't dead when I found him."

"He die later?"

"No."

"But . . . Del said he killed him."

"I thought he had, too, but Doc Harper saved him." She looked at me. "When you say this comedian fella mighta come back to have his revenge . . ." She shook her head. "I don't see how. He's lucky to be alive at all."

Lionel Cedric Harper, M.D., was now retired from medicine, and had moved to northern Idaho. Sheriff Sissy called him and made introductions by phone. She showed me where New Meadows, Idaho, was on the map. I called the rental company and told them what had happened to my car. Sissy had what was left of my automobile towed to the sheriff's office. There was going to be some paperwork for me, but luckily I'd checked all the little boxes and paid the extra fees for all kinds of insurance, even, apparently, against rednecks with baseball bats. I left the battered remains for the rental agency to recover. We checked a bus schedule and it looked as though I was going to be taking the Greyhound all the way to Boise. That was fine by me. I was so sore I could barely walk and had had only half a night's sleep, and that was in the backseat of a car.

Sissy dropped me off at the bus stop, a gas station along the main street of Alandale.

"You let me know what you find out," Sissy said. She had changed out of her sheriff's uniform and into civilian cowgirl clothes—jeans and a flannel shirt. She was a muscular woman but built in proportion. Her hair was loose and streaked from the sun. She kept a shotgun on a gun rack in her own personal pickup. "The last I seen of Chad Karp was when Doc Harper took him to the hospital over in Talmadge."

"Harper ever tell you what happened to him?"

"He said he never came out of his coma," Sissy said. "Not even after someone came to move him."

"Who?"

She shook her head. "Doc might have known, but I didn't ask. I was already well into running my campaign." She looked outside at the chilly landscape as cars intermittently passed by.

The morning light at this altitude had no smog to dilute the blue sky. "Took a lot of stumping for a woman to become sheriff, you know."

"You got my vote," I said. "Thanks for saving my life."

She looked at me and smiled. "Well, I couldn't let them mess up a good-lookin' fella like you, now could I?"

Her bright eyes sparkled in her tan weathered face. She smiled. Out of uniform and off the job, it came easily to her. I was going to say something flattering in return but I heard a low diesel rumble from down the street and turned to see the bus slowing down to make its stop.

"You better get out," she said. "They only stop for five minutes and if the driver doesn't see you he might leave without you."

I opened the door, letting cold wind into the cab of the pickup. She didn't wince at the sensation. She was used to it. Me, I could feel the icy air on my fresh bruises. "I'll let you know when I find him."

"Hope he doesn't find you first."

"One other thing Del said still bothers me," I said.

"What's that?"

"He said something about killing Chad Karp 'just like the work order said.' You were married to him. Was that a phrase he used often?"

Sissy's face grew more lines around the mouth and eyes. "He used to say that when someone hired him to go beat someone up or trash their rig or do some other mischief. This isn't Vegas, but it's still Nevada. A lot of shady characters needing some dirty business done, and Del was the man to do it."

"You saying you think what he did to Chad Karp was a job for hire?"

"I'm saying it could have been."

"Who would have wanted that done?"

"You got me," she said, "but next time I get Del in jail for a Saturday night bust-up I'll ask him."

I nodded once and stepped out of the truck, looking at her as I closed the door and she drove away.

I got on board and bought my ticket from the driver for less than a hundred bucks. I found a seat in the back. I used my overnight bag as a pillow and had drifted off to sleep before the bus even started moving again.

I woke up in Idaho. The sun was the same distance from the horizon, but on a different side of the sky there were mountains. If there had been stops to refuel and pick up more passengers, they hadn't awakened me. I looked at my watch. I estimated I'd been out six hours. No dreams to report. No nightmares, either.

I shook my head to clear my thoughts and stumbled toward the bathroom. Lavatory facilities on board moving vehicles are not known for their aesthetics of sight, sound and odor, and this one was no exception. I felt like I needed a bath when I sat back down.

I sat and gazed dazedly out at the scenery wishing I was back home in Hollywood, getting ready to take a shower before hitting the clubs along the Sunset Strip. It was Thursday night. I'd have a spot in the Original Room at the Store, maybe another one at the Improv. I'd spent plenty of time on the road. As Dan Fogelberg put it so eloquently, the audiences were heavenly. The traveling was hell.

I saw a sign for Boise. Thirty miles. I'd slept through the stop in Twin Falls. I folded my arms against the chill coming off the window and waited for us to stop. When we did, I was in a city I'd never been in surrounded by people I'd never know. I stood in the bus station with my two bags and collection of body bruises and tried to figure out what to do next. I found another car-rental agency and laid down my plastic. I'm from L.A. Without a car I feel naked.

I was tired, dirty and hungry so I decided to give myself some recovery time. It was well within the budget allowed me by Louie Baxter and Max Gottschalk. I found a nice motel room and checked in. A long hot shower led to a change of clothes and a platter of down-home cooking at a restaurant within limping distance. Not low-fat or low-sodium, but quite tasty.

I got back to my room and looked in the local paper for the

Boise channel that carried *Page One* and watched that day's edition. I wanted to see if Sheryl Franklin had dug up any more dirt on Louie. No word of Louie. No sign of Sheryl. Just Ted the anchor. Hm.

I checked the time and realized that Max Gottschalk was probably out of the office by now and Louie was off the set. I had some other numbers I could have called—cell phones for Dirk Pastor and even Sheryl Franklin—but I left them alone. Instead, I called in to check my answering machine messages and see if anyone had left me any new information while I was out on the trail getting my head beat in.

I had three messages.

"Biff, it's Mike at the Comedy Store. I got a fallout tonight. You in town?"

Beep.

"Hi, Biff. It's Sheryl Franklin. I wanted to know if you'd like to get together for a drink or . . . or something. I'm on my cell phone. Here's my number."

The next message started with hissing silence. Some breathing.

In my hotel room in Boise, Idaho, over a thousand miles away I pressed the receiver closer to my ear. What was this?

"They . . . will . . . all . . . die."

I jerked the receiver away from my ear involuntarily. That voice. It felt like a nail was being twisted into my head.

I looked at the instrument in my hand and watched the sound come out of the plastic shallow circle full of little black holes.

"You . . . can't . . . save . . . them . . ."

Dave at the Comedysino had described the voice that had called him after he had received packets of money to give him instructions. He said that caller used an artificial larynx to disguise his voice, buzzing a tone against his throat to shape words instead of using his vocal cords.

Or perhaps he didn't have one to disguise. Perhaps his voice had been taken from him two years ago while chained to a post, savage bullies crippling him before leaving him for dead. Their mistake.

"I . . . swear . . . revenge."

Then the line was disconnected and my answering machine recorded ten seconds of dial tone before informing me in its own synthetic tones that there were no more messages.

I hung up. The message would be saved automatically.

Someone had ratted me out. He had gotten my number from somewhere, and, more important, the knowledge that I was investigating him.

Suddenly I wasn't sorry I was on the road anymore. That was my advantage. No one, at this moment, knew exactly where I was. If I chose, I could stay hidden for as long as I liked.

And find the Heckler before he found me.

Doc Harper lived in a cabin two hours north of Boise near the town of New Meadows, Idaho, population 600. I drove up there the next day, having checked out of my motel room in Boise. Although the size of the town was the same as Alandale, the scenery was markedly different. Mountains. Streams. Trees. Fish. Beautiful. Serene. No wonder so many hate groups located here.

His cabin turned out to be a two-story house sitting in a clearing right by a small creek, with a brand-new sport utility vehicle sitting on the recently paved driveway. Doc Harper had done well with his retirement funds. I parked my rental car and got out to breathe the clean air, my hands on my hips, back to the wind, until I heard a sturdy voice hail me from somewhere in the piney woods.

I turned. Doc Harper came into view, in hip waders over jeans, wearing a floppy fishing hat with lures stuck in it and carrying a rod and reel and tackle box. He had a pink round face, stood about five-five and had packed on a few pounds since he'd gotten out of medical school. He had a white mustache waxed into a slight curl at the ends and was breathing heavy as we met in the driveway.

"You that comedy fella?" he said by way of greeting. He had bright blue eyes that held a constant smile.

"Biff Kincaid," I said and extended my hand. Harper awkwardly shifted his rod and reel to shake.

"Lionel Harper. Please don't call me Doc. Everyone in Alandale called me that and now I'm retired. I don't even put the M.D. on my checks anymore. My shingle's down for good."

"All right, Lionel."

"Come on inside."

I followed him as he opened the front door without using a key. He didn't need to. There was no lock.

Inside, the cabin was lined with wood, with a living room big enough to house a small aircraft. There was a stone fireplace, a stuffed trout hanging over the mantel, and memorabilia from a lifetime of medicine mounted on the walls. Windows looked out onto the creek in back and a deck shaded with trees that rustled in the breeze.

"Nice place," I said. "Hate to think what it would cost me back home in California."

"Hell to heat in the winter," Harper said as he stripped off his waders and set down his gear. When he took off his hat I could see he was bald except for a fringe around his skull. "Spend a lot of time upstairs, where the warm air goes."

"Must be pretty with all the snow, that time of year."

"Pretty all year around up here," he said. "You say you're from California?"

"L.A."

"Christ, I hate California. No offense, son. But you people are crazy to live in that hellhole."

"You ever been there?"

"I went to some medical conferences there. Sat on the freeway for an hour in air I could literally see, trying to go from the airport to downtown. I mean, I could *see* the air. Someone asked me if I wanted to go to the mountains, I said what mountains? The damn smog was so bad I couldn't even see the mountains."

I nodded. "Must have been in the summer."

"Before the riots and OJ," he said. "After that crap, I never set foot there again. Beer?"

"Sure." It was three o'clock in the afternoon.

"Have a seat."

I eased my aching bones down on an overstuffed couch with cowhide pillows. Harper came out of the kitchen carrying two amber bottles with no labels and handed me one. We toasted. "Here's to swimming with bowlegged women."

"Live long and prosper."

We drank. It was a hoppy brew, with a sharp aftertaste. I held the bottle away from me and studied it. "What's this?" I asked.

"You don't like it?"

"No, it's good," I said. "I prefer stout and ale over lager."

"Good."

"But where'd you get this?"

"From the cellar," he said. "Made it myself."

"So you're a B.D.," I said. "Beer doctor."

He laughed a little bit at that, thought about it some more and laughed again. "That's funny," he said.

"You can use it."

He set his beer down and folded his hands across his stomach. He looked like Santa Claus on summer vacation, minus the beard. "So you're in show business."

I nodded. "A stand-up comedian."

"What's that like?"

"I travel a lot," I said.

"Ever have one of those shows when nobody laughs?"

I nodded again. "Sure. More than one, I'm sorry to say."

"Do you just forget about it and say that was just one night, or do you ever think about quitting altogether and getting into something else?"

"I've never thought about doing anything else," I said.

"Ah." He grinned. "A man of purpose."

"That's what's brought me here," I said.

His turn to nod. "Sissy told me. You wanted to know about a patient of mine. A comedian as well, if I recall." He let a breath go in and out. "Chad Karp."

"Sissy told me that you helped her cut him down from a tree where Del and Clayton had chained him."

Harper shook his head. "I had to get my bolt cutters out of my truck to snap the links. He pitched forward and would have hit the ground if Sissy hadn't caught him. He was . . . I have never seen a human being in worse shape in all my years of medicine that lived. I saw some oil-rig accidents where I had to be told I was looking at the remains of a man. But this young fella . . . God, people can be so cruel. There is no more savage beast than man."

"How severe were his injuries?" I asked.

"I don't have my records handy," Harper said. "They're in storage downstairs. But . . . what I can recall . . ." His hand went to the top of his head. "He had been scalped, like an Indian. But that's a misnomer. Indians learned to scalp from white men, did you know that? No? Well, Del had cut his hair off so it was dangling by a strip in the back. His skull was exposed. His larynx had been crushed."

"So he couldn't talk?" I was thinking of the synthetic voice I had heard last night on my answering machine.

"I guess they wanted to make sure he would never be able to stand on a stage and tell jokes again. Or they were trying to hang him."

"Any damage to his arms or legs?"

"No, they weren't even broken. There were severe burns and knife cuts on his hands. Pliers had been used on his fingernails, I think. It was like something I'd heard about happening in wartime. Like I said, I'd seen industrial accidents that were more severe, but I'd never seen anyone deliberately do this sort of thing to another person."

"What happened to him?" I asked. "After you cut him down, I mean."

"I had already notified the hospital in Talmadge that I'd need an ambulance. We got him to my office in town and I stabilized him there. I had to give him an emergency tracheotomy as he was having trouble breathing. Then the ambulance came and took him away. I followed in my car. Not that I could do anything; I just wanted to make sure that he arrived alive. I called a trauma physician I knew there and alerted him to the situation and he got . . . Chad, did you say his name was?"

"Chad Karp."

"He got Chad right into surgery. I waited around some. When Chad got out of surgery I talked to Dr. Ross—Wallace Ross, that was the attending—and learned he was in critical but stable condition. Then I went back home. Called a few times to make sure he was hanging in there. Word got back to Clayton Hollister I'd found their victim and he came to see me. I'd had enough of Clayton Hollister and his bullying ways behind a badge. Nothing in the Hippocratic oath about lying to a corrupt stupid lawman. So I told him the patient died. He wanted to see the death certificate so I mocked one up, showed it to him, and destroyed it after he left. He's so gullible it was easy to fool him. He said he'd look into the matter. Investigate it. Idiot. If he wanted to investigate it, all he had to do was look into the mirror. Charges were never brought."

So that's why Del Lacey told me he'd killed him, I thought. And . . . Louie Baxter, too. Hm.

"I say something interesting?" Harper asked.

"It's all interesting," I said. "What happened after he was admitted to the hospital in Talmadge?"

"He stayed there for three weeks while we tried to find his family," Harper said. "I'd call and talk to Wallace Ross to check up, but the patient never came out of his coma. Then Dr. Ross called to tell me the patient was being moved."

"Moved where?"

"All I knew it was somewhere out of state. Next of kin had claimed him."

"What next of kin?"

"I couldn't tell you. I could call Dr. Ross and ask him, if he's still at the hospital. I've been retired for over a year now. He might have moved on himself." He set his beer bottle down. It was empty. "What's your interest in this Chad Karp fellow?"

I took a deep breath. "Of the two other comedians who witnessed the attack on Karp, one has been murdered. Another is being threatened. Clayton Hollister, Del Lacey and Jim Parkins, the owner of the Payroll Saloon, were kidnapped and left to die inside the Payroll Saloon after it was torched. Del Lacey barely escaped. The others burned to death. There have been notes and writing on a wall left as clues, enough to make me think these crimes are motivated by revenge. It's possible Chad Karp survived his injuries and recuperated enough to take retribution on those responsible for his fate."

Harper looked at me. "That's a rather romantic notion," he said. "A scarred and tragic figure exacting just vengeance. Sounds like the Phantom of the Opera."

"I hadn't thought of it that way," I said.

"And what's your part in it?"

"These threats have hit a little close to home," I said. "They're heckler remarks—'get off,' 'you suck,' that kind of thing. I filled in on a show for the comedian who was killed. The one who's being stalked is a friend of mine. Along the way some other people have paid the price for being at the wrong place at the wrong time." I was done with my beer. "Last night, a threat was left on my answering machine back in L.A. And I've never been one to let bad enough alone."

Lionel Harper stood. "Let me call Dr. Ross," he said. "I'll see what I can do to help."

"Thank you."

"I do remember him telling me one thing about the patient's family, though."

"What's that?"

"They were extremely well-off. All bills were paid in full. We're talking critical care, around the clock, for several weeks. Over six figures. So that may help narrow your search."

"It also would explain a few things," I said.

"Like what?"

"Why he's so confident he will succeed."

"Most madmen are."

SEVENTEEN

Dr. Ross did still work at the hospital in Talmadge, but he was not able to get back to Lionel Harper until later that day. By five o'clock in the afternoon I figured it was time that I took my leave despite Harper's generous offer of a night's lodging. I tooled my rental car back down the mountainside to Boise.

I called Harper that night around eight.

"I heard from Dr. Ross," Harper said. "He's going to have the information overnighted to me in the morning from the medical records department."

"What information, exactly?"

"The patient transfer form listing the facility Chad Karp was transferred to and which doctor."

"Will the next of kin's name be on there?"

"Maybe. It doesn't have to be. But he's sending that and some effects from Karp's wallet."

"Wallet?"

"Yes. He left his wallet behind. Next of kin never claimed it."

"You mean like his driver's license and things like that?"

"Yes. I mean, I don't know specifically. I told Dr. Ross you were a private investigator working with the police. You're not licensed or anything are you?"

"I'm in the Screen Actors Guild," I said. "Does that count?"

He didn't get it. Industry humor is only good within Southern California area codes. "So I'll call you when it arrives and you can come back up and see what we've got," Harper said.

"Can I have another one of those beers?"

"Sure," Harper said. "Even a few for the road."

"Sounds great."

"See you tomorrow."

I hung up and called Max Gottschalk's office. I got voice mail. I left a message, including the number where I was. I hung up and started looking for an old movie to watch on TV when my phone rang.

"Biff, it's Max Gottschalk."

"That was fast," I said. "You still in the office?"

"I'm at the studio. It's tape day for *Baxter's Place*."

"How's it going?"

"Slow," he said. "You see *Page One* tonight?"

"No."

"Sheryl Franklin aired a story a few hours ago on how the script was rewritten to accommodate Louie's absence earlier this week, and they were giving lines to Larkin Thomas, the kid who plays his younger brother," he said. "So I'm here in my capacity as executive producer to investigate."

"I see," I said. "Did she put in there that you've signed Larkin Thomas as a new client?"

There was a tight silence on the other end of the line. "No," he said, through teeth ready to grit. "And it is my associate who represents Larkin Thomas."

"Drew Carruthers?" I asked.

"Andy," Max said. "I like to call him Andy. We already have a Drew."

"So let me ask you something," I said. "Did Gottschalk Entertainment sign Larkin Thomas as a client to sit on him and keep him from stealing the spotlight from your star client Louie Baxter—because, you know, I hear that happens—or are you covering your bases in case Louie Baxter goes off the deep end and has to check back in to rehab, you still have a show to executive produce and shepherd into syndication?"

The teeth were definitely gritting now. "With a mouth as big as yours," Max Gottschalk said, "I can see why you're still working the clubs."

"Instead of what? Getting played like a chess piece by someone like you? It's the managers, executives, agents and lawyers who control most of television. The suits. I've met plenty of them, and they all want me to kowtow to them like they're the keepers of show business heaven. The only problem is I'm not impressed by their money, their power and I sure as hell am not impressed by what I see on TV, especially what's supposed to be comedy. So why should I waste my time kissing the ass of some overpaid meeting-taker and memo-writer who does a shitty job? It doesn't make sense to me."

Silence. He was right, though. If I could play the game a little better, I'd probably be a rich man. I'd seen plenty of other comedians do it: Take the money, make the faces, say the lines other people had written. Stop doing stand-up and start hosting awards shows. I'd just have a slight problem shaving every morning without wanting to cut my own throat.

"Explain to me why I returned your phone call," Gottschalk finally said.

"I'm on the trail of a comedian Louie worked with two years ago," I said. "A fresh-faced emcee that nearly got lynched by a bunch of rednecks on a road gig. Louie was the headliner."

"Uh-huh," Gottschalk said. "And you think this may be the guy after Louie?"

"Louie thinks so," I said. "The assault left the poor guy in a coma. Someone claimed him three weeks later and had him moved out of state."

"When?"

"I get that information in the next twenty-four hours."

"So what were you doing talking to Sheryl Franklin at the Comedy Store the night before you left?" he asked.

"I'm trying to let her down easy," I said. "She keeps calling me. Even when I'm on the road."

"You call her back?"

"Not yet," I said. "I thought I'd check in with you first."

"I've tried calling her," Gottschalk said. "Even had Dirk trace her steps. No such luck."

"What are you saying?"

"I'm saying that since Sheryl Franklin turned in her last story about the scripts being rewritten on *Baxter's Place* she hasn't been heard from," Gottschalk said. "That was yesterday. They haven't seen her at *Page One*, she's not at home, she isn't visiting her mom, she's not at the hospitals or airports. She's vanished from the face of the earth."

I didn't say anything.

"Remember, we both saw that story she did naming this guy as the Heckler," Gottschalk said. "So I'm thinking maybe he first took notice, then took her."

Silence.

"Kincaid? You still there?"

I met Lionel Harper, Beer Doctor, at noon at a roadside diner, halfway between Boise and his cabin. I had coffee and a chicken salad sandwich while mist clouded the pines outside and trucks rumbled by carrying loads of felled shorn trees.

"Here's the copy of the patient transfer form," he said, handing me an already-opened FedEx envelope. "And the other stuff."

He went back to eating his bowl of soup while I looked at what was inside. The patient transfer form was originally on colored paper, so the copy was dark, but I was able to make out the name "Chad Karp." He was being released to a Dr. Steven McCandless at Saint Angela's Medical Center in Bearclaw, Washington.

"That's a private hospital," Harper said. "Don't know much about it. Never been there. To the hospital, I mean. Seattle's beautiful, though."

I nodded. "I played some clubs in and around it," I said. "Where's Bearclaw?"

"Outside of Seattle. North. I looked it up on a map."

The transfer form was dated three weeks after Chad Karp had

been assaulted. "There's nothing on here about what relation the person who claimed him was," I said. "It only says 'Matthew Karp.'"

"Doesn't have to say," Harper said. "That and the attending physician's name is enough."

I pulled out the next sheet of paper. It was a photocopy of Karp's social security card and driver's license, found in his wallet when he was admitted to the hospital in Talmadge.

"One-oh-two-eight-eight Knispell Drive," I said, "Bearclaw, Washington."

Harper nodded, dabbing at soup dribbling down his chin. "Sounds to me like someone in his family came to take him home."

"Yeah, me too." I squinted at the license photo. It was my first look at what Chad Karp looked like—or used to look like before Del Lacey and his cronies got through with him. He had long sloping features, big round eyes, a thin nose over a weak chin and a goofy smile fixed on his face as his picture was being taken. Brown lanky hair. A prominent Adam's apple. He looked like the funny guy in math class who knew when to shut up before the teacher sent him to the principal's office. Hey, guys, how's it goin'? Wanna hear a joke?

I checked the stats. Five-ten. Brown eyes. A hundred and sixty pounds. I imagined him against a mob of strangers. He didn't have a chance.

I set the envelope aside. "Thanks," I said.

Harper looked over at the envelope. "You didn't see the pictures."

"What pictures?"

"Of him and his girlfriend."

I looked back in the envelope. For some reason, instead of a copy, Dr. Ross had sent us the original of a strip of photos that must have come from Karp's wallet. It was four pictures from a photo booth, color, folded at the borders so they unfolded like an accordion. Chad was squeezed inside the booth with a lovely young girl of no more than twenty, long ash blond hair falling about her face as she and Chad mugged and kissed for the camera. She had perfect white teeth so big they almost went buck, framed by rose-colored lips, dancing blue eyes, high cheekbones and a long elegant neck. The pictures had been stained by water, but the moments of love and laughter were still preserved.

In one photo she held up her hand to touch Chad's face. On that hand was a diamond ring.

"Engaged," I said, looking up at Harper.

He nodded at me grimly. "Left her standing at the altar, I bet."

"She's beautiful."

"Yeah." Harper finished his soup. "Someone loved him. Someone found him and took him back home. Maybe it was her."

I put the photos away, treating them with extra care. "Want to know what I find out?"

"Sure," Harper said. "My guess is you're off to Washington."

"Today."

"Then come on. I got more home brew for you in the car."

I flew into Seattle later that afternoon. I looked out from my window seat and saw that over the islands and inlets it was raining. What a surprise.

I landed and remembered the first rule of visiting Seattle for anyone from L.A.: always rent a car, even if you drove there. California license plates got your windshield bashed in, got you cut off in traffic, pulled over and honked at. Ever since Californians began buying up real estate in and around Oregon and Washington so rapidly that home prices were now out of reach of the natives who had grown up there . . . well, I couldn't blame them for being a little hostile. And Angelenos with our big-city attitudes and show business manners often don't travel well or leave a good taste in people's mouths.

I drove my rental car out on the freeway and rolled down the window and breathed in the scent of the air through the rain. Clean and sweet. I'd done some weeks up here, even knew a few comedians who'd stayed on after, playing the Pacific Northwest and Canada, growing out their hair and beards and taken to wearing flannel shirts and boots and paying cheap rent.

I found Bearclaw on the map, at least an hour away from any comedy club I'd ever heard of. When I got there the freeway gave away to long wide residential streets, stately homes and lush green trees. It was midafternoon as I drove through peaceful neighborhoods, watching paper boys deliver the afternoon editions, kids come home from school, the rain letting up just in time. No graffiti. No gangs. No gunshots.

Saint Angela's Medical Center sat on a block by itself, surrounded by a high wall of trimmed hedges, the three-story building peeking over the top. In front there was only a pale statue of the Virgin Mary, her arms outspread, her eyes as blank as marble disks.

I circled the block and found the entrance in the back. A curved driveway led me in from the street to a parking area of less than a hundred spaces. I parked and walked in and presented myself to the wimpled nun behind the visitor's desk. I said I was there to see Dr. Steve McCandless about a patient of his. Chad Karp.

I was a long way from Los Angeles, and was somewhat surprised when Sister Evelyn—as her name tag said—picked up the phone and paged Dr. McCandless without any further inquiries about my business except to ask my name. I gave her all three, dropping the Biff: Brian Francis Kincaid. Made myself sound as Irish as a policeman's wake.

I took a seat and paged through a copy of *Catholic Digest*, feeling as though I had been taken back not to my own childhood, but that of a previous generation. *Och, now, the Lard woiks in mysterious ways, Young Biff. Ye're better off not knowin' His great 'n' grand plan. . . .*

"Mister Kincaid?"

Sister Evelyn was waggling a phone receiver at me. "Dr. McCandless is on the phone," she said. "I'll ring him through here."

I got up and picked up the wall extension she was pointing at.

"Dr. McCandless?" I said. "I'm sorry to disturb you without an appointment."

"That's all right," he said. "I'm only doing paperwork in my office. What's your interest in Chad Karp?"

"I'm trying to find out what happened to him," I said. "I learned he was transferred to Saint Angela's as a patient."

"Well, he's no longer here at Saint Angela's," McCandless said. "He left us two years ago."

So he *was* here. "What happened to him?" I asked.

"You mean you don't know?"

"No," I said. "I was referred to you by a Dr. Ross in Talmadge, Nevada. Your name was on the patient transfer form. When he left there he was in a coma."

"As he was when he arrived here at Saint Angela's," McCandless said. "An awful thing. A brutal crime. The worst of its kind." He sighed. "A tragedy, really."

"So . . . when you say he left you . . ."

"Yes?"

"Do you mean he died?"

"No," McCandless said. "He woke up."

Dr. Stephen McCandless's office was on the second floor of Saint Angela's. On the half-open door to his office was a plaque that read: STEVEN MCCANDLESS, M.D., DIRECTOR TRAUMATIC BRAIN INJURY UNIT. As soon as I arrived there he suggested we go for a walk. "If I stay at my desk, someone will drop by or the phone will ring," he said. "It's best if we're undisturbed. I'll just take my pager."

He was a big man, over fifty, with a florid face and wide fleshy features and icy green eyes. He had red hair like me, but it had gone white around the sides and even started to yellow in the back. He was barrel-chested under his lab coat and had big thick hands with wide knuckles. He spoke under a broken nose with thin wine-colored lips. In one hand he held a thick folder labeled: CHAD KARP. His chart.

"Doctor," I said, "you'll have to forgive my ignorance, but what's your area of specialization?"

"I'm a neurologist," McCandless said. "I'm director of the Traumatic Brain Injury Program we have here at Saint Angela's.

I think it's one of the best in the state. Most patients brought here have suffered some type of severe head injury. Most of our patients have received their injuries in car accidents." He paused. "With severe head injury—from a car accident or a beating such as Chad had suffered—during the first week of hospitalization the brain can swell. If it doesn't get enough oxygen then parts of it begin to die. Dr. Ross had the sense to monitor the intracranial pressure on Chad and perform the necessary surgery to drain it. They have a lot of accidents out there in that part of Nevada—oil workers, loggers, ranch hands—so he knew what to do. He followed the same guidelines we do here, and did a ventriculostomy on Chad so pressure from his brain could be relieved. The first weeks—or even months—are the riskiest for coma patients because what you are looking for are signs of conscious behavior. In movies and soap operas, someone's in a coma for months and then suddenly they're awake. It's actually a matter of degrees, degrees often measured in single digits."

We'd gotten off track. "Who put you and Dr. Ross in touch?" I asked. "Did you know each other already?"

McCandless shook his head. "No, we didn't. Ross knew Chad's older brother who still lives at the home address listed on Chad's driver's license here in Bearclaw: Matthew. It was Matthew Karp who decided to bring Chad to Saint Angela's. Both boys were raised in the Church, Matthew more so than Chad."

"Matthew lives here?" I said. "In Bearclaw?"

Dr. McCandless nodded. "He's in the computer gaming business and has done quite well at it. When Matthew contacted me and told me about Chad, he assured me that expense was not going to be a problem. He told me he wanted to move Chad here to Saint Angela's as soon as the swelling in Chad's brain was stabilized. Matthew had gone to Talmadge to see his brother, but he was unnerved by what he'd seen: tubes running in and out of his brother's skull, his head swollen to half again its size." He cleared his throat. "I think this was more upsetting to him because there had been some friction between Chad and Matthew before the accident. Matthew had essentially been raising

Chad since their parents died ten years ago and Chad had pursued a career choice that Matthew found . . . frivolous."

"Show business," I said.

"Specifically stand-up comedy. And now this was the result."

"This doesn't happen to every stand-up comedian," I said. "This is something unusual."

"Matthew didn't see it that way. He felt he'd let Chad walk on a path of . . . sin. And this was their mutual punishment."

My turn to shake my head. "This Matthew must be a real piece of work."

"He's quite devout," McCandless said, "and an extremely generous benefactor. Saint Angela's cared for Matthew and Chad's mother before she passed away."

We were walking on the grounds, behind the high hedge I'd seen from the street. There was thick full grass coating a yard as big as a high school football field. Patients were brought out to get some fresh air. Some were in wheelchairs. The nuns watched over them like nesting flightless birds. The outside world was kept at bay. It had done enough to these people.

"What happened after Chad arrived?"

"I saw him for the first time two weeks after the attack, and treated him for six weeks until he recovered enough to leave our care," McCandless said. "In all my years of medicine, I'd never seen a human being in such a condition: his hair scalped away from the skull, his face and hands burned and scarred, his larynx crushed so he couldn't talk even if he wanted to."

"So what did you do?"

"He was already in stable condition. We have a coma stimulation plan where the staff—as well as family members—continually stimulate the coma patient through their sensory modalities. We don't just feed and turn the patient. We encourage family members to come and talk, touch, feed and interact with the patients. They play their favorite music, read from beloved books, engage them in conversation. In this way patients can be encouraged to react to stimuli. It's been proven very effective in coma recovery."

"Did you try that here?"

"Yes."

"Who came to see Chad? Matthew?"

"Matthew came to pray," McCandless said. "It was Helen who gave Chad the necessary stimulation therapy."

"Helen?"

"Chad's fiancée."

I pulled the wallet-sized photo booth pictures from my pocket, the ones that showed Chad kissing a beautiful young woman. "Is this her?"

McCandless took the photos. "Oh, yes. Oh my God yes. That's . . . that's the two of them, isn't it?"

I nodded. "These photos were left behind at the hospital in Talmadge," I said. "Dr. Ross sent them on."

McCandless smiled with sad delight. "Oh, they were so in love. That's what Helen told me. They were going to get married." He handed the pictures back to me. "She was such a lovely girl. Every day she came for weeks, with a little portable stereo so they could listen to music together, books on tape for when she wasn't there, tapes of his old comedy routines. She would come on weeknights and watch TV with him. Comedies, mainly. Ones with stand-ups like him. As a matter of fact, that's when he first started communication, was during a TV show. He couldn't speak, so he started writing notes. Within the hour we got him an artificial larynx that he could hold to his throat and form words with. It was a remarkable step."

I had a funny feeling. "Which one?"

"Which what? What artificial larynx did he use?"

"No," I said. "I mean, which TV show was he watching when he woke up?"

"Oh, well . . . I don't watch TV much myself."

"Do you have the date?"

"I'm sure it's written down in here . . ." For the first time, Dr. McCandless consulted the chart. It was as thick and heavy as a telephone book. "Here we go: October 21. Almost two years ago—12:15 A.M."

The *Tonight Show*. Chad had woken up during the *Tonight Show*, six weeks after the accident.

That could have been the night Louie Baxter was on.

"What is it?" McCandless asked. "Something wrong?"

"No," I said. "Everything's fitting together." I turned to him. "You said Chad left Saint Angela's after being here a month?"

"Two. He woke up after a month. After another month he had recovered to the point where we thought he could continue therapy at home."

"Where was home?"

"His brother's house. We arranged for physical therapists to treat him there. Along with his initial injuries, his muscles had atrophied. He needed to exercise them just to get to the point where he could walk again."

"Dr. McCandless, how much can someone recover from a coma?"

"Mentally or physically?"

"Both."

"It can be almost a complete recovery. I've had coma patients who can walk and talk normally, and unless they told you, you'd never know that they had been in a coma. Others still have memory and coordination problems."

"Could a patient like Chad Karp ever hope to regain his full strength?"

"It depends on what you mean by full strength. Do you mean where he could compete on the college track team, no, but—"

"Enough to where he could attack someone."

Dr. McCandless looked at me strangely. "Exactly what are you saying?"

I stood and looked out at the parade of wheelchairs and walkers on the lawn. "The reason I'm here is that someone has found the perpetrators and witnesses of the attack on Chad Karp and is killing them off. One comedian has been stabbed to death, another comic is being threatened. Two of the men at the nightclub where he was assaulted were burned alive. A third is scarred for life."

"That's awful."

"What I want to know is whether it is possible for Chad Karp to be the man that did all this? Could he be up and about, traveling over the western part of the United States, carrying out threats and exacting revenge on people, like some Phantom of the Opera?"

McCandless consulted the chart again. "I haven't monitored his recovery for quite some time, but . . . it's possible. Chad was very determined to make progress."

"Why?"

"He didn't say. He just had to walk again, had to move again, had to get better. He was a man with a mission." McCandless blinked at me. "I hope this wasn't it."

I stood to go. "Where can I find Matthew Karp?"

EIGHTEEN

On its little curve of Knispell Drive, 10288 was the biggest house on the block. It didn't say that on Chad Karp's driver's license. All it listed was his address.

I drove by the house once, turned around and drove by it again. A colonial mansion, Chad Karp's home address sat on a parcel of land bigger than the entire street I lived on back in Beachwood Canyon. The house was set several dozen yards back from the curb, its white pillars silent and imposing. I looked for a name on the mailbox. There was none. No cars in the curved driveway. The garage door was closed. A lone light was on in a single room upstairs, glowing softly in the afternoon gloom.

Whoever Chad Karp had been, wherever he had come from, there had been money. When he had come out of his coma, it had been waiting for him. I wondered what else in his life had shown that kind of patience.

I parked on the street and walked up the driveway, looking for dogs, alarms or gardeners. I didn't find any. I reached the double doors and they were each ten feet tall. The world I was stepping into was outsize to the one I lived in.

It took me a while to find the doorbell. It was a solid brass button set inside the mounted head of a gargoyle. I pressed his tongue and listened to bells ring through the door.

I waited while someone came to answer. I heard steps along the front hallway and then one of the doors opened and I saw someone new.

He was tall, about six-two, just on the other side of thirty in muscular fashion, wearing a white monogrammed dress shirt over linen pants. His initials were MWK. He had prematurely graying hair, large eyes, and a nose that had been under the knife, bobbed to less than the family length. I recognized the big eyes and the long jaw. Another Karp. "Who are you?" he asked me.

"My name's Biff Kincaid," I said. "I'm looking for Chad Karp." I paused. "You must be Matthew."

That took him back. "How did you know who I was?"

"You look like your brother," I said.

"Why are you looking for Chad?"

"I'm a comedian," I said. "It's . . . a bit of a story after that."

He looked outside, at the sky above. "It looks like rain," he said. "You'd better come inside."

With that, I stepped through the door.

Matthew Karp kept an office upstairs, one that looked out over an acre of land behind the house. There were horse stables and a guest cottage: a mare was grazing in a pen. He *had* done well.

The office was decorated with posters for computer games. Some I'd seen advertised on television. A digitally created ninja dressed entirely in red brandished a sword made of light in "Archangel" and struck a slightly different pose for "Archangel Returns." A buxom beauty sporting angel's wings—with a dozen similarly endowed accomplices—struck a karate pose for "Heaven's Raiders." Somehow I was getting the idea that Matthew Karp did not have a good relationship with the marketing department.

Also on the walls were certificates from martial arts institutes, curved knives and short swords mounted behind glass and photos of Matthew Karp wearing a karate *gi*.

Once seated in a very comfortable chair, I told him about the chain of people and events that had led me to him: Tiger Moore, Louie Baxter, Sheriff Sissy, Lionel Harper and Dr. McCandless.

When I was done he shifted in his high-backed black leather swiveling chair behind his desk and looked out at the plants and animals that he owned. A collie marched around the horse pen, concerned only with the affairs of animals.

"So you think my brother has decided to seek revenge on those who have done him wrong?"

"It's possible," I said.

He nodded. The sole light I had seen burning from the street was from this room, in this office. It sat on a writing desk by the window facing the street. We were sitting in the gray gloom that filtered in from outside.

"What makes you think that?"

"I would," I said. "Wouldn't you?"

"I like to think my brother found it in his heart, through the grace of God, to forgive those who had injured him."

"Did he say anything to that effect?"

"My brother is unable to speak due to his injuries," Matthew said. "He uses a device he holds against his throat to talk, and he doesn't like the way it sounds."

"Did he ever show any desire to get even with those who had done this to him?"

"Not to me."

I felt I wasn't getting the full story with a Q and A. I needed to let Chad Karp's brother tell it to me on his own terms. "What happened after Chad left Saint Angela's and he came here?"

"I remodeled a room to accommodate the physical-therapy equipment my brother needed so he could recover here. He didn't want to stay in the hospital one more day than necessary."

"I can imagine."

"No, you can't, Mr. Kincaid. None of us can imagine what Chad's torment was like. At first, he hobbled around here on a cane, barely able to stand upright. His face was so scarred that he wore a mask to cover it. I took down all the mirrors in the house, even in the bathroom. He didn't want to see what he looked like."

He looked down at the polished wooden surface of his desk, as if it were an oracle showing him pictures from the past. "But the worst part was to see what had been done to him on the inside," Matthew said. "My brother . . ."

He fell off into silence. I prompted him gently: "Tell me what he was like before."

He looked up at me, dry-eyed. "He was . . . not like me. We're ten years apart. I was always the serious one, in church or school when Chad was out playing with an army of his imaginary friends. My father died at age forty. A salaried accountant. He didn't leave us much money. My mother had to go to work as a secretary in his old firm. She put me through school that way, and then I started working—first as an intern at that same firm. We were too poor to afford a computer at home, so I stayed after hours and started messing around on the ones left on at work. This was back when CD-ROM games were just starting to sell. I found a few lying around in some desk drawers and stayed up all night playing them. I wrote one of my own and sold it to one of the up-and-comers in the industry. They gave me a big enough check that I went back to my father's old accounting firm and told my mom to quit, that same day. She never worked again. I wrote and sold more games and started to buy her everything: a new house, a new car, a new wardrobe . . . coming back from shopping once on her way to the new house in the new car a semi hit her and she was critically injured. Took her a while to die. She lay in a coma for months. At Saint Angela's. That's how I know that facility. She died within a year. At twenty-five, I was alone in the world except for my little brother, Chad."

He took a deep breath and let it out slowly. "It was tough. I didn't know anything about being a brother, much less a surrogate parent. Chad was much more emotional than I was. I guess that's why he was always into books and trying out for school plays and putting together assemblies. I thought all of that was so . . . eccentric. A waste of time. Child's play."

"It's not all play," I said.

"Lucky for me I kept writing new games and upgrading the old ones as they sold over and over again." He continued as if I hadn't said anything. "For Chad's eighteenth birthday I offered to fund his college education. He said he wanted to major in theater. I had no idea what was involved with that, other than lots of pretty girls at rehearsal. I'd been to maybe two plays in my life. But . . ." He spread his hands. "It was his life. I let him do what he wanted. He went to Washington State over near the Idaho border. We saw each other at holidays and over the summer. I used to visit him there. He got cast in a production. And . . . I hadn't seen many plays, I don't even go to that many movies or watch TV— but I went to see him." He lifted his eyebrows. "I couldn't believe what I saw. I came back the next night and sat through the same play again, just to see Chad's acting again."

"How was he?"

"He was terrible. He was nervous, he forgot his lines, and his voice came out funny. The rest of the people had varying degrees of talent. Chad didn't have a very big part and I could see why. When I went backstage to see him, I put on a happy face and told him I enjoyed myself. He seemed to be friends with everyone. They all liked him. He just had no natural talent. I thought, maybe with time he'd get better. But it's such a competitive field, if you don't jump head and shoulders ahead of the pack right out of the gate, I'm not sure it's worth everything you have to go through. The rejection and so forth."

"When did he start doing stand-up comedy?"

"In college. Professional comedians would come through on the college circuit and he would see them perform: comedians from New York and Los Angeles and San Francisco touring across the country. That was where he began to get the idea that one could make a living as a stand-up comedian. He began doing amateur nights and talent shows . . . he had some other name for them. I can't remember what."

"Open mikes."

"Yes. Open mikes. He started to get some material together and make the rounds. This was in his senior year. Graduation was looming and his friends outside the theater world were interviewing for jobs."

"Did you ever see him perform?"

"Once, at a student bar. He wasn't any good at that, either. The frat boys booed him. This time, I didn't put on a happy face and tell him I thought he was great. I gave it to him straight. I told him he had no job, no marketable degree and no future in this business. I would fund him going to graduate school, but only if I got to approve his course of study this time. I wasn't going to throw my money away on his daydreams anymore. I'd spoiled him because Mom and Dad weren't around to see us grow up, but this—I said, pointing at the stage—wasn't what they wanted."

"What did he say?"

"He said, 'I'm getting married.' "

"Married?" I couldn't keep the surprise out of my voice.

Matthew nodded. "Exactly what I said. He had met a girl: an actress in a play. They were going to move to L.A. and try to make it big together. It sounded so impractical to me I just blew up at him. I lost my temper. I told him he was a dreamer, that he was wasting his time, that I wasn't going to spend my life bailing him out of bankruptcy. He told me I was just jealous, and I said how could I be? He didn't have any talent.

"I said, 'You're no good, Chad. I've seen you time and again and whatever it takes, you just don't have it. Save yourself the heartbreak. Give it up.' "

"That *was* laying it on the line," I said. "What was his reaction?"

"He lost his temper in return. He said he would pay me back, every penny, for all the money I'd used to fund his education, but he didn't need me anymore. He was going to live his own life. He was going to marry Helen. He was going to make it big. I'd be sorry. Then he said . . ."

I waited. It came.

"He said he never felt like we were brothers. I was like a stranger to him. He never understood me and my world of computers. He thought my games were hypocritical and pretentious. I'd always judged him. I'd never loved him. And he had never loved me back. He said it was time we stopped pretending we meant something to each other and just go our separate ways."

There was more. I waited for that, too.

"And I said . . ."

Silence.

"I'm not proud of my temper," Matthew said.

I nodded.

He cleared his throat. "I said, 'That just cost you the rest of your college money. You're on your own from now on. I'm cutting you off.' "

He looked up at the ceiling. This time his eyes weren't so dry.

"Money," he said.

I let some time pass, about the length of a school prayer.

"When did you see him again?" I asked.

His eyes worked their way across the ceiling and down toward me. "Lying in a hospital bed in Talmadge, Nevada, with a tube draining fluid from his brain. His face was swollen so badly I didn't recognize him. The doctor told me this had happened at some comedy performance."

"It was at a bar called the Payroll Saloon," I said. "In Alandale, Nevada."

"I know where it happened," Matthew said. "In a bar full of people where no one saw a thing. Apparently everyone is too scared of the town bullies to give a statement to the sheriff."

"Things are different there now," I said. "So's the sheriff."

"It was my fault that he ever ended up there in the first place," Matthew said. "When he took those dates in Nevada Chad had been nearly destitute, living in a flophouse hotel where he paid rent by the week. He wasn't prepared for the real world. He'd gotten fired from a series of minimum-wage jobs—he'd never had to work before—and scuffled about at . . . what did you call them?"

"Open mikes."

"Open mikes, trying to get something that paid. When he got these three nights in Nevada and his most recent boss wouldn't let him off work, he quit. He went on the road with twenty dollars in his pocket."

"Chad tell you this?"

"No," Matthew said. "Helen did."

I stood up, reaching in my pocket for the wallet-sized pictures I had of Chad and the beautiful blond girl in the photo booth. "This is Helen?"

Matthew looked at the pictures, and I looked at him. "Yes," he said. "That's her."

I sat back down. "You meet her before or after Chad was attacked?"

"After," he said. "She called me to ask what had happened to him. I had to tell her."

"Dr. McCandless at Saint Angela's told me Helen visited Chad quite often," I said.

Matthew nodded. "Went to see him every day. Read to him. Talked to him. Played music. Touched him. It's a form of therapy for coma patients. Sensory stimulation can help a coma patient recover consciousness." His expression softened. "She would have done all that anyway, even if it wasn't part of his therapy. I looked at her with my brother and . . . he was right. I was like a stranger to him. This woman loved him. I learned more about my brother from talking to her than I did talking to him."

"Maybe it's because you listened to her better," I said.

He blinked that one over. "I think you're right." He looked at me. "You get along with your family?"

"Let me put it this way," I said. "They're a great source of comedy material." I used his smile in response as a chance to change the subject back to his brother. "Chad was in a coma for how long?"

"Weeks and weeks. At least a month or two."

"And you and Helen cared for him all that time."

"Helen cared for him. I paid the bills."

"That's still caring."

"I like to think so."

"Helen have family here?"

"No. She's from Oregon. Portland."

"So where did she stay while Chad recuperated?"

"With him. I put them both up in the guesthouse out back. Free rent to take care of the animals—the horses and the dogs. Helen got a job as a night clerk at a motel with lodging included but Chad's return visits to the hospital for therapy every other day wore her out so much I asked her to do some paperwork for me and I paid her a modest salary out of my own pocket. Basically it was a token gesture to let her know how much I appreciated what she was doing for my brother."

"How long did Chad stay here after he left Saint Angela's?"

"A year. I converted a room downstairs into his own recovery unit, full of equipment to help him exercise. We hired physical therapists to put him through a daily regimen. He left the hospital in a wheelchair, then graduated to a walker and then a cane. Within three months he was walking on his own and working with weights, getting his strength back. He started drinking protein shakes, bulking up bigger than he had been before. He wore a series of masks to hide the scars on his face. Before he left I could look out my window and see him pumping iron in the backyard, a black ski mask on his face, sweat running down his body. He looked like . . . an executioner in training."

Maybe that's what he was, I thought. "You said you hoped he had forgiven those who had brutalized him," I said. "Did he know who they were?"

"His memories of the *year* before the attack were gone, never mind the day," he said. "He didn't remember meeting Helen or ever doing stand-up comedy. It was quite a shock to us as well as him. Imagine that: a piece of your life, just . . . gone."

"Did he ever find out who the people were that attacked him?"

"I don't know," Matthew said. "We communicated through Helen, and that was mostly about his care."

"And did you and Helen ever speak about Chad outside of his presence?"

Matthew Karp sat back in his chair and folded his hands. "During the months of Chad's rehabilitation here at home, Helen came to me once when Chad was resting. She said she was worried about him. She said that the coma had damaged more than his body and his brain. It had damaged his soul, somehow."

I cocked my head, like a dog hearing a funny sound.

He kept talking: "She said he wasn't the same. He had scars of a different nature, and these didn't look as though they were going to heal anytime soon. They had tried to be . . .

intimate . . . again . . . and Chad had failed. Several times. There was nothing physically wrong with him there. It was all in his head. He knew he was disfigured. Hideous.

"She said he had become withdrawn, silent. A lot of it had to do with the artificial larynx he hated to use. But his sense of humor was gone, his playful nature . . . he was no longer kind or affectionate. It was like sometimes he didn't want her or anyone else around. He liked physical therapy, but other than that . . . he seemed to spend a lot of time writing in a notebook. I have a dozen computers here in the house and he never asked to borrow one."

"What was he writing?"

"He told Helen he was working on a script. His reasoning was no one needed to see what a writer looked like. When it was done he was going to move to L.A. and break into the entertainment business. He wanted her to go with him. She told me she had postponed her own move to Hollywood to take care of him. I immediately offered to take care of their expenses, to help them get started. Helen said that was very kind, but after she had gotten Chad settled she planned to move out on her own. She felt that the man she had fallen in love with was gone, and gone for good. This new person—a quiet watchful soul wearing a mask and building up his body—was no one she knew."

Matthew fell silent, looking into the polished wooden top of his desk before speaking again.

"So I waited for Chad to come talk to me about it and the days and weeks went by and he kept working out and writing and keeping to himself. Helen started to help me out more with my business and we . . . I guess you could say we became more friendly. I could see why my brother had fallen in love with her. She was kind, intelligent and beautiful. Very good sense of humor. I enjoyed being around her."

"So Chad wasn't the only one to fall in love with her?"

Matthew smiled. "I guess not. I was hoping she'd change her mind about moving to Southern California with him, but no. She wanted to pursue her dream." He said the last phrase with an airy sarcasm. "I didn't want to make a complicated situation even more so. I prayed for strength and God gave it to me." He smiled bitterly. "He certainly gave it to her. To resist my charms, I mean."

"When did they leave?"

"Six months ago, I think." He stopped and looked up the date inside an upper right corner of his brain. "Yes. Just about six months ago. I gave them ten thousand dollars and a car."

"When did you hear from them next?"

"I only heard from Helen. She called once from a pay phone during the trip south and then she wrote me a few letters. They found an apartment near the beach." He looked through his desk drawers until he found a small packet of less then half a dozen picture postcards and opened envelopes bound by an oversize plastic paper clip. He looked at the return address on one envelope. "In . . . Santa Monica?" He looked at me for recognition.

"I know where that is," I said.

He referred back to the letter. "She got a job with a catering service—laying out food for the cast and crew of TV commercials and music videos—and Chad continued to write. He spent a lot on postage sending out his scripts and getting them right back but he did find a personal trainer in order to keep up his physical rehabilitation."

"Any names in those letters?" I asked. "People I might be able to contact back in L.A.?"

Matthew looked at the letters one by one, front and back. "No," he said, but he kept the correspondence on his side of the desk.

"When did you receive the last one?"

"From Helen?" Matthew said. He gave a sad smirk. "That's what she called it, too." He thumbed through the short stack until he came to a powder blue envelope and slid it to me across the desk. "Here," he said.

I picked the envelope up, carefully taking the letter out and reading it.

Dear Matthew,
   This will be the last letter I write to you for some time. I don't think I should call either. I have left Chad. We no longer live together. I need to live by

myself, or maybe it's just that I need to get away from him. I told you that since his accident it's been like living with a stranger. I never knew how much until we were on our own and away from you. I don't feel I know who he is anymore, and it's getting harder and harder to remember who he used to be. Our situation has become too claustrophobic for me to continue. He never goes out and never speaks to anyone or leaves the apartment unless he absolutely has to. He writes and watches TV. I am his only contact with the outside world, his caretaker, his only friend. Since we have stopped being lovers I don't know what I am anymore and I need to find that out again.

I know Chad might contact you, and I don't want you to have to lie to your brother so I won't tell you where I'm going. But I do hope someday when we meet again, it will be as friends. You have always been so good to me. God bless you and love always to the horses.

Helen

I looked up at him. "That was it?"

"For her, yes."

I put the letter back in the envelope and noted the address: On Euclid Street, apartment number 3A. I knew where that was. I looked at the date on the postmark. Three months ago. She'd moved out during the summer.

"You ever hear from her again?"

"Not her, no."

"What about Chad?"

"He called before the letter had arrived. I think she had mailed him a note, too."

"What did he say?"

"Not much. Just *'where-is-she?'* I knew it was my brother because of that buzzer he used to speak." Matthew held a fist to his throat to illustrate and imitate Chad's voice. "He sounded-like-a-robot."

"What did you tell him?"

206

"When I realized Helen had left him I said I didn't know where she was. He told me to call if I heard from her, then I got the letter and I called him and left a message on his machine—Helen's voice was still on it—and I never heard back from him. Called twice more with no response. The second time the answering machine was off and replaced by voice mail that did not use his voice and simply stated to leave a message."

"Did you ever try to contact him by mail?"

"A few times, but . . ." He spread his hands. "No answer."

"Not even a call back?"

"No." He shook his head. "I still thought I had an idea of where he was. Up until now I thought he was simply nursing a broken heart. Then you showed up."

"You still have that number?"

"Sure." He opened a drawer, put the letters back, and pulled out an address book. He read the number to me. Area code 310. I wrote it down in my organizer, next to the address.

"Helen have any family?"

Matthew nodded. "In Portland. Her parents. John and Cynthia Pratt."

"They ever hear from her?"

"I don't know."

"You know how I can get in touch with them?"

"Uhhh . . . I never called them myself . . ." He got up and went to a wooden file cabinet and opened a drawer. "But I bet if I looked at my old phone bills . . . from when Helen was here . . . ah-hah." He turned to me, phone bill in hand. "Try this number." He read it to me.

"So you've heard nothing from your brother since then?"

"No."

"Ever try to find him?"

Matthew shrugged. "I always thought I knew where he was." He looked at me as I stood up. "But what about you? Are you going to try to find him—and Helen?"

"I'm going to try."

"Do you think you'll have any luck?"

"Found you, didn't I?"

He stood and began to walk me downstairs to the door of the

house. "If you do—find Helen, that is—let her know that I'm worried about her. She can come back here, if she wants. I just want to make sure she's all right. Tell her that . . . I'll be glad to help her out."

"I'm sure if she needed your help she would have called."

"Do you think . . . if Chad found her . . . he might have done harm to her?"

"I don't know," I said. "He's your brother. You know him better than I do."

"No, he's not my brother anymore," Matthew said. "He's not Chad. I don't know what he is anymore. That attack changed him into someone or something else. Something new. Something not . . . good."

We were done talking. I walked out the door and back into the world.

NINETEEN

I left Seattle.

I got on a plane and flew to Portland. I rented a car and drove to Haskell's, which was downtown near a used bookstore. It was almost show time when I arrived. I bought a ticket for five bucks and went in. No one recognized me and the three headshots out front advertising the night's entertainment didn't ring any bells. They were making new comedians all the time.

I took a seat in the back and watched the club operate. There were pretty waitresses carrying heavy trays and bored bartenders making the drinks too sweet. The house was half-full and the stage was dark and the mike was cold, but all that was going to change soon. I sat in the back and had a local beer and wished I was going on tonight.

The show started and the emcee took the stage. His name was Aaron Logan and he did about fifteen minutes of local and topical material. The local stuff went over particularly big. Then he brought up the middle act and when he went offstage I found him by the bar.

Aaron Logan was tall and skinny and had a big throat with a large Adam's apple. He had light blond hair that seemed to grow only from the top of his head and thick glasses he wore offstage. His teeth were so big they showed even when he wasn't smiling. He looked like a Don Martin character from *Mad* magazine come to life. I knew that the comparison wouldn't hurt his feelings because it was one of his opening bits.

"Funny stuff," I said. "I liked that bit about the first day of school."

"Thanks."

"It's clean," I said. "Ready for TV."

"All my stuff's clean." He looked me over. "You a comic?"

"Yeah," I said. "How could you tell?"

"You talk like one," he said.

"I do a better job of that up there," I said, pointing at the stage with the open end of my beer bottle.

"Where are you from?"

"L.A."

"You looking for some stage time?"

"Another night," I said. "Right now I'm looking for a booker."

"Who's that?"

"Mark Roper," I said.

Aaron's beer slowed halfway between his mouth and the bar. He looked me over again. "You're not looking for a booker," he said. "You're looking for trouble."

"How's that?"

"Roper's not booking a lot of dates these days," Aaron said. "He got busted."

"What'd he get busted for?"

"Drugs. He sold some coke to a cop. They tried to get him to squeal on his connection. He says he didn't, but he got out after just a year."

"So you think he cut a deal with the law?"

"He had a high-priced lawyer from somewhere," Aaron said. "It *looks* like he talked. When I go through my Rolodex at home I cross off the names of people who've squealed to the fuzz, because I don't think they're going to be around long."

"Doesn't he book this gig? Haskell's."

Aaron shook his head. "Not anymore. He lost it when he got arrested. I think he's on probation. Can't go in nightclubs anymore. Can't go in nightclubs, you're not going to get much new business as a comedy booker. He still books a few road gigs."

"So do you know where I can find him?"

Aaron looked me over again and this time he didn't look so goofy as he did onstage. "You're not listening to me, friend."

"I am," I said. "Every word."

"You ever deal with Mark Roper?"

"He booked me in here once," I said. "Never met him."

"He is not an hombre you want looking at you too long."

"Just have a few questions for him."

Aaron Logan shrugged and drank some more beer. We both watched the middle act—an Asian-looking fellow who was doing bits about his Mexican mother and Korean father—and listened to the laughs swell and break like waves on a shore.

"I know some comics that used to get pot from him," Aaron said. "That was in an apartment about a mile from here. I can get the address from the manager's office. If I was him I would have moved. But maybe he's still there, waiting for people to kill him."

"I promise I'm not here to do that."

Aaron laughed darkly. "If you were, you wouldn't be the first. He's leaned on a couple of comics in his day. I think some of them he might have used as mules for his drug pickups. I know a few who met up with the wrong end of a baseball bat."

He put his beer down. "I'll go get that address for you. If you're still alive this time tomorrow, let me know if he isn't. I got some buddies that would like to use his headstone as a pissing target."

I found Mark Roper's apartment in the basement of the building. His door was in the back by the laundry room off a street that had gotten a few months behind on its taxes. It was marked with potholes and the streetlights were sputtering and dim. It looked like Hollywood just below the Boulevard, but cleaner and colder and with less traffic.

The overhead bulb had been broken and so I stood in the

dark knocking on the door. I could feel the paint peeling under my knuckles. I was a long way from home. I could disappear here and no one would find my stiff and bloated corpse for a while.

There was a faint glimmer of light underneath the doorway, and after I knocked a second time I saw shadows move within. I stood there for another ninety seconds and I'd raised my hand to knock again when I felt cold steel pressing against the back of my head, so firm and hard I could almost guess the caliber.

"Who are you?" the gun holder asked. I recognized the low rumble of Mark Roper's voice. I could smell sweet incense on him.

My hands automatically went up in the air by the sides of my head. "Biff Kincaid," I said. "I'm a comic."

There was a pause. The gun barrel shifted slightly against my scalp. It was pressing against the base of my neck. From there it would start renovating my skull from the hairline out.

"Kincaid?" Roper said. "From L.A.?"

"That's me."

The gun's touch left my neck. "Didn't I book you?"

"Once," I said. "For a week. Into Haskell's."

A large strong hand reached out to turn me around and I faced Mark Roper's silhouette. He was big, at least six-five, and his hair hung like dried dog turds off his head, giving him a Rastafarian look. He had a beard that fell halfway down his chest and mixed in with the incense was a tangy body odor. I couldn't see his eyes or his mouth. The only light was from a streetlight in the alley over his shoulder. The gun in his hand was like a silver piece of shadow, still pointed at me. "You here to kill me?" he asked.

I shook my head. "Pat me down," I said. "I don't have a weapon."

He turned me around again and I leaned against the front door with my palms kissing the splintery wood frame. His hands spot-checked the folds in my clothes and then he stepped away. "Okay," he said. "What do you want? I do my business by phone and computer."

"I have a few questions," I said.

"About what?"

"Chad Karp."

That got me some more silence and his shoulders lifted and fell as he took a deep breath. "Let's go inside," he said, and as I turned to face the front door quickly he caught my shoulder and said, "Not that way."

He led me into the laundry room, twisting a timer switch on the wall outside to turn on a light so yellow and feeble it wouldn't draw a moth. One washer had its lid up and was filled with garbage. The other one was sitting in a fetid pool of water. A scrawny cat lived in one dryer that had been used for batting practice and was cracked with rust. Behind one of the water heaters was a man-sized hole in the wall with a blanket over it. Roper lifted the blanket and stepped through. Just as I was about to ask where we were going I followed him in and saw that I was in an L-shaped passageway that he had hollowed out in the building's aging infrastructure by knocking down a few walls.

The blanket fell behind me and I saw that the walls held more than just bare beams, bent nails and cracked plaster. There were soft violet lights from inside half a dozen glass boxes. The glass boxes were lined with gravel and decorated as miniature landscapes of desert terrain. Roper gave me a moment to adjust my vision long enough so I could see in one of the terrariums was a squat furry tarantula whose bristly body was as big around as an empty coffee cup, and just as animated.

I looked at the other glass boxes. One of them had a visible occupant, this arachnid bigger than the first, and with yellow markings. He was at Roper's eye level, and since Roper was taller than me I could look up and see the spider's fangs. There was a piece of masking tape on which a name had been written in faint pencil:

BORIS.

"My pets," Roper said.

"I take it you're allergic to cats," I said, "and dogs bark too much."

Roper's scowl retreated, in the dim light, and I took that as something toward a smile. "Keeps the neighborhood kids out," he said. He opened a well-oiled door and walked into a room.

I followed. The apartment wasn't much of a living space, more of a storage-slash-office area. I saw no bed or sink, just lots of cardboard boxes stacked around where furniture should be. The light in here was from halogen floor lamps. There were chairs and a couch to sit on, but this was more like a laboratory than a home. On a metal desk sat a computer hooked up to the internet, and an open e-mail I couldn't help but see was from Mister Silly's in Salt Lake City.

I nodded toward the computer screen. "Bobby Lee Garnett told me where to find you," I said.

"When?"

"Just a few days ago," I said. "We'd just worked together at the Comedysino in Vegas."

"Last night at Mister Silly's he got so drunk he threw up onstage."

"That must be his new closing bit," I said.

"Still a smart-ass, huh, Kincaid?"

"I do my bit for the war effort," I said. "But I know all I need to know about Bobby Lee Garnett. I want to ask you about Chad Karp."

Roper indicated I should have a seat. I lowered myself into an unpadded metal chair that looked like it had been put together out of an ammunition locker. Next to me was a lighted terrarium with a snake the size of a sewer main coiled on a branch. A terrified white rat crouched in a glass corner, his pink eyes bulging and white whiskers twitching.

Roper reclined on a black leather couch that hissed as he sank into it. In better light I could see that his eyes were baggy and lined. He had a small paunch beginning to show. He wore baggy black jeans and a black T-shirt that had a pentagram on it. The death rocker at home. He opened the lid on a glass cage next to the couch and scooped out another tarantula, petting the eight-legged friend as it sat in his hand. I had the feeling this was done for an intended effect, and I don't know what the effect was intended to be other than I wished he would put that big hairy spider back in its cage and let me get the hell out of here.

"Chad Karp is dead," Mark Roper said.

"No, he's not," I said. "He's alive."

Roper looked at me, the tarantula now crawling across his

hand and up his arm in slow measured mechanical motion. This one had bits of red in its fur. "I booked him on some one-nighters in northern Nevada a few years ago," Roper said. "He got in a fight with some local rednecks. They left him to die out in wilderness."

"Ever wonder why no charges were brought?" I said. "No police officers came around asking questions? He didn't die. He lay in a coma for a while but he woke up and recovered to the point where he's now finding some of the people involved in the attack and taking revenge on them."

"What kind of revenge?"

"Murder," I said. "Tiger Moore is dead. Louie Baxter has been threatened. Two of the principals involved in the attack in Alandale are dead, one badly mutilated. Karp sends threatening notes to his intended victims. One syndicated tabloid show that's been covering the story has nicknamed him the Heckler."

Roper plucked the tarantula off his T-shirt and dropped him back into the glass cage, closing the lid. "And you think I might be next?"

"I don't know," I said. "All you did was book him, right?"

Roper leaned forward and ran his hands though the caked links of his hair. "Damn, I knew I never should have stayed in comedy." He shook his head and looked at me. "Ten years later and I can't get out of it. Now I'm trying to set up my own Internet business."

"Selling what?"

He stood up and crossed over to an open cardboard box, reaching inside and pulling out a black wax cylinder. "Satan," he said.

He pulled out another candle, this one red. He held them both up. "This is your devil-worshiping starter kit. I call it Candle Power. I get these wholesale for fifty cents each, slap a couple of labels on them, throw in a Dark Prayer Scroll that I wrote myself and pack it in bubble wrap and ship it out for fifteen dollars."

"To who?"

"Kids," he said. "Remember when we were fifteen and into

Kiss and Alice Cooper? Same idea. I hate my parents, my school, I can't get the girl I want. Might as well make an offering to Lucifer."

"In the form of MasterCard, Visa or American Express," I said.

Roper snorted. "Yeah. Payable to . . ." He crossed to the computer and closed his e-mail to reveal a home page with a horned figure sitting on a glowing hot rock. "Satan's Throne." He waved an arm around the room. "That's what all this is about. Candles, T-shirts, books, pentagrams. Just launched last month. My site is getting two hundred hits a day and twenty orders a week, each week showing a growth of five percent. Pretty soon I'll be able to move out of this dump. Finish out my probation in style."

"We keep getting off the subject," I said. "And that subject is Chad Karp."

Roper sat back down on the desk by his computer. "See this?" He picked up his computer mouse to show it to me. It was a miniature human skull. "You click on the eye sockets to make it work," he said. "I get 'em for five bucks and sell 'em for thirty-nine-ninety-five."

"Two years ago, did you book Chad Karp into the Payroll Saloon in Alandale, Nevada, with Louie Baxter and Tiger Moore?"

He gnawed a fingernail and spit out what he could bite off. "What if I did? That make me an accessory or something?"

"You seem to think it does."

"Why do you say that?"

"Because you don't want to answer my questions," I said. "I'm working with the Las Vegas police on this. I can get Detective Charles Gregory to call you and ask you some questions. Get in touch with your parole officer." I lifted the top of the glass cage next to me and stuck my arm inside between the mouse and the snake. Neither of them were expecting this. I'd seen something interesting inside.

"Hey," Roger said. "He's dangerous. What're you—?"

"He's not poisonous," I said. "Neither are those spiders. I watch Discovery Channel." My fingers probed the gravel at the bottom and came up with a packet wrapped in aluminum foil. "Oh-ho-ho. What have we here?" I brought the packet out and laid it on top of the glass cage, unfolding the foil like it was a linen napkin. "Very clever, Mark. You get these cages filled with all kinds of creepy crawlies to guard your stash of . . . what?" The last lifted layer revealed the contents. "Some good old leafy green bud." I picked it up by the stem and turned it in the light. It was a small stem of the Northwest's finest homegrown marijuana crop, packed with dense fibrous growths. I drew it under my nose, sniffing it like a cigar. "Good body, nice aroma. What does this go for on the open market?"

Roper looked at me like he wanted to feed my head into the snake cage with another white rat tied around my neck. "That's a thousand bucks you have in your hand, Kincaid," he said.

"Not to mention another two years in the pokey," I said.

"It's yours to keep if you'll just walk away."

I rewrapped the pot in the aluminum foil. "Relax, Roper," I said. "I'm not here to bust you—unless I have to. What do you say you start telling me what you know about Chad Karp?"

Roper slumped in the chair at his desk. "It was a setup," he said.

"What? The booking?"

Roper looked at me. "The whole thing. The gig, the attack, what those guys did to him. They weren't just some drunk rednecks. They were local hired muscle." His gaze fell to the floor. "They were just supposed to scare him, though. Rough him up a little. Not do all the stuff they did to him." He sighed. "That's what you get with amateurs. My part was just to get him there."

"How did it happen?"

"I got a phone call. One of my regular customers for grass knew someone who was looking to get a comedian taken out of action. All I needed was to get him to a certain place at a certain time and they'd take care of the rest."

"Who was this customer?"

"Kyle Watson. He's a private detective. Worked for some of the local law firms, checking out accident fraud and stuff. He said he had a special job to do for a local bigwig and my share of it was five grand."

"Five thousand just to book Chad Karp into Alandale, Nevada," I said.

Roper nodded. "I asked for a name. He told me. Showed me a headshot. Told me where he was playing: an open mike at a coffeehouse. I was to approach him as the local comedy scumbag that I was and put him on the road. Get him into my Alandale gig in Nevada. Once I had him booked I was to tell Watson what night Chad was going to be there and with whom; he would take care of the rest. I asked what 'the rest' was and he wouldn't tell me. But I could tell it was a setup for something bad."

"So you went and found Chad?"

Roper shrugged. "Who was I to turn down five grand? This was a new one on me. The first week I had coming up was that string of one-nighters in Nevada with Tiger Moore and Louie Baxter. I didn't even normally put an opener and emcee on the bill. I went down to the coffeehouse and saw Karp's act. He was terrible. He had maybe five minutes that would go over only within a block of a college campus."

"So then what happened?"

Roper shrugged. "I booked him. I said can you do a week in Nevada next week. He said great. He was very excited. I realized this was his first road gig. Didn't know it was going to be his last."

"What else do you remember?"

"I only met him that one time. He was young, just out of college."

"He have any friends with him?"

"Just his girlfriend. I met her."

"What was she like?"

"Beautiful. I remember that. I couldn't understand what a dweeb like him was doing with a knockout like her." He looked up at the ceiling, trying to remember details, but they wouldn't come. "When they made the first gig I called Watson and said, 'They're on the road; where's my five grand?' I had it within the hour. Cash. Good thing I had it, too. I got busted a few months later selling gram to a cop and paid it all to my lawyer and then some."

"When did you hear about what happened at the Payroll Saloon?" I asked.

"Tiger came to see me when I was in jail," Roper said. "He asked if my bust had anything to do with that Karp kid, and I said no. Then he told me the whole horrible story."

I sat back. I had all I was going to get.

"You going to find out who set him up?" Roper asked.

"I'm going to find out a few things," I said. "Where can I find this Kyle Watson?"

"I don't know," Roper said. "Don't see him anymore."

"He ever tell you who was behind the setup?"

"No," Roper said. "I didn't know this kid from Adam, Kincaid. Ask yourself who would want to do this guy in—an openmiker? For what?"

"One more thing," I said, and reached back inside the glass snake cage.

"Hey, you want more stuff—"

"Nope," I said. I closed my hand over the white mouse in the corner and gently lifted him out, cupping both hands over him. "I'm taking this with me."

"Sure," Roper said. "Go ahead. I get them from a pet store."

I nodded and stood. "I can find my own way out."

"You sure? I'll turn the lights up a notch. It can be hard to see in there." The mouse squeaked in my hands. "What are you doing, Kincaid? Playing animal liberator as well as comedy detective?"

"See you, Roper," I said. "Don't tell anyone I was here."

I walked through the hallway lined with tarantula cages and out into the laundry room. As soon as I got to the street I found an alley lined with garbage cans. I bent down and let the mouse go. He stopped, unsure of his newfound freedom, sniffing the ground, whiskers twitching, wondering what had just happened.

"Go," I said. "Die free."

Then I turned and walked away.

TWENTY

I stayed in Portland another day. I called the number that Matthew Karp had given me for John and Cynthia Pratt. I got an answering service that referred me to Mr. Pratt's legal office. So he was a lawyer. I called that number and by noon I knew where to find Helen Pratt's father.

Just after one in the afternoon I walked into a redbrick-and-brass building downtown, the kind that houses financial institutions, medical offices, and legal firms where men amassed wealth and power either on a local, state or national scale.

I took a gleaming elevator, its interior doors polished to a shine, to the tenth floor. The doors opened on a lobby that was bigger than some nightclubs I'd played. The receptionist was a middle-aged woman who looked like she'd never had to throw anybody out before. That was about to change.

"May I help you?" she asked.

"Yes," I said. "I'm here to see John Pratt."

"Junior or senior?"

That threw me. I didn't know there were two of them. "Senior," I said.

"Did you have an appointment?"

"No."

"Can I have your name?"

"Biff Kincaid."

"And what is this regarding?"

"Helen."

"I'm sorry?"

"Helen Pratt," I said. "That's his daughter."

"I see." She didn't like that. "I'll notify Mr. Pratt's assistant, Linda. She handles Mr. Pratt's appointments."

I turned around and took a seat in the antique waiting chair, next to the glass table stacked with magazines. Lately I seemed to be in nice places only to tell someone bad news.

"Hey, *you*."

I turned to see a stocky handsome young fellow about ten years younger than me standing in a white shirt and blue tie with shoulders that strained at the yoke. He was an inch taller than me and had piercing blue eyes over a sharp nose and a full mouth that was thinking about starting to snarl. His hair was ash blond and his jaw was square. I could see the family resemblance from the photos I'd seen of Helen. He had an athlete's build and it was barely held in by his business clothes. He looked mad and he looked mean.

"What do you know about my sister?" he said.

"Not much," I said. "I'm trying to find out more than I know. Right now, I just found out she has a brother." I looked around me. "And her dad has a good interior decorator."

"How did you get in here?"

"They have these new things now," I said. "They're called elevators." I pointed.

"Quit being a smart-ass and answer my questions," he said.

"I'll do my best on the second part," I said, "but I'm afraid we're stuck with the first."

"Where is she?"

"I was going to ask your father the same thing."

"You a cop?"

"No," I said. "I'm a stand-up comedian."

He took a step toward me and brought his hands out of his pockets. They were thick and meaty and one knuckle had been flattened. His already smallish eyes narrowed under his jutting brow. I might as well have said I was a child pornographer. "We don't have much use for comedians around here," he said. "Why don't you hit the bricks?" He used his thumb like a referee to indicate I was to head for the showers.

I didn't move. "I'm just here to ask your father a few questions," I said. "I'm not trying to cause your family more problems."

He took a step closer. "Why don't we step outside and talk it over?"

"That's not a good idea right now," I said. "Actually, that's not a good idea anytime."

"What kind of a name is—" He turned toward the receptionist.

She responded. "Biff Kincaid."

He turned back to me. "What kind of a name is Kincaid, anyway?"

"American, last time I checked."

He looked me up and down, flicking one hand out so it grazed the side of my head. "You're a Mick, aren't you?" An ugly silence filled the air. The receptionist looked down at her desk top. "A dirty potato-eating Mick." He looked at his fingertips as if my red hair had left a residue and wiped them on his pants.

"I've laid off potatoes because of the starchy carbohydrates," I said. "But you put another finger on me and you won't get it back."

He thought that over as if it might make some sense. Then he spit in my face.

"Johnny!"

A booming older male voice filled the lobby and stopped my hand in mid-punch as it flew up from below my waist. John Pratt Junior had an open spot just below the right side of his jaw. I was going to nail him like a board and he was going to go down and then I was going to let him get up just so I could knock him down again.

But when he heard his father's voice, Johnny turned his head and I would have hit a man when he wasn't looking and that wasn't fair—not that I ever cared about fighting fair—but his father would have ejected me from the building and I never would have gotten to talk to him. As it was, I was now the wounded party, with spittle running down my brow, and was owed some recompense. If I played it right, I could get my wounded honor back in information.

John Pratt Senior was not quite as tall as his son, but barrel-chested with a quick powerful stride. He stepped forward, drawing a silk handkerchief out of the breast of his dark wool suit and handing it to me. "I apologize for my son's behavior," he said.

I looked at him and then at his son and back at the father again before taking the handkerchief and wiping my face with it. "You should," I said.

John Pratt Senior turned to Junior. "Johnny. Go home."

Junior's lips pressed together. He had wanted to fight.

"Go home and check on your mother, Johnny. Right now."

Junior looked at me as he turned away. "Another time, Paddy," he said.

His father stepped forward to say something but I held up a hand to quiet him.

"Count on it," I said.

Junior turned away, his shoulders moving like a bull's beneath his dress shirt. I did a final wipe of my face and neatly folded the handkerchief before handing it back to Senior. "Thank you, Mr. Pratt."

"Would you like a chance to wash up?" he asked.

"I'm fine," I said.

He was a tan, good-looking older man with bigger eyes than his son, a rounder nose but just as strong a jaw. He hadn't added too much weight since he was Junior's age. His hair was black, gone slightly duller since his youth. Helen's fair and blond genes must have come from his wife's side of the family. I put him at fifty, with still plenty of punch and kicking left in him. I caught my reflection in his polished black shoes on the new carpet. An atmosphere of deference surrounded him, and he had spent a lifetime building it. He was a man in control of every aspect of his environment except his family.

"Who are you here to see?" he asked.

"You," I said.

Pratt turned to the receptionist.

"I'd just phoned Linda," she said. "Then Johnny showed up."

Pratt nodded once to himself. "Linda's my assistant," he said to me under his breath, "and Johnny's latest . . ." He looked around for a word. "Conquest."

"I think your son was alerted by the fact that I'd come to see you about Helen," I said.

The urgent concern in John Pratt's face dimmed, and his large eyes focused on me. "What do you know about my daughter?" he asked.

"Not much," I said.

"Do you know where she is?"

"No," I said. "But you just answered my first question. Apparently you don't know where she is, either."

"Who are you again?"

"Biff Kincaid," I said. "I'm a comedian."

"Did you say . . . comedian?" He didn't like that word much either. And all these years I thought the world loved a clown.

"Yes," I said. "Perhaps it would be best if we talked in private."

"Marilyn," Pratt said to the receptionist. "We'll be in the library."

"Yes, Mr. Pratt."

He took me by my elbow in a firm grip to guide me through the offices and toward a solid wood door. "How did you find me?" he asked as he opened it. A fresh-faced clerk was seated at a polished oak table, perusing an open tome from the four walls of bookshelves that surrounded him. He looked up, saw who was walking in the room, and scurried out the back door without a word.

"It's not that hard to find people who have their own law firms," I said.

"I mean, how do you know about Helen?" He indicated I should sit on one side of the conference table in a padded black leather chair. He took another.

I told him the whole saga of the Heckler, ending with Mark

225

Roper's assertion that he was hired to book Chad Karp into the Payroll Saloon in Alandale by a private detective named Kyle Watson.

"I know Kyle Watson," John Senior said. "He's done work for this law firm."

I waited.

"You don't think that . . . that *I* hired him, do you?"

I spread my hands. "I'm here to learn," I said. "But judging from the reception I got just a few minutes ago, I'd say it's more likely someone else in your family might have made the deal."

"You mean like Johnny? Because of what he said?" John Senior shook his head. "He gets that from his mother."

"His temper?"

"His . . . politics." He tried to smile and it came out a grimace. "Africans, Jews, Asians . . . he feels they can't be trusted." He looked at me. "What was his problem with you?"

"I'm Irish," I said.

"And especially Catholics," he said. "My wife calls them Pope-lovers."

"Like Chad Karp?"

"I don't know if my wife or son ever met Chad," Pratt said. "Helen never brought him to the house. Her other boyfriends had never met with her mother's approval. She always felt Helen was reaching 'beneath her social station,' as she put it. She wanted Helen to marry a boy like Robert Osgood."

"I like the name," I said. "Who is he?"

"He's someone my wife met in her . . . group."

"Group? You mean like a therapy group?"

Pratt sighed. "I wish. My wife is not well, but she refuses to see a psychiatrist or take any medication. About five years ago she began developing these delusions about how the world was being taken over by unholy forces—aided and abetted by the United Nations, of course, and the Pope. She joined this group she heard about on the Internet that call themselves the Crown of Thorns. They advocate racial and spiritual separatism. No mixing of the ethnic groups. Any money I let my wife have access to she gives to them so they can spread their message of distrust. She's tried to get me to read some of their junk but . . ."

He shook his head. "I had to drop out of local politics because I was afraid some reporter would find out my wife was mentally ill and that was why she never showed up with me at public functions anymore." He looked at me. "She's not the woman I married. I'd divorce her, but the vows say in sickness and in health and she is quite sick."

"So when your daughter Helen started dating Chad Karp . . ."

"She had Kyle Watson dig into his past," Pratt said. "He found that he was Catholic and that Karp is not his real name."

"What is it?"

"I can't pronounce it," Pratt said, "but it's Croatian. Not one of the five peoples acknowledged as spiritually pure by the Crown of Thorns. Joan told Helen she couldn't see Chad anymore and that she was never to bring him to the family house."

"And what did Helen do?"

"She packed up her bags and left," Pratt said. "She and Chad had just moved into a one-room apartment on the outskirts of town. She'd gotten a job as a waitress and he was going to—I don't know, learn to drive a cab or something." A hint of a smile. "It was completely foolish and totally impractical and they were utterly broke. I could tell it was love."

"Did you ever meet Chad?"

"Certainly. I'd call Helen, ask her if she needed any money or a hot meal. A lot of times I would get Chad on the phone. I remember when he told me about getting this comedy job in Nevada. He was very excited. I congratulated him."

"And then what?"

"And then she didn't hear from Chad on the road when he was supposed to call. She became worried. When he didn't come back on time she got very concerned. I got in touch with the state authorities to try to learn what happened, but Helen found out from Chad's brother," he said. "When she called to tell me, she got her mother and told her that something had happened to Chad in Nevada. An accident. When her mother said it was God's way of punishing a Pope-lover, Helen hung up on her. She called the house next Sunday morning, when she knew her mother was at church. That was when she told me she was in Seattle, and Chad was in a coma. I offered to help her financially, but she wouldn't take it. Apparently Chad's brother was quite well off, and grateful for Helen's assistance in his medical care. Then she told me Chad had woken up and was starting to recover. She even came to visit me once. On her birthday."

"But she never told you the real nature of his injuries?"

Pratt shook his head. "When we were together, she wanted to hear news about her own family, not that it was any better. We joked about that, how she was qualifying for her nurse's license. Our visits were private. She wouldn't see her mother or her brother. It's odd, but even though my son is called Junior, I don't feel as close to him as I do Helen."

"When was the last time you saw her?"

"Six months ago. She told me she and Chad were moving to Los Angeles and she would call me from there."

"And?"

"And I never heard from her again. I have been unsuccessful in locating her or Chad Karp since."

"L.A.'s a big town," I said. "Easy to get lost in."

"Especially if you don't want to be found," he said.

"Did your wife or son ever express interest in finding Helen's whereabouts?"

"All the time. They said they were praying for her return. Every now and then my wife would spout off some nonsense about how God had sent her visions of Helen in biblical times as the prodigal daughter. I think they tried to get Kyle Watson to find out where she was but he was unsuccessful." He blinked a few times. "I have to say that the news I find most disturbing is that this comedy booker—"

"Mark Roper."

"—Mark Roper, says that it was Kyle who approached him to get Chad into the hands of those thugs."

"He could have not known what was going to happen to Chad once he got him there," I said. "But I'd be interested to hear Watson tell his side of the story in his own words."

"Would you like for me to arrange a meeting?" John Pratt asked.

"That would be helpful," I said.

"How long are you in town?"

"I'd stay until tomorrow if he's unable to meet with me today," I said. "There's someone else I'd like to speak to as well."

"Anything I can do to help find my daughter," he said.

"All right," I said. "I'd like to talk to your wife."

TWENTY-ONE

I went back to my motel room. I'd picked up some local papers at a coffeehouse on my way back and was going to scan the pages looking for a comedy night I could crash while I was in Portland, but that plan went out the window when I opened the door to my room and saw two large strangers standing inside.

One was tall and thin, with waxen skin and hair so black it looked dyed. He wore jeans and a green sweater with a brown deer embroidered on it. He had a toothbrush mustache beneath a bird's beak of a nose and thin fingers that were currently paging through my day book.

My luggage had been searched and my clothes were spread out across the bed, my other belongings scattered on the floor. The other intruder looked slightly older. His sandy hair was cut short and stiff as if he'd joined a rather stylish military unit. The 'do didn't make his round squat face look any more handsome. He was wearing a tan trench coat and was ripping a pair of my khakis apart by the pockets.

"I told you light starch, and on hangers," I said. "This is the last time I use the in-house laundry here, I swear."

When I came in, the door had hidden a third member of the party and he had remained in the corner until I stepped in the room. I found this out when the door swung hard against my left side, crashing into my elbow. I fell to the right, rolling back to my feet against the same wall as the bed. I was unhurt, but now I was inside the room. The door closed behind me, and I saw who had been hiding there in the corner.

John Pratt Junior.

"Hey, funny boy," he said, his fists bunched like heads of lettuce. "See how you like these odds: three against one."

"Actually, I'd say with you it's more like two and a half."

His small eyes went piggish and crimson flared along his jaw. He had changed out of his work clothes and now he was wearing a black sweat suit and jogging shoes. Under the sweatshirt he had a flat hard bulge. A gun. "Eat shit, you filthy Mick." And then he charged me.

I was standing in a corner made by the double bed and the wall. I'm sure he thought he had me trapped, and I would have been if only he'd thought ahead enough to take the lamp off the nightstand. As it was, he'd left it there and when I picked it up it was nice and heavy and hard and the cord snapped right out of the wall as I flipped the shade off, grabbed it by the bulb socket and crowned John Pratt Junior on the head with it.

"Lights out," I said. "The captain's turned off the no smoking sign."

He staggered back, blood gushing from a spot on his head he couldn't find, and since he was probably seeing at least two of everything he stumbled back and fell down. He wouldn't be any trouble for at least another thirty to forty-five seconds.

I hurled the lamp at the dresser mirror which was just between the other two. It shattered the silvered glass and the thug with the Hitler mustache ducked while the one in the trench coat came over the bed at me.

I threw myself on top of John Junior and pulled his sweatshirt over his head to find his piece. A .45. Not my favorite, but I couldn't afford to be picky. A gun is only as good as its user. Junior had done me one favor. He'd left the safety off.

I whirled around, still on the floor, just in time to stop the trench-coated bed sprinter cold as he stepped off the mattress and onto the floor. He froze, one foot on the bed and one on the carpet, like a cartoon character.

"Want to be dead?" I asked.

He stayed still. I guess that meant no. I got to my feet as the thin one with black hair straightened up. I stepped away from John Junior as he lay moaning on the floor until I had the door just behind me. I reached behind and opened it until I could feel outside air on my back. Good.

"We don't have time for twenty questions," I said. "So I'll start with asking just who the hell you gentlemen are."

The one in the trench coat slid his other foot to the floor so he was no longer doing a balancing act. He glanced at the one with the toothbrush mustache and said nothing.

"All right," I said, "let me guess." I pointed my gun at the one with the Hitler mustache. "You. Adolf. He looked at you before answering, so you must be the boss. That means you're the only one who thinks he's irreplaceable. I'll make a deal with you. Anything goes wrong in the next three minutes, I'll drill a slug right into that funny little face of yours."

"You can't cover both of us at the same time," Adolf said.

"Now, there you're wrong," I said. I could see the trench-coated wonder tensing by my side. I swerved the gun so it pointed right between his headlights. They went on high beams as he looked down the barrel. "You must be a private detective."

"How did you—I mean, what . . . ?"

"Because most private dicks used to be cops and you look like you used to be a cop before you decided you wanted to dress better and take a regular lunch," I said.

"I retired," he said.

"Then let me see your buzzer and your piece," I said. "Piece first."

He shrugged off the trench coat to reveal a shoulder holster and took a nine millimeter out by the barrel and tossed it on the bed. I made him back up against the wall so I could pick it up. "Ah-hah," I said, as I trained a gun on each of them. "Now that's more like it. See? Now I can plug either one of you at any time. Oh, and since you used to be a cop, then you

233

probably have a backup piece stored in the slash pocket of your pants. So I'll take that one, too."

He winced and did as I said, placing a .38 on the bed. "And don't forget your peeper license," I said. "You're leaving that here with me."

He laid it out on the bed pillow like a mint. "Stealing a firearm is—"

"It's not stolen until it leaves the room," I said. "Yours I'll leave here, but I'm taking the clip with me." I nudged John Junior with my foot. "And maybe you missed it, but he gave me this other one as a gift."

"What do you want?" Adolf asked.

"Just a little more mileage on the information highway I seem to be lost on," I said. "You, the private eye, crawl back over the bed and stand by your boss there."

He did as I said. I made a show of making sure they were both in my sights like I was at a carnival attraction. Then I looked at his license.

"So you're Kyle Watson," I said to the private eye. "I thought so."

Kyle nodded once, mute.

"Kyle, you know Mark Roper?"

"Yes."

"You tell him to book Chad Karp two years ago?"

"Yes."

"In Alandale, Nevada, right?"

"Yes."

"You know what was going to happen to him?"

"Something bad."

"Who paid you to do this?"

Silence.

"I'm willing to bet it's the guy standing next to you. Maybe Junior threw in a little folding money."

Watson dropped his eyes to the floor. Junior was still only semiconscious.

"OK, Kyle, we're done." I stepped to the side. "You can leave. Empty your pockets so I know you're walking home and don't call the police. When you hear from John Pratt Senior tell him we already talked on the phone and I seemed like a real nice guy."

Kyle followed my instructions and left. He'd had a gun held on him before.

I turned my attention to Adolf.

"How do you know he won't call the police?" he asked.

"And say what? I had my gun taken away from me? He might as well tell his buddies on the force I sewed him a dress and called him Mary." I kept the gun on him. "Now it's just you and me, sweetheart."

"You are a homosexual?" His face was so pale I could see the blue in a temple vein.

"No," I said. "They have this new thing now. It's called comedy. It often involves jokes."

"Comedy is the tool of the Africans and Israelites," he said in his froggy voice, "to pollute the minds and bloodline of the white race."

"Not only that it's a great way to meet babes," I said. "Take your wallet out and toss it on the bed."

"Why?"

"So I can see who you are," I said.

"And if I refuse?"

"I'll shoot you in the foot," I said.

He didn't move. "You haven't the nerve."

"You know what? You're right," I said and whipped the pistol barrel across his mouth.

He went down on one knee and an elbow, a hand going to his teeth to see if any had come loose. His fingers came away red. "You will pay for that," he said. He sounded like he'd just come back from the dentist's and they were having a sale on Novocain.

"I'm looking at the bed and I still don't see your wallet," I said, and brought the gun butt down on the base of his spine. He went sprawling on the carpet and started to crawl away, but then he remembered why I was hitting him and brought out his calfskin billfold and threw it back at me.

I opened it up with one hand and thumbed out his driver's license. Robert Osgood.

"I know you," I said. "You're the guy Helen's mom thought would be perfect for her." I dumped the rest of the carrying plastic out onto the bedspread. He slowly righted himself to a sitting position against the bathroom wall. "You're in that group of wackos. What's it called?" I found a laminated membership card, complete with official seal. "Ah. The Crown of Thorns."

"The white race cannot be allowed to die out," he said, staring at a point in space.

I squatted down in front of him. "Listen, Osgood," I said. "I don't care about your personal politics. You want to worship Adolf Shitler, go right ahead. The First Amendment is my best friend."

He glanced up at me. He was running his tongue around in his mouth to see if the bleeding had stopped.

"But I'm looking for the reason why an open-miker like Chad Karp was tied to a wooden post and left to die," I said.

"What concern is it of yours?"

"It's my concern because Chad Karp didn't die," I said. "He lived. And now someone is taking revenge for what was done to him. Now it's either him, or someone who wants a lot of people to think it's him. That's another story." I gestured with the bloodied end of the barrel. "Right now I've got a few questions for you. You're either going to answer them straight up, or I'm going to have to hurt you some more."

He looked at the gun and then at me and then he nodded.

"Who paid Kyle Watson to set up Chad Karp?" I asked.

"I did."

"How did you choose Alandale, Nevada?"

"We had a member there."

"A member of what?"

"The Crown of Thorns."

"What was his name?"

"Clayton Hollister."

I searched my memory for the name. "The former sheriff?"

Osgood nodded.

"So he must have introduced you to Del Lacey."

Osgood nodded again. "The three of us met with Jim Parkins,

the owner of the Payroll Saloon, and we told him what we wanted."

"Jim Parkins seemed like a good man to some people up there," I said. "Why did he decide to go along with a couple of thugs like you?"

"I paid him five thousand dollars," he said. "And he was having an affair with Del Lacey's ex-wife. Didn't want Lacey to find out. Hollister threatened to tell him."

"So Parkins let Hollister and Lacey take Chad Karp out into the wilderness and tie him to a post and torture him half to death."

Osgood nodded dully. "First, they dragged him behind a truck." He closed his eyes. "They were only going to scare him a little. But Del Lacey . . . he went crazy. No one could control him. I thought I was hiring a professional. A fellow soldier. But he liked inflicting agony for its own sake. I mean . . . Chad Karp was no one to him. He was just a convenient target for his rage."

I didn't say anything.

"After a few hours, Karp passed out. Lacey couldn't revive him anymore. He'd . . . he'd scalped him, for the love of God. Torn out his fingernails. Put a blowtorch to his feet. Taken a hunting knife to his face and neck." He opened his eyes and looked at me. "You're telling me he's recovered from that?"

I nodded.

"But I was there," he said. "I saw what was done to him. He couldn't do what you say he's doing, for God's sake. I would be surprised if he could ever walk again."

"It might not be him," I said.

"Then who?" Osgood asked. "Why?"

"I don't know."

Osgood dropped his gaze. "I loved Helen Pratt," he said. "I still do. I'm from a family with money, far more wealthy than her own. We own entire blocks of downtown. Instead, she went with a good-for-nothing Croatian. A Catholic."

I let him talk. "I thought if I scared Chad Karp enough, he would leave her alone. I just wanted him to stay out of Portland, get a few bruises, maybe a black eye, not . . . murder."

"Why were no charges ever brought in the assault on Chad Karp?" I asked.

"I paid the sheriff off for two years," he said. "Tens of thousands of dollars. He kept a lid on it. Until now, I suppose." He touched a finger to his mouth. The bleeding had stopped. "As for Helen . . ." He shrugged. "I never saw her again."

"She went to take care of Karp," I said, "after he got out of the hospital."

"I still believe she has a greater destiny with me," he said. "We would make many fine children."

"Not in this lifetime," I said. "Get up."

He was momentarily confused. "You're letting me live?"

"Sure," I said. "You surprised?"

He stayed seated. "The Irish kill children and expectant mothers in the name of their Pope," he said.

I sighed. "Osgood, none of this has anything to do with race wars or international banking conspiracies or any of that crap you believe. Now get on your feet. We're almost done."

He righted himself and I walked him over to stand in front of the fragments of the shattered dresser mirror. "Look at yourself," I said. "I want you to see what you look like one last time."

His eyes widened. "Before what?"

"Before I do this," I said and brought the gun barrel down across his face.

He screamed and his hands went to his face as fresh blood filled his eyes. He curled up in a ball and started breathing sobs through his open mouth. I bent down and grabbed his shirt collar so I could whisper fiercely in his ear.

"Now you think twice before you pick on a comedian again," I said. "Black, brown, white, yellow, Jewish . . . whatever. We come in all shapes, sexes and sizes. We may act the fool but we are nobody's victim. We drink too much and talk too loud but I guarantee you the toughest man in the room is the one with the microphone. So now every time you look in the mirror you remember it was a comedian that broke your nose. A comedian."

I dropped him back on the floor so his head thudded against

the baseboard and left him alone. I got my suitcase and gathered my belongings, stuffing them inside in a matter of minutes. The last thing I did was toss the key on the bed. I was checking out.

On my way out of the hotel room I saw that John Pratt Junior had gotten to his knees and was struggling to bring a sap out of his back pocket. "Thanks for the gun," I said, and clocked him over the ear with the butt. If you're not going to shoot anybody, a gun is a handy thing to hit people with. Junior went back down like a sack of pork chops and I stepped on his stomach. He went *oof.*

I stopped in the doorway to survey the damage. The hotel room was torn apart. Furniture was overturned. There were spots of blood on the carpet. The mirror was shattered and the lamp was broken. Two men lay hurting on the floor. They were both still conscious. They could both hear me.

"The Irish," I said, "have left the building."

TWENTY-TWO

Cynthia Pratt lived at home with her son and her husband, in a six-bedroom house on Bayless Drive in a neighborhood called Arden Oaks, Portland's most affluent suburb. Around eight o'clock that evening, I pulled up into the circular drive in my rental car and parked. I seemed to be meeting a lot of rich people these days, and none of them were in show business. Coincidence? I think not.

I rang the doorbell and waited. Before I'd left his office in downtown Portland, I'd made arrangements with John Pratt Senior to come to his house after dinner and speak to his wife. He said she was usually "alert" until about ten o'clock.

Pratt himself answered the door. He had changed out of his office garb into a flannel shirt and jeans that looked like they had been tailored for him. "Mr. Kincaid," he said with a bit of a flourish, "you're right on time."

I caught a whiff of distilled sprits as I walked past him into the hallway. As he closed the door I saw he was carrying a small glass of something the color of furniture polish.

"Can I make you a drink?" he said.

"Do you have Guinness?"

He smiled and shook his head.

"Murphy's?"

"Sorry. Junior keeps some ale in the kitchen fridge, though. I can get you a bottle of that."

"Sure."

He led me into the kitchen and opened a refrigerator the size of my bedroom closet. "You haven't seen Junior today, have you?"

"No," I lied. It had been about four hours since I'd kicked his ass all over Main Street, but no father likes to hear that about his own son. "Was he looking for me?"

"He called to ask if I knew where you were staying." Pratt turned to me with a bottle of Fuller's ESB in his hand. Apparently Junior's xenophobia did not extend to his taste in brewski. "Since you two didn't seem to hit it off, I thought it best to play dumb. He might try to find out through Kyle Watson, though."

"I'll keep an eye out."

"Would you like a glass?"

"Please," I said. "I like to see what I'm drinking."

He found me an imperial pint glass, the kind with the Queen's markings on the rim, and uncapped and poured me a half pint. "Here's to it, then," he said.

I tasted the Fuller's, and it was just as good as the last time I'd had it—straight out of the tap at a pub in Santa Monica. Junior was a better bartender than he was a brawler. "Where's your son now?"

"Spending the night at a friend's," Pratt said. "I have the feeling it's my secretary."

"Did you speak to him?"

"He sent me an e-mail." He freshened his own drink with a bottle I didn't recognize. "Sure you won't join me in a scotch? I get this sent over from Glasgow. Tough to find Stateside."

"I'm fine," I said.

"Let's go into the library," he said.

He led me out of the kitchen, into a hallway as big as a television studio and opened the door to a windowless room lined floor to ceiling with books. Flames danced in a fireplace, and a love seat and two padded chairs were arranged in a semicircle.

In the love seat sat Cynthia Pratt.

Although it was midevening, she was still dressed for high

tea. She wore a silk blouse under a linen jacket and skirt. Her blond hair was swept up into a bun. She wore hose and heels, and diamond rings adorned her fingers. She looked like a human doll of her own making, someone painted and poised to be viewed and not necessarily designed to talk. She had porcelain skin and the high cheekbones and full lips and large blue eyes that were the hallmarks of her daughter's beauty.

"Cindy," John said, as he led me into her line of sight, "this is that young man I was telling you about."

"Hello, Mrs. Pratt," I said. "My name is Biff Kincaid."

She moved her head like a Disneyland animatronic figure, using her neck to move her eyes. She kept one hand on the arm of the love seat and one hand on her knee.

After she blinked at me a few times I sat in one of the padded chairs. John took the other.

"I don't know what your husband told you," I said, "but I'm looking for information about your daughter's whereabouts."

"I have not spoken to my daughter in two years, Mr. Kincaid." Her voice was soft and mellow. "She ran off with that dirty Catholic boy."

"Chad Karp," I said. "To be honest with you, that's who I'm really looking for."

"She might as well cut my heart out, mixing her bloodline like that."

"Mrs. Pratt, I spoke to Chad Karp's brother, Matthew," I said. "He told me Chad and Helen had moved to Los Angeles."

"California? Where they're letting the city be overrun by the illegals?" There was no invective in her delivery. She could have been discussing the recipe for apple crumb cake at the next picnic for her church group. "Might as well call it the United States of Mexico down there."

"The entertainment industry is located there," I said. "Your daughter wanted to be an actress."

"I told her to stay in the theater," Cynthia Pratt said. "That's where the quality writing is done: for the theater. I don't care what anyone says, it's still true."

I nodded.

"The Jews run the TV and the movies and look at the filth

they put on. Blacks chasing after everything in a skirt. Cartoons swearing at each other. I had my cable disconnected."

"That'll show 'em," I said before I could bite my tongue. I felt John Pratt's look dig into my side.

"Well, someone's got to take a stand, Mr. Kincaid," she said. "The world is going to hell in a handbasket as our president sells off our country to the English, the Japanese and the Dutch when he's not over in Rome kissing the Pope's ring." She found a wrinkle in her jacket and smoothed it out with the palm of her hand. "You ask me, we should take some of those missiles we had pointed at Russia and fire them straight at the Vatican."

"I was hoping I could get the names of some of Helen's friends that you know of—fellow drama students—who might have moved to Los Angeles and run into her there," I said.

"Joan Stafford."

I nodded and repeated the name. "How did she know her?"

"They were college roommates," Cynthia Pratt said. "They were going to move to Los Angeles or New York—they hadn't decided which—as a kind of team, you know. Then she met that Croat and he filled her head with all kinds of lies. They're a gypsy people, the Croats."

"Do Joan Stafford's parents live here?"

"They're dead," Cynthia Pratt said. "She was raised an orphan. I checked into her parentage, though. Good clean bloodline. No mixing of the faiths there. Beautiful girl."

"Do you have a picture of the two of them?" I said. "Or of her?"

"I do," John Senior said. "In my home office upstairs. I can give it to you. Sorry I didn't think of it before."

"Did you keep in touch with Joan Stafford?" I said. "Ever hear from her again?"

"No," Cynthia said. "Not after Helen ran off with the Pope-lover. I like to think Joan knew the only thing to do was to turn her back on Helen: let Helen know how disappointed we all were in her betraying her own kind."

I stood. "Thank you for your time, Mrs. Pratt," I said. "If I find your daughter I'll ask her to call home."

Cynthia Pratt looked me up and down. "What did you say your name was again?"

"Biff Kincaid," I said. "The Biff is short for Brian Francis."

Her eyes narrowed. "What kind of a name is Kincaid, anyway?"

"It's a dirty Catholic one," I said, and left.

I spent one more night in Portland, at a hotel next to the airport. If Kyle Watson were smart, he had paid for the damage I'd caused to the last room I'd stayed in plus a few grand to keep anyone from calling the police. By the time I got back from talking to Cynthia Pratt it was nine-thirty at night and I tried calling Louie Baxter, Dirk Pastor, Andrew Carruthers and Max Gottschalk in that order. The only person to answer his cellular phone was Max Gottschalk.

"Kincaid, where are you?" Gottschalk asked.

"Portland, Oregon."

"What's going on up there?"

"I think I solved half of our little mystery here."

"You found out who's been stalking Louie?"

"I already had a good idea of the who," I said. "What I found out was the why."

"Tell me."

I did. "So what I'm bringing back to L.A. are the names of two wanna-be actresses who may or may not still be in Hollywood. One of them may or may not be in touch with the other. One of them may or may not still be in the company of Chad Karp. Who may or may not be calling himself and acting as the Heckler."

"That's a lot of may or may not bes," he said.

"It's what I've got," I said. "And now I need your help. Or someone's help."

"How?"

"Call the agencies that cast extras," I said. "See if either Helen Pratt or Joan Stafford are listed with them. They've only been in town six months so they're probably still trying to get their SAG vouchers to join the union. If you can't get their personal information, book them for the next episode of *Baxter's Place*. We'll talk to them that way."

"I'll have Andy do it," Gottschalk said. "First thing."

"No," I said. "You do it. And you alone."

"What's the matter, Kincaid? Don't tell me you decided to trust me all of a sudden."

"Will you do it?"

"Sure."

"How's Louie?"

"Not good."

"What do you mean?"

"He didn't show up for work again today."

"Uh-oh."

"He's holed up in his Malibu house on a bender."

"Where's Dirk Pastor?"

"Dirk quit. I hired another bodyguard but Louie refuses to let him in his house. Andy went out to Malibu today. Says Louie's coked up, drunk and used a gun to chase him off."

"What's going on with the show?"

"We're shooting . . . something. A show where the other cast members—Larkin Thomas, Ralph Waters, Sheila Fell—are planning a surprise birthday party for Lou, so they all tell their favorite stories from previous episodes and we go to flashbacks. There's a three-minute scene at the end where he shows up. Hopefully, we can get him to do it." He blew out some air. "We gotta do something, Kincaid. The network's stepped in and started making some big changes I'm trying to talk them out of. We're supposed to be shooting our shows for November sweeps."

"Maybe if I'm able to get some answers on this end . . ."

"Yeah. Maybe Louie'll straighten out." He didn't sound optimistic. "And that's the biggest may or may not be of all."

TWENTY-THREE

I left Portland the next morning.

In my bag was the picture John Pratt had given me of Helen Pratt and Joan Stafford, a backstage color photo taken when they were both out of costume, their hair up, stage makeup still on their faces. Both were very pretty young women, full of life and dreams. That's the way you could be in your senior year of college. Reality had yet to hit you in the face like an iron pancake.

I arrived at LAX by noon. I breathed the smog and got in my car and felt like I was home as I inched my way up La Cienega towards the Hollywood Hills. The Pacific Northwest was beautiful and peaceful, green and uncrowded. Southern California was none of those things. It was full of wackos and crazies, a lot of them with fast cars and loaded guns and loud voices in their heads telling them how to use both. It was where people came from all over the world to find a little magic and instead wound up looking for spare change. If you lived here, you couldn't love it. It was too scary a place to love. You showed your affection by not moving away.

I drove home to Beachwood Canyon and unpacked. There was a message from Max Gottschalk. He had done better than book Helen Pratt on that day's episode of *Baxter's Place*. He had her home phone number and address. He read them to me over the phone—she'd moved from Santa Monica to the Valley—and said if I wasn't able to get her she was due on the set at four that afternoon. He was headed out to Louie's house in Malibu if I needed him. There was a drive-on pass for me at the studio gate.

I put on some sweats and walked down Gower to the gym and spent an hour lifting weights and running in place. I walked back to my apartment, stopping by to pick up a chicken plate at the Middle Eastern deli on the way. I showered at home, toweling off in front of the TV and reheating my food to eat as the local news started at four in the afternoon and that was how I learned Louie Baxter was dead.

I ran out the front door as soon as I could pull on some clothes, my hair still wet from the shower. I got in my car and headed north on the 101. Helen Pratt lived in the Valley, out in Toluca Lake. If I could get to her before the police did . . .

I kept the radio on an all-news channel. Every ten minutes the top local story was repeated: Comedian Louie Baxter had been found dead in his Malibu home. Police were investigating. No cause of death had been determined, but that information would be forthcoming.

I headed north on Cahuenga off the 101 freeway and turned left after I went under the 134 on Blix Street. Houses turned to apartments along the tree-lined street. Not a bad neighborhood. I found a gated complex and a parking spot on the street right in front of it.

I got out and matched her address to a button on the telephone security system. The name there was SMITH. Either she hadn't changed it or she didn't want to be found.

The entrance was set above the street on half a dozen steps. The ground level of the complex was ringed by a set of metal bars that showed a dim parking garage half-full of cars. The sign out front read NO VACANCY," but it advertised a sundeck, laundry facilities, an exercise room and air-conditioning. I pressed the button for Helen's apartment and listened to her phone ring. She might have had another job waiting tables but if she'd gotten an acting job she might have taken the day off or arranged for someone else to take her shift . . .

"Hello?" A female voice.

"Helen Pratt?"

"Who is this?"

"Helen, you don't know me," I said into the security speaker. I glanced around for passersby. I was alone on the block except for an old man walking his miniature poodle and he wasn't looking up from watching his pet sniff the grass. "My name is Biff Kincaid, and I'm a stand-up comedian."

"You're right, I don't know you."

"I'm here because I'm looking for Chad Karp," I said.

"He's not here," she said quickly. "Look, I don't know who you are or what you want, but I have to get to work . . ."

"The job on *Baxter's Place?*" I said. "As an extra?"

Silence.

"I got you that job through Louie Baxter's management so I could talk to you," I said. "And there's no need for you to go to the set today because they're not shooting anything because Louie Baxter was found dead this morning. If you don't believe me, turn on the news."

"Dead how?" she asked in a small urgent voice.

"I don't know yet. If he was murdered the police may think Chad had something to do with it. You can either hear it from them or you can hear it from me, but I might know more about what's going on. I would think that's obvious because I found you first."

Silence. The old man with the poodle looked up at me, picked up his dog and scurried back home.

"You can talk to me out here on the sidewalk or I'll go to a pay phone and call you back if you want, but your parents talked to me, your brother tried to beat me up, and Matthew Karp gave me your name, so I think you at least owe me—"

The front door buzzed open.

I stepped inside.

The complex was made up of at least two dozen apartments set in a red-tiled courtyard with a dried-out fountain. She lived in number 11, which was up a set of metal stairs and along a metal railing to a door painted a light turquoise. As I knocked I looked down the railing and saw a metal elevator door, its buttons smudged and unlighted. It must lead to the parking garage.

The door opened and I saw Helen Pratt in person for the first time. She had the same ash blond hair and delicate features I'd seen in the photos found in Chad Karp's wallet: the large eyes, the full mouth, the high cheekbones and clear fair skin.

She stepped away from the door to let me in. She had the television on and a local on-air reporter was doing a stand-up on the Pacific Coast Highway in front of Louie's house in Malibu.

"I want you to know," she said, "that I have this." In her hand she held a shocking device with four metal prongs. She pressed the button once and a thread of blue lightning traveled between the two top posts. And here I thought I looked like such a nice guy.

"You won't need it," I said.

She kept the door open. "Come on in and sit on the couch over by the window," she said. "I'll stand here by the door."

She wanted to be able to make a clean getaway in case I went psycho on her. That was fine by me. I sat on the couch, keeping my hands out of my pockets and looking as harmless as I could. I nodded at the TV set as they went back to their regularly scheduled program. "What's the latest report?"

She found a remote and switched the television off. "No evidence of foul play," she said. "Could be a heart attack or an overdose."

I nodded. "Louie was bingeing pretty hard on coke and booze."

"Who are you again?"

"Biff Kincaid."

"And you're a stand-up comedian?"

"Yes."

"Here in L.A.?"

"Yes."

"You talk like you know Louie Baxter," she said.

"I do," I said. "Or I did. He's the one who told me about Chad Karp. I've spent the last week trying to find him."

"What are you, like a private detective?"

I shook my head. "Just a fellow comedian," I said. "I guess I was trying to keep what just happened from happening. Louie never did handle pressure very well."

"Then he was in the wrong business," she said.

"When was the last time you saw Chad Karp?" I asked.

She sighed and looked at the metal shocker in her hand. She set it on a shelf next to her house keys and sat in a dinette chair. "He left two weeks ago," she said.

"To go where?"

"I don't know," she said. "He . . . disappeared."

I waited.

"We'd moved down here six months ago," she said. "After he'd recovered enough from his accident—you know about that, right?"

"Enough to know it wasn't an accident," I said.

"What do you mean?"

I told her about meeting up with Robert Osgood and Kyle Watson. She sat listening, riveted to her chair until I was done.

"You mean . . . this whole thing was a . . . like a hit or something?"

I nodded. "Apparently Robert Osgood thought if he could scare Chad away, you would be his to marry."

She let out a small puff of air through her open mouth, then slowly began to shake her head side to side, looking around the apartment as if it threatened to tilt like a carnival fun house. "I met him maybe three times," she said, "on trips home from college. I knew he was part of my mother's nutty religious group, but . . . he started calling and writing me so much I finally told him I was in love with someone else. That only seemed to make it worse. He came to school and tried to find out where I lived . . . I had to call the campus police. I almost got a restraining order against him. When he found out who Chad was he started calling and threatening him, saying he could never have me but I never thought he'd . . ." She put her head in her hands and shook her head to herself for a moment, then lifted her face, dry-eyed.

"When did this become my life?" she said. "I remember my senior year of college; I thought Chad and I were going to get married and we'd move to L.A. and become famous actors known for our independent artistic integrity." She laughed to herself, a sound that held as much mirth and humor as ice cubes hitting a metal tray. "I keep waiting for someone to tap me on the shoulder and tell me that all this hell was meant for another Helen Pratt." She made a gesture with her hands. "I feel my life is really out there somewhere, waiting for me to resume it."

"If it's any consolation," I said, "I broke Robert Osgood's nose."

"Oh, that's an improvement," she snapped. "He'll be able to afford the plastic surgery, believe me. He's richer than Chad's family and mine put together. No wonder I could never find out what happened. No wonder no one up there would talk. They had all been paid off."

"What was Chad able to recall?"

"He couldn't remember anything about the attack," she said, turning on me with a simmering rage. "He didn't remember who he was there with or how he got the gig. The trauma to his head was so severe that his memory was affected. He knew his name. He knew his brother. But he didn't remember that he had ever been a comedian and he didn't remember . . ." Tears sprung to her eyes and her hand flew to her mouth. It took her a moment to compose herself. "He didn't remember me."

I blinked. "He didn't know who you were?"

She shook her head. "No. I showed him pictures, videotapes . . . everything to remind him of our life together. He remembered nothing of the past two years. It was bad enough that he couldn't talk, that he had been disfigured, but to be damaged on the inside that way . . . it was like he had died and a stranger had taken his place."

Her eyes were seeing only the carpet, as if the fibers had begun to weave and move, clearing like a mist to reveal the unspoken. I'd learned that when someone zones out like that it's like they're hypnotizing themselves. Memories become clearer. Truth is told. Suggestions can be followed, but they must be gently made.

"A stranger," I said.

"Yes." Her voice was as soft and low as a priest in confession. "A man with no face. No voice. No memory. Almost . . . no name. He wore a mask to hide his scars. Used a buzzer to talk. It was like Chad's corpse had been . . . reanimated. There was no life to him. No joy. No . . . laughter."

Her right eye welled and a single tear felt its way down her cheek.

"It was like I was his nurse. I was the one who brought him home from the hospital. Home to Matthew, the only family he had left. Matthew . . ."

Another tear. Different eye.

"Matthew saved him. Saved us. Saved me. And in the end, let us go."

"Matthew's a good man."

She looked up at me. "You've seen him?"

"Yes."

"Is he well?"

"Yes. Can I tell him I found you?"

"Yes. I . . . I should call him." She looked around, as if trying to find the phone.

"He was concerned when he hadn't heard from you. So was your father."

She nodded and sniffed and wiped the tears off her cheeks, chin and neck, looking at her fingers. "I know I should have let them know. But I didn't know how to tell them what happened after we moved down here." She chuckled. "You know, Matthew reminds me of my father. I used to tell him that. And I guess I've just realized they've never met."

I nodded as if the conclusion was obvious. Good men in bad times are bound to appear similar. "What did happen?" I asked. "What didn't you want anyone to know?"

"We moved down here . . ." She looked around the apartment. "To a place in Santa Monica first. Before we had left Portland, I wasn't sure if I could stay with Chad, but L.A. was so big and complex . . ."

"I know what you mean," I said.

"I clung to him, a little bit, I guess," she said. "It was better than being alone. Chad was like a rescued animal, silent and wounded, never wanting to venture past the front door.

"We had money Matthew had given us. I got a job. Chad bought a computer and started writing. TV scripts. Screenplays. He thought if he couldn't break into show business with his face or his voice he'd try working behind the scenes. We weren't happy but we were fine. It was fine. He couldn't talk but sometimes he would listen as I bitched about my day. That's all we really want at the end of the day, right? Someone to listen?"

I smiled. "I'm a comic," I said. "I need a roomful of people if I can get it."

She nodded. "He took one bedroom and I took another. He had his own bathroom. So did I. I did the shopping, the bills. He stayed in his room mostly. That's so creepy, you know? Someone who won't come out of his room.

"We saw each other at mealtimes, although he ate in his bedroom so he could take his mask off. At night, when it was empty, he went to the exercise room downstairs in our apartment complex and lifted weights and stretched for hours, doing physical therapy, until someone called the police and reported a masked burglar. Then he bought equipment and moved it into the apartment. I found myself making new friends and staying out late so I didn't have to be there at night when he came out of the bedroom and lifted weights in front of the TV. His body was better and bigger than ever, but it ... it didn't attract me. We had tried resuming our sex life up north and it didn't work. One time I came home and I'd had a little too much to drink and he had finished working out and I asked him if he thought we could ever, you know, try it again. He said only if he could keep his mask on."

I winced.

"So I wrote Matthew a letter and said I was moving out. I found this place and told Chad I was leaving."

"What did he do?"

"He followed me. I had a week in here by myself and then he showed up at midnight with all his belongings in a rented van. He said he . . . shouldn't be alone. He thought he might hurt himself." A weak frown flickered on her mouth. "Notice he didn't say anything about being without me. Just not being alone."

"What did you do after he moved in here?"

"I got busy, just to avoid being here with him. I took acting classes, got photos made . . ." She smiled once, briefly. "Started getting extra work. Callbacks on some commercials. Got a non-union gig on a Saturday morning TV show."

"Which one?"

"*Thunder Sword.* I wore a lot of makeup and a headdress and . . . well, not much else. Saturday morning TV's sure changed since I was a kid." She smiled a little longer than the last time.

I hated to make the smile go away. "And what went wrong?"

Her mouth straightened. "Chad . . . changed. Even more."

"When?"

She took some air in and let it out. "I told you he was writing scripts."

"Yes."

"For TV."

"Yes."

"He decided to try his hand at sitcoms."

"Okay."

"So he started to watch some."

"Yes."

"And that was how he saw *Baxter's Place.*"

"Louie's show?"

"Yes."

"And what happened?"

"He recognized Louie's voice," she said. "He remembered his face. The same thing had happened when he was back at Saint Angela's, but I didn't put any importance on it. He woke up when Louie Baxter was on the *Tonight Show.* His memory hadn't come back before. This time it did." One hand went up in the air, as if she was trying to stop something that had already occurred. "It all returned to him in a rush. The trip. The gig. The night in Alandale. Who he was with. Who attacked him.

What they had done to him. It came back into his memory with such force he was rolling on the carpet, his hands to his stomach, sobbing silently as he remembered. He spent an entire night like that. It was as if they were doing it to him all over again."

"And the next morning?"

"The next morning he told me he was going to get them all back," she said. "He would have his revenge. He would make them pay."

"When did this happen?" I asked. "When did he remember?"

"Two weeks ago yesterday," she said. "A few days later he left. And I haven't seen him since."

"You just came home one day last week and he was gone?"

"No," she said. "Someone took him."

"Who?"

"I don't know."

"Did you see the person?"

"Yes," she said. "On the top of our building is a sundeck. After Chad said good-bye to me I took the elevator to the roof and watched him get in a car with someone. Someone who got out and helped him with his bag."

"Male or female?"

"Male."

"Can you describe him?"

"I just saw him for thirty seconds," she said. "And I was looking down from the roof."

"Try," I said. "I'll ask you some questions and you answer them as best you can."

"Okay," she said. After ten minutes and twenty questions I had a rough mental sketch based on height, weight, hair color, clothing and automobile. She had gotten a good look at the car. When we were done she looked at me blankly. "Does that help?"

"Yes."

"Do you know who that is?"

"I might."

"Anything else you think might be important?" She looked around.

"I'd like to see Chad's computer."

TWENTY-FOUR

At ten minutes to nine that night I picked up my drive-on pass at Radford Studios. It was still waiting for me when I got there since Max Gottschalk had called it in. No one had bothered to call and cancel it, and the security guard was watching a Dodgers game on a small black-and-white TV. I knew where to park. I left my car and walked to Stage 9, where *Baxter's Place* was taped. This hour of the night, there was no security guard outside. The red light above the video camera was dead. I was the only person in sight.

The door to the stage was already unlocked. My appointment had shown up early. It was a little creepy, but it was too late to turn tail and run. I was the one who had asked for this meeting.

I stepped through the doorway and onto the soundstage. It was dark except for the work lights, which had been set at extra dim. The set was about as bright as a Hollywood alley, and I'd learned to stay out of those.

I stepped forward, leaving the door open behind me, listening for the sound of another human footfall. All I heard was the pneumatic hiss as the exit door closed softly closed behind me, sealing me inside with a pneumatic *thump*. The red exit light glowed on my back.

I walked across the stage floor as slowly as I could, letting my eyes adjust to the darkness. My vision was greatly hindered by the fact that I had not been born a cat. I reached the limits of what I could see very quickly. I felt the muscles in my face as I opened my eyes as wide as they would go.

Ahead of me was the comedy club set, a familiar setting made all the more eerie by its displacement. In the dim light, it looked as authentic as if it had been cut out of another part of the city and set down here by airlift. All the pieces were in place: tables, chairs, stage, microphone. I stepped my way through the tables and onto the stage, tapping the microphone with my fingers. It was off. Louie had insisted on having the club set built with live sound, to make the atmosphere in the stand-up scenes as realistic as possible.

I found the amp and turned it on. A red light glowed and I heard an electric hum over the speakers. I touched the mike again, my finger taps coming out like thuds over the P.A. system. Next to it was a lighting board that was supposed to control the lights set around the stage. I wondered if that was rigged up, too. I touched a control, barely moving it. One single light just above my stage right glowed. I moved the stool over to where I could reach it and stood on its wobbly wooden legs while I turned the light around to face the audience. I found another light that worked and did the same. Half the lights now hit the front row of the audience as well as where I stood on stage. Good to know. I shut them off.

I heard a door open and close in the darkness behind me.

I turned and saw that it was the double set of swinging doors that led to the dressing rooms. A sliver of fluorescent light from the hallway beyond glowed where the doors met, and enough light shone through so I could see Dirk Pastor's shaved head. He took two steps, then stood, blinking in the near darkness. He looked around. He didn't know where the controls for the stage lights were.

I stood up. "Over here, Dirk." I stepped off the stage and onto the audience part of the set.

"Hi, Kincaid," he said. He sounded tired. "Just went and got a few last personal things out of the dressing room."

We walked toward each other, meeting under a dim stage light like a city streetlamp in a bad part of town.

He put out his hand. I shook it. In the dim light, I could see his angular hairless features were weary with grief, his eyes swollen and red. He looked five years older than the last time I saw him.

"You have any trouble getting on the lot?" I asked.

"No," he said. "My pass is good until the end of the week and I still have a key to this place. Guess I should turn those in now. Not that anybody'll be needing them anytime soon."

"How'd you hear?" I said.

"Same as you," he said. "The news." He looked over my shoulder. "You by yourself?" he asked.

"Not since you showed up," I said.

"So what did you want to ask me that was so important?" he said. "You find anything out on that little trip Louie sent you on? Too bad he didn't live to hear about it."

"Just a few questions," I said. "When's the last time you saw Louie?"

"Two days ago," Dirk said. "When I told him I quit."

"Why'd you quit?"

"Because I couldn't take it anymore," he said. "Kincaid, you saw what he's like. Going off on binges for days at a time, not caring when or if he made it to the set. I was the one getting yelled at by Max Gottschalk because I couldn't keep his client off whatever drug he got his hands on." He wiped his face with his hands and shook his head, as if he'd just thrown cold water on himself. "Louie was going to get fired or get caught drunk driving or something, and since I couldn't get him into a rehab I walked away. I got tired of being the whipping boy for an entire network show."

"So what happened to Louie?" I asked. "You must know more from talking to the police than the news channels are telling."

"He OD'd," Dirk said. "Coke, booze and pills. It all caught up with him. Gottschalk found him on the floor of his bathroom around ten o'clock this morning and tried to revive him with CPR. He was pumping his chest with one hand and calling 911 on his cell phone with the other. Paramedics came, but they couldn't do anything for him." He looked down, at something between my face and the floor. "He's dead."

"News says the police ruled out homicide."

"Is that why they questioned me for four hours?" He looked back up at me. "When you called I'd just been released from custody, right into the waiting arms of the press. Jesus, there's a lot of TV channels these days."

"Was there anything at the scene?" I said.

"Like what?"

"Like a note," I said. "Like writing on the wall."

"Oh, you think . . ." He shook his head. "No, nothing like that."

"Had he gotten any notes since I last saw him?"

"Not that I know of," Dirk said dismissively. "One night when he was high Louie told me the whole story about what happened in Nevada and how he'd asked you to go check it out. Some comic got beat up, right? I wondered where the hell you'd gone, but I had my hands full just finding Louie after he pulled another one of his disappearing acts at the Comedy Store. He went on a tear after he found out he was being let go."

"Let go from what?"

"From the show," Dirk said. "The producers had already fired him. Since you've been out of town he's missed two rehearsals and a taping. They just hadn't made a formal announcement yet. He was off the wagon big-time. He'd been on a drunk since Thursday. Coke to counteract the booze, pills to counteract the coke. He started playing with a loaded gun, going outside on his balcony and yelling at whoever he thought was out there to come and get him. After I walked away there was no one there to watch over him. That's all. End of story." He snorted. "The Heckler can go away now."

"He won't," I said. "He can't."

Dirk wasn't sure what I'd just said was important. "What?"

"Because there never was a Heckler," I said. "Not the way we thought there was. He doesn't exist."

"You think it's that Chad Karp guy Louie let get fucked up two years ago?" Dirk said.

"No, it isn't," I said. "My guess is that Chad Karp is already dead."

That got his attention. "What?"

"Chad Karp's injuries were too severe for him to do all the deeds the Heckler did," I said. "Someone else met Chad Karp, learned his story and adopted his appearance and motives for their own purposes—and they had help."

"You're saying it's someone else?"

I nodded. "It's more than one person. Think about it: How could anyone get on this set and plant those notes? Who would know where Louie was going to be at certain times?"

"But what for?" Dirk said. "That's what I don't get."

"Because they also knew if they frightened him badly enough, they could get Louie to kill himself with booze and drugs," I said.

"Who would want to do that?"

"The person who paid you," I said.

Dirk's jaw twitched, but his eyes didn't move. "Kincaid, what the hell are you saying?"

"Who else could get those notes inside Louie's dressing room?" I said. "They showed up when the set was full of people. You've got so much extra security in here an ant couldn't sneak into the coffee sugar."

"Kincaid—" He stepped forward like he was going to silence me.

I stepped back and held up a hand. "I'm not asking you for a name because I know you don't have one," I said. "He approached you. Maybe he had something on you, something from your past or present that you wanted no one else to know. That's how he works, through bribery and blackmail."

Dirk swallowed but he held his ground.

I kept talking. "I'm thinking someone offered you money. Maybe hundreds, even thousands. All you had to do was leave a note. How were you to know who it was from or what it meant?"

I'd laid it out there, and now I let my statements hang in silence. Dirk's mouth worked noiselessly and his eyes left my face to look somewhere else for a while.

"I still don't know who it is," he said.

I waited.

"I thought it would just be an easy way to make some extra money," he said. "I thought they were fan letters."

"Not after the first one you didn't."

He looked back at me. "No."

"So why? Why not tell Louie or Gottschalk?"

Dirk blinked. "Because I hated him."

"Louie?" I asked. "Or Gottschalk?"

"Both," Dirk whispered. "But Louie most of all."

"Why?"

"I was hired to keep Louie clean." Dirk snorted. "The DEA couldn't keep that guy clean. He was a party waiting to happen. He had the big break everyone dreams of in this town and he was just pissing it away. I knew he was going to screw up and soon I'd be out of a job—just like the last guy. Everyone else seemed to be looking out for themselves, making all this money while I got nickeled and dimed on my salary and expenses.

"I was supposed to be his bodyguard and ended up being his flunky. That was deliberate, planned humiliation on his part. The truth was, he didn't want me around. You saw what it was like, and that was just one night. I have to get the car, greet visitors, make sure he has plenty of water and snacks . . . even pick up his clothes. Too bad you didn't see me get dressed down in front of the rest of the cast and crew because I brought him the wrong kind of diet soda.

"You know why all those other bodyguards quit? Louie drove them away. It's Gottschalk who keeps hiring them. I go to him for a raise and all I hear is about how tight money is: 'It's not in the budget. This is coming out of my own pocket.' Meanwhile, this show is getting ready to rake in millions. I knew I wasn't getting any of it."

He was getting worked up. "So I took the money from whoever this guy was and . . . and I was the one who sold stories to Sheryl Franklin, too. At first. I didn't know it would lead to this . . . Heckler business."

That made sense. "How did he contact you?"

"A delivery. An overnight package. Sent to me here. I don't know how he got my name . . ."

"What was inside?"

"The first envelope with Louie's name on it, and ten thousand dollars."

"That's all?"

"That's all. Later that same day there was a phone call on my cellular. A voice . . . like a machine talking . . ."

"What did it say?"

" 'Did he get it?' I instantly knew who he was and what he was talking about. I said no. The next day, another ten thousand. No note. Something else." He looked at me. "He did have something on me, Kincaid. Something you don't need to know about. Something no one needs to know about why I left the LAPD."

I nodded.

"I got another phone call. The same question: 'Did he get it?' This time I said yes."

"And the same with the second note?"

"The same with the second note," Dirk said, nodding along. "Do you have any idea who this is? Because I'd like to—"

I saw a piece of the shadow against the wall begin to move.

"Wait a minute," I said.

"What?" Dirk turned to look.

The shadow stepped away from the wall and disappeared behind a wall of the set.

"We're not in here alone," I said. "We've got company." I nodded toward where I'd seen the shadow move.

Dirk's hand flashed under his jacket and suddenly there was a gun in his hand. "We need to split up," he said. He pointed toward the dressing rooms. "Go that way. See if you can draw him into the light."

"What about you?"

"I'll nail the sucker right between the ears as soon as I get a bead on him," he whispered, and then he was gone, vanishing under the audience bleachers.

I had no choice but to do as he said. I headed for the dressing rooms, the lone fluorescent light that peeked around the edges guiding my way. I was halfway there when I saw a part of what I thought was one of the double doors take a new shape and move toward me.

I turned around. I'd been foolish to come without a weapon. "Dirk!" I yelled.

With a whoosh of air I felt something heavy and hard crash down on the base of my skull. I hunched my shoulders and dropped my head to deflect the blow, but it still packed enough punch to knock me down to my knees, tropical colors blooming in front of my eyes. I pitched forward, my hands slipping ahead to brace my fall. My head suddenly weighed as much as an engine block, and I struggled to lift it and clear my vision as I heard a hissing sound from beside me and Dirk cry out. He staggered out from under the bleachers, his gun dropping to the floor, one arm spasming away from his side, suddenly useless, what looked like a long thick dart piercing one biceps.

On my hands and knees, I felt more than saw a presence race out of the shadows beside me toward Dirk.

I started crawling toward the set, toward the comedy club stage. I had only one chance.

Dirk and his attacker struggled in the darkness in front of me. I heard grunts and groans, blows exchanged, cries of pain as Dirk was wounded, a huffing, wordless sound as the other one was hit. They were evenly matched, now that Dirk was wounded.

Something clanged on the floor, spinning to just within my sight: a dark deadly weapon, its single loaded arrow discharged, but a quiver of them left. A crossbow. What the . . . ?

My hands hit the carpet of the comedy club stage. I pulled myself up, the pain in my head now fading to where I could think again. I had to reach the control board. I had to reach the light switch.

"No, no, *no* . . ." I heard Dirk plead behind me, each syllable rising in pitch and volume until his voice was choked off. He was losing the battle. I clenched the microphone stand in one hand and the performer's stool in the other and pulled myself upright, using them as crutches. I turned and saw what was happening.

Dirk was being held from behind, a black-clad arm looped around his bald head, his eyes wild with fear even in the dark. His attacker's form blended in with the darkness, so it was hard to tell what he was doing to him, but I saw the gleam of a blade being withdrawn from a belt and disappear behind Dirk's back. Dirk jerked with each knife thrust into his back: in-out, in-out, in-out, screaming silently until the veins in his skull stood out, beyond any help, beyond hope, beyond healing, as his blood began to spatter the floor like leaking paint.

He was let go and he fell to the floor.

I was now standing upright on the comedy stage.

The figure in black was unhurt. He walked swiftly toward his crossbow and picked it up.

I fumbled in the dark for the controls of the lighting panel, looking for the switch I'd found before. I kept hold of the mike stand. It was the genuine article, not a dummied-up prop, the metal shaft long, the base heavy. Very heavy.

I heard him breathing as he loaded an arrow into the crossbow and pulled it back, locking it with a wooden *click*.

I put my hand on the control panel blindly, hoping my fingers found the right buttons.

I looked out from the stage. He was there, five feet away, right in the front row, raising the crossbow like a medieval soldier. I saw the arrowhead, the edges razor-sharp, pointed at my left eye. That's where it was going to hit, shooting all the way through my brain.

No time left.

I closed my eyes and hit the lights, falling to the floor.

The two spotlights I'd set earlier blasted him full in the face just as he fired and his shot went wild, the arrow hissing through the air over my head and landing with a *thunk* in the wall of the set. In one sweeping motion I stood up, mike stand in hand, and swung hard. He was already moving away, looking for cover, but he couldn't see worth a damn and ran right into a cocktail table. He went over it hard, bending at the waist. I'd aimed not for his head but his back and I caught him right at the base of the spine.

He flailed wildly in wordless agony, bringing down the table and a couple of chairs with him as he fell to the floor. His legs lay useless beneath him, the crossbow dangling from the fingers of one hand.

I stepped over him and raised the mike stand again. I could see the mouth hole in his black leather hood, his lips wet and gasping, the eyes looking up at me in surprise.

I swung again and knocked him out cold. The flailing stopped. He slumped unconscious.

I kicked the crossbow away from his hand and tied his feet and hands with the microphone cord. Then I went and looked at Dirk where he lay. His eyes were open and staring, surprised to be dead. I picked up his gun and checked to make sure it was loaded, the safety off. I felt around on his belt for his cellular phone. I flipped it open and called 911.

After I hung up I could hear my captive breathing. I went over to where he lay and nudged him with my foot. He was still in the land of Nod. I set the gun and the phone aside and knelt over him. There was one thing I had to know for myself.

I lifted his head off the floor and felt for the metal snaps on the leather hood around the base of his skull. There were three of them. I undid them one by one, then used both hands to peel the mask off of his face and let his head fall back down to the floor.

I stood up, the hood in hand. The spotlights were still on, so I could see his face clearly. There was still something I needed to know.

"What have you done with Chad?" I asked aloud.

TWENTY-FIVE

The questioning of the suspect was held at the Central Valley office of the LAPD the next day. I wasn't supposed to be there, but Sergeant Charles Gregory of the Las Vegas Police Department had flown in and, despite the fact that he had come to regard me as a world-class pain in the ass, let me stand next to him and watch a monitor as the first interrogation was held of what the television and newspapers were now calling the Heckler Killings. Couldn't argue with the catchy phrasing.

Two LAPD detectives were inside the room with the suspect, now dressed in prison whites, seated at a small table and not wearing the leather hood I had taken off his head. Everyone could see his face. Clearly. He had indicated he would be cooperative. He wanted to confess.

Tape was rolling. One detective was seated, one standing. The seated one introduced himself as Jack Hampton and stated the date, time, location and purpose of the interrogation and that it was being recorded. Then he asked his first question of the suspect:

"Would you state your name, please?"

"Matthew Fitzgerald Karp," he said.

Gregory looked at me, and I looked at the monitor.

"He wasn't carrying any ID," Gregory said. "Is that who he is?"

"Yes," I said. "That's Chad Karp's brother."

The seated detective asked Matthew where he lived. The answer was the Bearclaw address.

"And what is your occupation?"

"I design computer games."

"Do you know a former police officer named Dirk Pastor?"

"I do," Matthew said. "I mean, I did. He never knew me."

"He's dead now?"

"Yes."

"How did he die?"

"I killed him."

"How?"

"With a knife."

"Why did you kill him?"

"I paid him to torment one of Chad's enemies," he said.

"Who was to be tormented?"

"Louie Baxter."

"Tormented how?"

"He was to leave notes for him in his dressing room," Matthew said. "Notes I supplied."

"And he did this for you?"

"Yes. Until . . ."

"Until when?"

"Until he learned about Tiger Moore's death. There was a third note, but that was a fake. I think that TV reporter Sheryl Franklin, made that one up herself."

"By Tiger Moore are you referring to a comedian also known as Lawrence Moore."

"Yes."

"How did Tiger Moore die?"

"I killed him. I broke into his hotel room at the Palace in Las Vegas and I stabbed him in the neck."

"Did you kill Clayton Hollister?"

"Yes."

"Did you kill Jim Parkins?"

"Yes."

"Did you attempt to kill Delbert Lacey?"

"Yes. To avenge my brother Chad, yes."

"When?"

"After Chad had left home. I tracked them down and I chained them together in the nightclub where Chad had last performed and I set it on fire."

There was a brief pause.

"I designed a computer game about professional killers," Matthew said. "It's called 'Assassin For Hire.' To research it I met some real-life mercenaries. Career soldiers. I paid them for their advice on how to design the game. They schooled me in the ways of murder. They took me with them on missions. They let me experience the kill, using people who would never be missed. When I learned what had happened to my brother . . ." He shrugged. "I asked these men to help me find those who had tortured and maimed him. I took my revenge on them. I never told Chad. I thought that was it. Then, when his memory came back, he told me other names. Names of the comedians who were there and let it happen. Tiger Moore. Louie Baxter."

"Chad sent his brother a copy of the e-mail he sent to Tiger as insurance," I said in whisper, Gregory standing next to me. "I first thought it was more than one person."

"It was," Gregory said. "They just happened to live in the same body."

The seated detective continued the questioning: "And where is Chad?"

"He's dead," Matthew said. "Tiger Moore killed him. He shot him. Tiger wrapped the body in plastic and dumped it in Ventura County. Tiger told me this when I found him in Las Vegas— right before I stabbed him."

The detective waited.

"What happens now?" Matthew asked. "Do I go back home and wait for you to call me when there's a trial?"

"No."

"I have money," he said. "Millions." He looked at the standing detective. "Enough to make all of you rich."

"Is that a bribe?" the seated detective asked.

"Yes. I mean, it can be."

The detectives looked at each other.

"Don't you get it?" Matthew said. "I design computer games, based around characters. The Heckler was just another character I made up. He's not real. The police and the press got hold of the name and just ran with it. I was thinking of putting him on the market—you know, the first game patterned after a real serial killer."

"You might want to change that to created *by* a real serial killer," Detective Hampton said.

"But he's not *real*," Matthew said.

"All neat and tidy," I said. "No loose ends."

"Yes, there are."

The Ventura County Morgue was in a one-story building a few blocks from the beach. I had been there before. Ventura itself was an hour up the Pacific Coast Highway from Los Angeles. I took the 101 freeway there. My personal presence wasn't required. I was giving Helen Pratt a ride.

"What did the LAPD tell you?" she asked.

"Detective Gregory is with the Las Vegas Police Department," I said. "He's coordinating with other law-enforcement agencies on this."

"So what did he tell you?" she asked.

"That Ventura County has a John Doe they want to see if we can ID."

"What's a John Doe?" she asked.

"A body that was found with no identification."

"I was told they want me to look at a dead body."

"If you're up to it," I said.

"Do they think it might be Chad?"

"There's a possibility."

"Why do they think there's a possibility?"

"Apparently this John Doe has some rather extensive facial scars."

"That's . . . that's what I was told." She was wearing large dark glasses and a hat. Her mouth had gone flat and her voice was dry and reedy. She was carrying a water bottle between her jeans-clad legs and seemed very thirsty.

"So how do I do this?" she asked. "Do I go into the morgue and they have a body on a table and someone pulls back the sheet and asks me if I think it's him?"

"That's pretty much it," I said.

"Have you ever done this?"

"Yes."

"Where?"

"The Ventura County Morgue, for one instance."

She turned to look at me through her dark glasses for the first time since I'd picked her up at her apartment. "I imagine you have," she said.

Several miles went by before she spoke again. "I've never seen a dead body before," she said.

"They can't hurt you," I said.

Another dozen miles.

"My father said he would meet me there," Helen said. "He didn't want me to do this, but I insisted. And . . . he had met Chad."

Another five miles.

"It'll be good to see my father," she said.

John Pratt was there, waiting in the parking lot with a car and driver. At first I thought the car and driver were police issue, but the car was a Lincoln Continental. When he saw Helen the two of them came together like the long lost family I guess they had become.

I hung back and nodded at Pratt's burly driver. Maybe he thought I was a driver myself. He nodded back. I looked at something else besides the sight of father and daughter hugging. I couldn't help but overhear their muffled moans turns to sobs and then the sound of sniffled tears.

I looked at the coroner's office and saw that a thin middle-aged gentlemen with a long hawk nose, glasses, a bushy mustache and Jack Nicholson hair had stepped outside to smoke a cigarette. He wore a plastic badge around his neck and a gun at his waist. I ambled toward him.

"You a coroner's deputy?"

He nodded. "That's right."

"We're here to ID a John Doe," I said. I moved my hand in front of my face. "The one that's all scarred up."

He looked over at Helen and her father, who were now holding each other at forearm's length, wiping tears from each other's faces. "Who've you got?"

"His girlfriend," I said. "And her father."

"No other family?"

"No."

The deputy snuffed out his cigarette and held out his hand. "Carl Wax," he said.

"Biff Kincaid."

"You a relative?"

"No."

"Family friend?"

"I guess so," I said. "What family's left."

"I don't mean to move things along too quickly," Deputy Wax said, "but I've got a seventeen-year-old kid who hung himself on Alta Mira Street, so . . ."

"Gotcha," I said. I walked over to John and Helen Pratt. John Senior and I greeted each other while Helen blew her nose.

"Are they ready for us in there?" John asked.

"Yes," I said. "Helen, you can still wait—"

She shook her head. "I'm going."

John took her hand and she gripped it fiercely.

"Let's go," I said.

We left the driver in the parking lot. I made the introductions to Deputy Wax, and Wax checked us in at the front desk. We walked down a long hallway where the temperature and the smell got well below the comfort zone. We walked through a set of double swinging doors into a room decorated in metal drawers: filing cabinets for the dead. It smelled like the day in school when the teacher had you dissect a frog, except ten times more pungent.

I stuck by Helen's side. Her complexion had begun to match the ceiling tile. She held on to her father by his whole arm.

Wax walked us over to one metal drawer big enough to hold a human body. "We found him three days ago after someone called in an anonymous tip, disguising their voice," he said. "He'd been killed a few days before that. He was wrapped in plastic and left in an abandoned building. Otherwise, the dogs and animals would have gotten to him."

"How was he killed?" Mr. Pratt asked.

"Shot in the chest." Wax put his hand on the drawer's handle. "Ready?"

"Is . . ."

Helen had a question.

Wax leaned forward and lifted his eyebrows to encourage her to speak up.

"Is he bad? I mean, does he look . . . messed up?"

"No," Wax said. "We just need an ID before we do a post-mortem."

All of us looked at Helen as she gave a final nod.

The drawer slid open.

Helen looked inside and turned away, burying her face in her father's shoulder. He held on to her. His lips went pale and pressed together wordlessly.

"Is this your boyfriend?" Wax asked.

Helen removed her face from her father's shoulder and nodded once. Then again. "That's Chad," she said. "You can close it now." She turned away, her father helping her out the door as her silence grew to a keening that echoed down the hallway.

Wax started to close the drawer but I stopped him. "May I?"

"Certainly."

I looked inside.

The body was in the drawer feet first. I stepped to the side so I wouldn't be looking at the face upside down.

"What happened to him?" Wax asked. "Why does his face look like that?"

"He was attacked," I said. "Some guys were hired by a hate group to beat him up, and they got carried away."

"Those scars look like burns."

"Some of them are," I said. "See? That's where they scalped him."

"Jesus," Wax said.

"You'll find other injuries in your postmortem," I said. "They worked him over pretty good. He was in a coma. Took him a while before he could even walk again."

I could see the bullet wounds in the gray clay of the chest, clustered together like three holes dug by a screwdriver.

"What's the story?" Wax asked. "Who was he?"

I looked up from the sight of Chad Karp's dead scarred face. I knew I'd be seeing it again, and the sight would wake me up in the middle of the night, on the road in a strange hotel room, years from now, and it would look just like it did now, even though it had long passed from this earth.

"He was a comedian," I said. "A stand-up comedian."

I went back home alone. When I got back to Beachwood Canyon I called Gregory on his portable phone.

"They ID'd the body," I said. "The Ventura County Coroner's office has Chad Karp."

"Already got that information, Kincaid," he said. He told me something else but it came out as a series of clipped syllables.

"You're phone's cutting out," I said. "Where are you?"

"Out in the desert," he said. "On the two-lane to Ridgecrest. Someone found Sheryl Franklin."

"What do you mean, 'found' her?"

"She's dead, Kincaid."

Sheryl Franklin had been killed inside her gold Mercedes, and either before or after she had been strangled the car had been driven off the road and left in a ditch behind a boulder, out of sight of the two-lane desert highway. A helicopter had spotted the car from the air and a highway patrol car had been sent out. She had been missing for three days. The windows had been left open and insects had gotten in. She didn't look quite as pretty as the last time I saw her, slumped over the steering wheel with newborn flies in her hair.

Across the inside of the windshield, in reverse, so it could be read from the outside, someone had written one word in large red smears:

HEKLUR.

"Looks like blood, doesn't it?" Gregory said. "It's not. It's paint."

There were a dozen officers from different law-enforcement agencies around the scene. It had taken me two hours to get there from home, and the first thing Gregory said to me was he wished I hadn't come. The lab techs were nearly done. Two county coroner's workers were there with a fresh body bag. The sun was still high in the sky and both Gregory and I were sweating. From the beach to the desert in the same afternoon, but that was California.

"Who did this?" I said. "Matthew Karp? Louie?"

Gregory shook his head. "Maybe neither."

I turned to him. "What?"

"It could be a copycat," he said. "We get those." He moved closer to the scene. Reluctantly, I followed.

"A copycat?"

"Yeah," Gregory said, his shoes sliding in the sand. "She goes on TV, she gives this killer a catchy name, some nut job out there thinks she's talking about him. Decides to do something about it."

"That happens?"

"Anything's possible," he said. "People are crazy."

A man in a short-sleeved white shirt with a surgical mask over his face reached into the car next to Sheryl's decomposing body and scraped off some of the paint on the inside of the windshield into a small glassine envelope. Satisfied, he emerged and nodded at the coroner's deputies. They moved in with the body bag. In the silence of the desert, its unfolding seemed particularly loud.

"So this could be just some other nut job," I said. "Nothing to do with any of the other killings."

"What I call media-inspired," Gregory said.

"Not even a comedian," I said.

"What?"

"He's not even a comedian," I said. "Maybe he doesn't know what a heckler is. Can't even spell it right."

One of the uniform officers on the scene gave up a shout. Everyone turned to look. He stood up from behind a cactus and held up something for all to see. A black piece of cloth he held on a stick. As he came closer, I could see what it was: a ski mask.

"If it's a copycat," Gregory murmured, "he's a clumsy one. We can get hair off that. If we get hair, we get DNA. They probably left other samples behind. It looks like they didn't kill her right away. Kept her alive and had some fun with her first." He turned to me. "It's over for you, but just starting for us. You can go back to being a comedian now."

He walked away from me and I stood in the desert sand while Sheryl Franklin was taken out of the car and loaded into the body bag.

"He's not real," I called after Gregory.

He stopped. "Who?"

"The Heckler," I said. "We all made him up. He's not real. He doesn't exist."

Gregory looked up at a police helicopter flying overhead, searching the area in ever-widening circles.

"He does now," he said.

He walked toward Sheryl Franklin's car. I stood where I was and felt hot sand fill my shoes and waited to feel funny again.

About the Author

Dan Barton is a professional stand-up comedian. He has performed on television, in feature films and commercials.

He is the author of three previous novels. *Killer Material* is the debut mystery featuring the series protagonist, comedian-turned-amateur-sleuth Biff Kincaid.

He also works at E! Entertainment Television as supervising producer of the award-winning series *Celebrity Profile.* He was twice nominated for an Emmy for his work on *E! News Daily.*

A resident of southern California, Barton is working on the next Biff Kincaid novel. He can be contacted at www.killer material.com.